# RESURGENCE

Hell on Earth: Book 5

## IAIN ROB WRIGHT

Don't miss out on your FREE Iain Rob Wright horror starter pack. Five free bestselling horror novels sent straight to your inbox. No strings attached.

Visit the back of the book for more information.

# FOREWORD

So... if you are still with me, this is book 5 in the Hell on Earth series that began with The Gates. Book 6 will likely be the end, so things are now ramping up towards the end game. I hoped you enjoyed the previous book, although it was a slight departure. I needed to widen the scope of things before the final battle, which is why we visited the castle in the woods. This book will return to the main plot line, and book 6 shall bring everything together.

As with previous books, this one has a mix of old characters and new. I hope you enjoy every page.

Wit much appreciation,

Iain Rob Wright

Strong people stand up for themselves, but stronger people stand up for others.
— **Unknown**

Be careful when you cast out your demons that you don't throw away the best of yourself.
— **Friedrich Nietzsche**

Oh look, carnage!
— **Doug, Cooties (2014), Lionsgate Premiere**

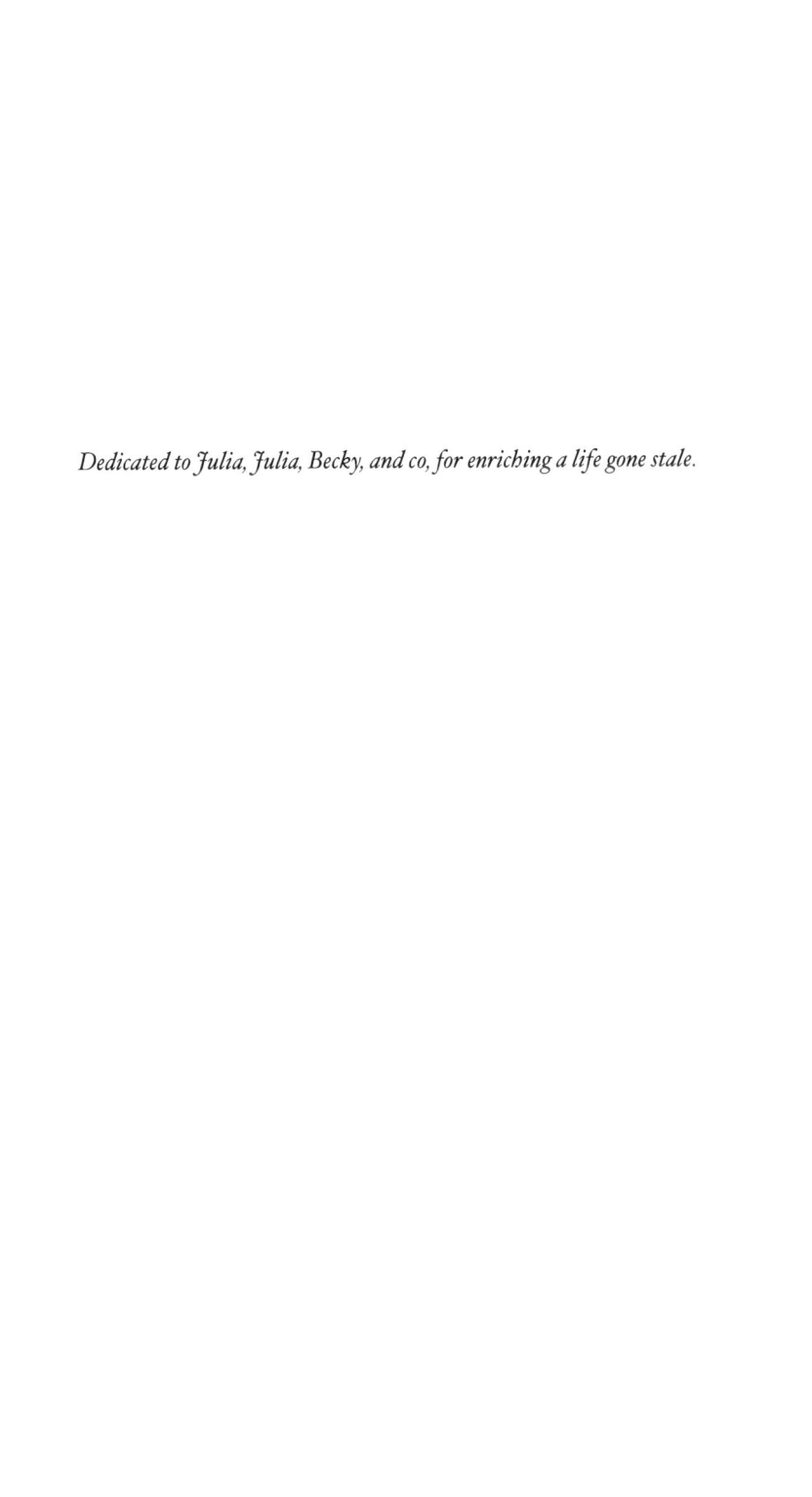

*Dedicated to Julia, Julia, Becky, and co, for enriching a life gone stale.*

# CHAPTER ONE

AYMUN AWOKE ON THE GROUND, sweating, blankets kicked aside. The winter had been tough, sleeping in unheated houses and outside around dwindling campfires, but the ground had finally thawed and the sun had started making brief appearances. Last night had even approached *warm, and* Aymun had taken the blessing with a smile.

Waking amongst the twigs and brambles didn't disconcert Aymun. He'd never lived a life of comfort or wealth, but over time he had come to enjoy the feeling of God's earth against his back. Whether it be the shifting sands of back home or the leafy forests of England. Something, however, was wrong this morning. It wasn't that a demon lay snoring three feet away from him. Or the fact that his tummy groaned from a lack of food. No, it was his missing companion that concerned him. Vamps never awoke first. He always needed stirring.

But this morning, Vamps had awoken and left their camp in silence. Or was it Crimolok – Red Lord and sibling to both Lucifer and Michael – who had left?

The archangel had found its way inside Vamps after a confrontation in Hell's throne room. Such tales would once have been the domain of Aymun's precious Quran, but in these times new chapters were being written out on blank pages. There was no way of knowing how mankind's story would end, or even what would happen next. God had abandoned His children and monsters fought in His wake. Crimolok was the worst of them all, but he was trapped inside Vamps' body.

Aymun reached out and shook the snoring demon to his left. "David? David, wake up."

The demon bolted upright, as he often did when woken. The small creature was a bag of nerves. "I am David!"

"Yes, you are David. I am Aymun, your friend."

The demon blinked and stared at Aymun. It spoke slowly. "Yes, Ay-mond. Safe Ay-mond."

Aymun patted David's sinewy thigh. "Vamps is missing."

David leapt up and started hopping anxiously. He'd been naked when they'd first started travelling with him, but now the demon wore loose-fitting black trousers and a Tottenham FC shirt. "Bad thing. Bad thing. We must find."

Aymun stood up. "Yes, we need to find Vamps and the abomination inside him."

"Vamps good. Vamps bad."

"Both. Help me look."

David stopped hopping and gave Aymun a serious look. "Yes. Help."

And so the two of them set off through the woods, a Syrian and a demon, both far from home. Which direction Vamps had travelled was unclear, but Aymun spotted some trampled leaves and a snapped branch that led him towards a nearby incline. He hoped he would find his friend at the top.

He hoped he would find his adversary too.

Truthfully, Aymun had been at a loss since surviving the battle at Kielder Forest. They had the Red Lord contained – imprisoned inside a mortal vessel – but the problem with human bodies was that they were fragile. Crimolok's current confinement was temporary, which was why Aymun eagerly sought a path that would take advantage of their current, brief reprieve. With the Red Lord contained, now was the time to act. But act in what way?

The incline steepened, and the undergrowth gave way to stony earth. Soon, they were trudging upwards towards the edge of a rocky outcropping. Vamps stood on the highest ledge, staring down at the stony ground twenty feet below.

Aymun slowed his approach, not wanting to startle his friend and cause him to fall. "Vamps? Vamps, my brother, what are you doing?"

Vamps didn't turn, but he gave a reply. "What d'you think would happen if I threw myself against those rocks? You reckon Crimolok would die with me?"

Aymun approached a few more steps, trying to see his friend's face, to see what was going on there. "If you kill yourself, who knows what would happen?"

"I'd go to Hell, right? That's what the Bible says. And the Quran."

Aymun chuckled, but it was from nervousness not humour. "They are just books. Words on paper written by the pens of men. The truth is deeper than mere words, and it is ever unknowable. We were not made to understand the workings of existence. I fear we have learned too much already."

"But there's a chance I could throw myself from this ledge and take Crimolok with me? We don't know, do we? I could end it all right now and this shit might be over."

"You would be gambling with the lives of millions. Perhaps billions."

Vamps finally turned to face Aymun. Despite his dark skin, he seemed somehow grey. Sickly. "I think you're being extremely optimistic."

Aymun shrugged and conceded the point. "Then I would tell you that even one life is too precious to gamble with. Vamps, you shoulder a great burden, but you have done so before with great courage. That courage is still inside you, as much as anything else might be."

Vamps clutched his stomach as if it ached and his face creased in misery. His impassiveness fell away, and his emotions took over in a flood. "I can feel him in me, Ay. Every day, it's like I'm getting more and more crowded out."

Aymun put out a hand and took the final steps between them. He wished he could take this burden from his friend, but that was not the way of things. "We shall win this fight, brother. Mankind shall prevail as it always has. The evil inside you shall perish and we will see brighter days. This I promise you."

Vamps nodded, tears in his eyes. "I... I didn't sleep well. I think I just need to rest."

Aymun took Vamps by the arm and moved him away from the ledge. "Then rest we shall, brother."

---

Wickstaff grew more god-like every day. Before the gates had appeared, Maddy worshipped strong-willed women like Dame Helen Mirren and Deborah Meaden, but they all paled compared to the woman standing in front of her now. In Maddy's mind, Wickstaff was the reason everyone at Portsmouth was still alive.

*She never stops for a second.*

Wickstaff caught Maddy staring at her and raised an eyebrow. "What are you staring at, woman? Do you have something to say?"

Maddy shook herself. "Erm, yes, ma'am, I have the reports from Field Team One. Mass is back on base after securing the southern outskirts of Reading, but he plans to head right back out after resupplying. He hopes to push our lines north to Oxford within three months."

Wickstaff slapped a bunch of papers on her desk and chortled. "We really must discover that fine chap's surname. It crawls the skin to keep referring to him as Captain Mass."

Maddy smirked. "Makes him sound like a superhero."

"He isn't far off being one. Half the ground we've regained is down to Field Team One. If Captain Mass does any more to secure our welfare, I'll marry the man. Sod it, have you seen his body? I'll marry him regardless."

Maddy had seen Mass working out topless one time at the docks, so she was more than aware of his physique. To be honest, though, the furthest thing from her mind was sex, which was why she merely nodded without comment.

"Have the captain meet with me when he has a moment," said Wickstaff. "I would like to thank him personally for his efforts."

"Understood. The other field teams are making progress too. We've taken back Bournemouth and Poole, but to the east we're struggling to break through demon forces at Brighton. There's a gate there. We've lost a lot of men."

Wickstaff moved aside the papers on her desk and perched on the edge. As strong as she was, she looked weary. The last year had aged her five. Dark bags hung from her eyes as she looked at Maddy. "Are there still demons coming through this gate in Brighton?"

"A steady stream. The only relief is that not all the demons want to fight. Most just wander off."

"We're still getting reports of their odd behaviour?"

Maddy perused her notes, knowing she had a direct quote somewhere. "Erm, yes, Captain Dawson reports th*ey are 'behaving like Arabs in the Arctic'.*"

Wickstaff frowned. "What on earth does that mean?"

"I think it means *confused*."

"With the fallen angels gone, they've become rudderless. That's why we must act quickly and direct them back to Hell."

"What are your orders, ma'am?"

Wickstaff rubbed at her eyes and breathed for a moment. "It's tempting to go all-in on the offensive – we finally have the buggers on the run, after all – but there's still too much stacked against us. The demons outnumber us ten to one, and it's only their recent confusion that's allowing us to pick them off piecemeal. If we overextend, we could find ourselves assaulted from multiple sides. While it pains me to leave people in need of rescuing, we must remain cautious in our efforts. Give the field teams a day of rest. Let them hold the line for a while instead of pushing to extend it. I don't want to lose any more men. Meanwhile, I want to know why the demons are changing, and what exactly that means."

Maddy cleared her throat. "What exactly would you like to do?"

"Use your head, woman. We need to capture one of the blighters alive and put him to the torch."

Maddy raised her eyebrows. "A prisoner of war?"

"Yes, although don't expect me to follow the Geneva Convention, because, last I checked, Switzerland is now a part of Germany."

"Speaking of the German Confederation, Chancellor Capri is still demanding his nuclear submarine back."

"He can whistle for it. Commander Klein has made it clear he

5

wishes to remain in Portsmouth. He's got quite the poker club going on Thursday nights, by all accounts."

Maddy chuckled. "That's what I told Capri, but he wasn't happy. Also, Diane neutralised another assassin last night. It was attempting to sneak in on the back of one of our supply trucks."

Wickstaff tutted. "Only one this week. They're starting to give up on me. Does that mean they no longer deem me important?" She picked her papers back up off the desk and resumed studying them. "Thank you, Maddy. Now, if you don't mind, I might treat myself to some light reading followed by a few hours' sleep."

"Yes, of course, but first there's, erm, one last thing I need to tell you."

Wickstaff eyeballed her over the top of her papers. "Yes? Well, spit it out, woman. What is it?"

"It's General Thomas."

"That blustering old fool? What about him?"

Maddy swallowed. She'd been struggling with this news all morning. They were a family at Portsmouth, and things were working just fine. They didn't need a headache coming along and screwing things up. "General Thomas has stated he'll be with us tomorrow afternoon. In the flesh."

Wickstaff straightened. Her dark eyes narrowed. "General Thomas is coming to Portsmouth?"

"He's crossing the channel as we speak."

Wickstaff reached around the back of her head and tightened the knot around her ponytail. "Then I suppose we'll have to roll out the red carpet. Wake me up at twenty-one hundred hours, please, Maddy."

"Yes, ma'am. Should I—"

"Twenty-one hundred hours, thank you!"

Maddy wheeled around and left the room. A sickening puddle had grown inside her guts and it left her feeling unbalanced. Her anxiety arose from a certainty that things were about to change.

And change always left casualties.

---

With trepidation, Aymun studied Vamps. After his two-hour nap, he was looking better but was still ashen-faced and stiff. It reminded Aymun of the cancer patients he had visited in Syria's run-down clinics, where he had offered them solace through Allah's teachings.

*Allah will help him who moves in the way of Allah.*

Thinking of that young man he'd been made Aymun chuckle. One never knew where destiny would lead them, but in his youth he had thought there was a plan for everything. Most of those clinics were bombed or abandoned in the years that followed, and Aymun had put down his Quran to pick up an AK-47. Had that been Allah's plan?

*Probably not.*

Allah's only want for humanity was for it to survive. If humanity met extinction, it would render God vulnerable to attack by malevolent forces. Mankind was the battery powering His heavenly barricade. Perhaps it mattered little beyond that.

Vamps grunted after a moment. "We're not achieving anything walking through the woods like this. We need to be *doing* something, Ay. We have to do something to help."

Aymun sighed. "We are. We are heading back to Portsmouth to inform General Wickstaff about the settlement in the forest. Combined, Portsmouth and Kielder can take control of this country's central region by attacking from the north and south. Then the two settlements shall become beacons, calling out to survivors across the land to cease their hiding and take up arms. Portsmouth and Kielder represent hope, my brother, and hope is many times more powerful than a bullet or a knife. Our journey is vital."

"Vital," said David, although the demon clearly didn't understand the word. It was strange he knew English, seeing as how he'd told them he'd been a Briton from Roman times. And just a boy at that.

Aymun gave David a friendly pat on the back and then looked at Vamps. "We shall find our true purpose. Be ready when we do."

Vamps reached out and snapped a branch that was threatening to whip him in the face. "That depends who's at the wheel."

Aymun nodded. He understood his friend's concern, even if he could not fathom the horror of it. "Crimolok hasn't appeared in eight days. He appears to have gone dormant. Perhaps he will remain so."

"He hasn't gone dormant," said Vamps. "I can feel him scheming and pulling resources from my mind, trying to escape."

"Then you must thwart him."

Vamps smirked, which was a welcome sight even if it wasn't a complete smile. "Thwart?"

"It is indeed a word, no?"

"Thwart," said David.

Aymun nodded. "You see?"

Vamps left the smirk on his face, and for a moment they traversed the woodland in silence until Vamps lifted his head again to speak. Dark blood vessels invaded the rims of his eyes. "Look, Ay. I know I haven't been myself these last few days but... cheers for having my back, yeah?"

"You are my brother."

"More like a distant cousin but, yeah, we family."

"Family," said David. "Family good."

Vamps frowned at the little demon. "D'you remember your family, David? Back in the old days."

David smiled, which was horrifying on his twisted, skeletal face. "Family, yes! Big sister. Nori. Nori love David bad."

Vamps frowned. "What does that mean?"

"Nori big sister. Not wife. Should not be. Bad to love."

"Are you... David, did you screw your sister?"

Aymun tutted. Vamps possessed many good qualities, but tact was not one of them. Even in the dimly lit woods, Aymun instinctively looked around, embarrassed that someone might have heard the vulgar talk.

David frowned. "Nori love brother David. David love big sister Nori. But wrong way, they say. Family say. All say. I then young and understand not. Maybe understand now. Was wrong love."

Vamps pulled a face at Aymun. David's words were rarely straightforward, but they were obviously thinking the same thing. Aymun considered it, and was at first appalled, but then he realised that only his preconceived notions caused him to be repulsed. Deep down, he found himself unbothered by the revelation of incest. "There are worse things than love," he said quietly, "in whatever form it takes."

"Guess we know why David ended up in Hell," said Vamps. "That shit's proper banned, yeah?"

Aymun grunted. "Hell is a personal thing. David's damnation is not our business. If his older sister took advantage of him, then that is *her* sin. If the act was mutual, then who did it hurt?"

Vamps shrugged and seemed to let it go. "Who am I to judge what went down two thousand years ago? That shit was probably common. Hell, one time, I got off with a sixty-year-old down the pub for a bet. We all have a past."

David turned glum and stared at the ground as they walked. Despite his monstrous appearance, Aymun considered the demon a child. "David, you are with new family now, do you understand? Vamps and I shall protect you."

David looked up at Aymun and smiled. "David thanks. David protect too. Fight the bad."

Vamps patted the demon on the back, making him flinch. "You're a good dude for a demon, David."

David smiled again. "Demon, yes. Demon David."

Vamps shook his head and chuckled. Aymun laughed too, and for a moment life wasn't quite so dreadful. Brotherhood had always been Aymun's driving force – the thing for which he had always fought – and he was glad to have kept hold of it during his travails

*Brotherhood can take many forms, which is what makes it so precious.*

Vamps suddenly clutched his head and moaned. Blood started trickling from his nose and the blood vessels in his eyes widened. David yelped and leapt away, but Aymun lunged for Vamps and held him. "What is it? What is wrong?"

"I... there's something here. Something loud."

Aymun looked around but saw only trees and bushes. "I hear nothing. Only the wind and leaves."

"No, it's here. There's... something over there." Clutching his head with his left hand, he pointed with his right. When Aymun looked, he thought he saw a soft orange glow battling with the bright afternoon sun.

Aymun eased Vamps onto a patch of grass and told David to keep watch. "I'll be right back."

He set off through the bushes in the direction Vamps had indicated, and he soon became positive about what was making that orange glow. Something was lighting up the nearby forest, and a tenseness throttled the air like electricity before a storm. Aymun's stomach sloshed. Whatever Vamps had sensed, on a very minor level, he could sense it too. He parted the trees and stepped into a clearing.

The Hell gate existed over a shallow stream that was little more than a watery divot in the earth. The trees either side were sickly and dying, listing away as if they wished to get up on their roots and flee. This was an evil place, a wicked grove where demons had once spilled upon the earth.

But it was deserted now.

Aymun didn't know how the gates worked, but he was thankful that this one wasn't spewing demons. While both he and Vamps could fight, they were mostly surviving by staying hidden. They were ill-equipped for battle.

"Home," said David, creeping up behind Aymun. He spoke fearfully. "Bad home."

"That is not your home any more, David. It is an empty place."

"Yes," said David. "Empty."

"I can hear the howling of a million years of pain," said Vamps, stumbling through the bushes towards them. Blood gushed from his eyes and nose. "It feels like a part of me."

"It's not," said Aymun. "We must leave here at once."

Vamps shook his head. "No. This is what our mission is. This is what we're supposed to do. I see it now. It's clear."

Aymun frowned, even more so when Vamps moved him forcefully aside. "Please, brother..."

Vamps peered into the gate's translucent centre and spoke with a flat, emotionless voice unlike his usual street-influenced speech. "This is why Crimolok is dormant. Before, at the lake, he was stronger, but after the gate exploded at Kielder, it hurt him and left him weak. The fact I managed to recover is making him weaker too – more human than demon. Hell's influence is overwhelming him and I'm keeping him from healing. The screaming, the howling, all of it – it's suffocating him. He can't think. Hell is trying to drag him home."

"So he's powerless?" said Aymun, looking at the gate with a newfound appreciation. "This is good."

"Yes, but it's only temporary. If we close more gates, it could weaken him more." Vamps reached out and put his hand inside the gate. The otherworldly lens shimmered and twisted, then popped out of existence as if it had never even been there. Gone.

Aymun gasped. "H-How?"

Vamps wiped the blood off his face with the back of his hand. "Crimolok was the one who opened the gates. He can close them too. As long as he is using me, I can use him."

Aymun grinned. "You can close the gates at will?"

Vamps nodded wearily but then went rigid with pain. His face contorted, and his voice changed to a deep, rasping hiss. "It's so good to be back."

## CHAPTER TWO

Mass stayed in Portsmouth long enough to catch a full night's sleep and was back on the road the next morning. He only ever returned to refuel, rearm, and resupply, because his place was out on the road, reclaiming the land from demons. Saving people. His mission was the only thing that mattered. He was a warrior of the streets, leader of Field Team One. The Urban Vampires.

Mass had allowed half his team some downtime – leaving them behind at Portsmouth until the next mission – which left him with eleven men and a sergeant. Honeywell wasn't a bad bloke, but he was an ex-copper and a little too 'by the book'. That said, the older man was grieving the loss of his wife and son, and his burning anger was something Mass could use. Like him, Honeywell never took a break.

"You got us a route?" asked Mass, gripping the juddering steering wheel as their seven-tonne lorry drove along the weed-cracked roads. Honeywell sat next to him while six of the eleven men travelled in the back with the gear. The other five followed in a police-modified BMW X5. The lorry was the group's mobile base, packed with supplies and ammunition, but the Beamer was no slouch. It had a huge boot and a winch for pulling debris out of the road, as well as an engine that would be at home under the bonnet of a Porsche. Few obstacles got in the way of the Urban Vampires.

Honeywell consulted his map – satnavs rarely worked these

days – then looked at Mass. "We're near the Wessex Downs. When we checked the outskirts a few days ago, it seemed quite easy going. We might make it through to Oxford by tonight if we keep going, but I think we should exercise caution."

Mass grumbled. Honeywell was always pressing for restraint, wanting to reclaim each piece of land gradually. Mass preferred to push into the cities where there was a greater hope of finding people. The more souls they brought back to Portsmouth, the stronger they'd be when the next fight arrived. Despite their differences, Mass was mindful that Honeywell had both age and experience on his side. "Okay, Rich. What d'you reckon we should do?"

"We should focus on the Downs before moving further north. There's a lot of land where demons could hide, and the last thing we want is to overstretch ourselves. We might push into Oxford only to find ourselves cut off from behind."

If it was only him, Mass would've considered the risk acceptable – but it *wasn't* just him. There were twelve men for whom he was responsible. Caution sucked, but he owed it to his team to play things safe. "Okay, Rich, I hear you. We'll sweep the Downs before taking Oxford. We'll probably find people camped out in the woods. Plenty ran for the hills when things got bad."

"Exactly. Wherever we go we find survivors," said Honeywell. "Miraculous, really, that people are so adaptable. Just a pity that for every one person we find alive, we have to wade through a hundred dead bodies to find them."

To keep his mind from drifting into misery, Mass concentrated on the road. The way ahead was clear because they had hauled aside the wreckage and rubble in earlier days. Scavenger parties could now use the newly opened routes to bring back supplies to Portsmouth – but it wasn't enough. Canned food and dried pasta couldn't feed the thousands now living in the city, and new teams would soon have to be dispatched to establish rudimentary farms in the countryside and fishing fleets on the coast. People in Portsmouth would starve, but eventually they would get a handle on things. They would begin to rebuild civilisation. The Wessex Downs was perfect farming space for that future development and Honeywell was right to want to secure it.

*Maybe one day I'll stop fighting and grow potatoes. Ma would piss herself at the thought of that, but it would be honest work. Soil and sweat beats blood and death.*

"Just keep following this road," said Honeywell. "We can turn off in two miles."

Mass shifted in his seat and nodded. Being cooped up inside the lorry made him claustrophobic. He wanted to be out in the fresh air, slicing the breeze with his machete and obliterating demon flesh with his Uzi. Travelling always gave him a horribly tense feeling in his gut, like he was dying to take a piss and shit at the same time.

*And throw in a side order of puke.*

"I heard a rumour back at base," said Honeywell. "I was speaking with Diane, and, apparently, Maddy is scurrying around in a panic because of some incoming visitor."

Mass glanced sideways at Honeywell. "A visitor? Who?"

"Some general from the Middle East. The most senior officer in the British Army."

"There a*in't* no British Army any more."

Honeywell huffed and shook his head as if Mass was an annoying child. "In what *was* the British Army then. Anyway, Maddy worries that General Wickstaff might be relieved of duty. She was never officially a general from what I've heard, just a major who inherited command when there was no one else."

Mass sneered at Honeywell, not liking what he was hearing one bit. "Wickstaff is the definition of general. Without her, we'd all be dead. She's our leader." He looked back at the road, grunting as he steered to avoid a half-rotten corpse staining the tarmac. "The only leader I'm willing to follow."

Honeywell nodded, but said nothing else. His interactions with the general had been minimal compared to Mass's. Perhaps that was why he didn't see how vital Wickstaff was.

They travelled in silence for the next ten minutes until they reached a turning for the Downs. Mass rounded the truck onto a narrow country lane, and it didn't take long before they reached a gravel car park set beside a vast stretch of nature. The way the rolling green vista suddenly appeared from nowhere was breathtaking.

Aside from a brick building containing some toilets and an

overflowing bin, the car park was empty. A smashed-up vending machine lay empty and forlorn.

"The lorry won't make it into those fields," said Mass, peering out at the undulating hills and valleys. "We'll set our base camp here. Sound good?"

Honeywell nodded and exited the lorry. Mass switched off the engine and joined him around the back just as the X5 parked. Eleven men exited the vehicles and got to work at once, and in less than an hour, the team had erected four large tents in a nearby field and a gun emplacement on top of the brick building. Gross, a young lad from Brighton, took first shift behind the LMG while his buddy, Tox, handed him a flask full of hot tea. The Urban Vampires were a family. There were no ranks among them, other than Mass and Honeywell being in charge. All else was equal. They were family.

The men armed themselves and stood to attention beside the tents. Mass checked his watch and saw it was still only mid-morning. They'd made good time. "Okay, lads. We'll be on it all day, so take an hour to eat and get your minds right. I need three Vampires keeping watch, and we'll swap out every twenty minutes."

The men grinned. It had saddened them not to spend more time in Portsmouth, but an hour taking in the calm scenery might lift their spirits.

Honeywell took a flask of tea from the lorry and poured some for himself and Mass. Mass sipped from the plastic beaker with thanks and made sure to saviour it. There was a time he had thought he might never again get to enjoy something as simple as a cup of tea. If it hadn't been for his best friend Vamps' determination in the early days, Mass would've given up and died along with the millions of others in the UK – including his other friends, Ravy and Gingerbread.

*I miss those guys.*

He didn't know what had become of Vamps, or those who went through the gate with him, but after they left, the demons changed. Their threat lessened. They became confused. Mass could only assume Vamps and his companions had done something. They had taken the fight to the enemy and struck a blow. Now Mass had to do his part. He had to honour the memory of his friend – the bravest mofo he'd ever known.

*I hope you're still kicking arse somewhere, mate. Kick one for me.*

"I used to love it here," said Honeywell, staring off at the distant hills. A smile warmed his face, but it was as sad as it was happy. "We used to bring Dillon all the time, let him run through the fields for hours. Ha! He was like a dog off the lead. The energy that boy had... My boy."

Mass looked at Honeywell and saw the man's sadness. It was like staring at the sun, too painful to endure, so he looked away as he spoke. "Tell you the truth, Rich, I never really saw anything growing up besides concrete. I might've realised there was more to life than getting a rep if my old man had taken me to places like this. Too late now."

"Why is it? You're here now, aren't you?"

"Yeah, after the world ended."

Honeywell turned sideways to face him. "Did it? This place is just as I remember. The demons might have taken many things, but not this. Enjoy it."

Mass understood what he was saying. With the world in ruins, there was more reason than ever to stop and enjoy what remained, so he sucked in the crisp, clean air and stared off into the distance to enjoy the view. Yet, Mass knew that if he ever had come here as a child, he wouldn't have appreciated it – not then. Now, he appreciated it with his entire soul. To be alive and see a patch of earth so untouched... a blessing. And if he had something to do with it, future generations of kids would not miss out as he had. "I'm sorry you lost your family, Rich. I would've liked to have met them."

Honeywell gave a tight-lipped smile. "As much as it pains me, I'm glad Dillon isn't here. He was far too innocent to have coped with the things we've had to deal with. This war isn't over, Mass. We'll never get back what we were. There'll never be a place for innocent boys like my Dillon."

Mass sighed, knowing Honeywell was right. As much as humanity had withstood its extinction, the land still teemed with monsters. People still died every day, and as long as there were still portals leading to Hell, the war would never end. This was a mere cessation of hostilities while both sides licked their wounds and restrategised. That's why Mass was so eager to push on. The more land and people they reclaimed the less of a platform the enemy would have to launch future attacks – because the demons were still out there somewhere, remobilising, regrouping, and getting ready to wipe out what remained of mankind. Humanity needed to entrench itself as deeply as possible. This time they would be ready.

*Fuck me, when did I start sounding like a soldier? This time last year, my only responsibilities were smoking weed and pulling birds.*

*Honeywell is right. We can never go back.*

An hour passed and Mass assembled the men. The car park was isolated and quiet, so he left two men behind to guard base camp – Gross and Tusk. If they needed help they had signal flares, but the LMG atop the brick building was more than enough to handle any straggling demons that might find their way there.

Honeywell turned up the bass on his voice like a Bang & Olufsen stereo. "You all know the drill. Form a line and keep your eyes on the horizon. You see something, don't shout, signal. Well, come on then! Move it, move it!"

Mass took up the line's left. Honeywell took the centre. The fields were wide open for a mile around, which made an ambush unlikely. If an attack did come, they would see it early. Moving out in the open wasn't ideal, but the odds were in their favour.

The fields sloped, forming an overgrown valley in the centre, the incline of which caused everyone to trot as gravity gave them a push. It was only a few minutes before one of them grabbed the body next to theirs, who grabbed the body next to theirs. The entire line halted and dropped into a crouch.

Had they spotted something already? So soon?

Mass studied the line until he saw Addy, the group's only female, making hand gestures and indicating she had seen something ahead. Mass followed where she was pointing until he saw it too. A large shape in the valley, dark against the green and yellow grass. The shape didn't move, but it was out of place in the field.

*What is that?*

Mass gave the hand signal to engage with caution and the line moved forward with their various weaponry at the ready. While Portsmouth had a military armoury – and several warships had donated small arms and munitions to the cause – most of the Urban Vampires wielded weapons taken from Portsmouth's main police station – specifically its confiscation lockers. Shotguns and sporting pistols mostly. While every man and woman in the line had killed a demon with a knife or blunt instrument before, their shotguns made short work of most threats. They could have used the rapid-fire combat rifles from the armoury, but none of them were marksmen, or even professional soldiers. The Urban Vampires was home to the brave and broken; those who had achieved nothing in the old world but were passionate about fighting for the new. They did things up close and personal.

Mass couldn't help himself as the line neared the dark shape ahead. He picked up speed and broke out on his own, taking point. Usually, Honeywell would have hissed at him to pull back, but the strange object in the grass was clearly not a threat. It was just *something*.

Mass caught a smoky whiff as he got closer and the shape began to discern itself. It wasn't a single shape but several smaller objects lumped together. Charred bodies.

A funeral pyre.

The scene of a massacre.

Mass froze. Honeywell came up beside him, and then placed a hand over his nose. "Jesus Christ!"

Mass stared at the pyre in horror. Multiple blackened bodies were encased in what appeared to be rings of melted rubber. The substance had fused with their bones and made their skeletons appear inhuman, more alien.

"Tyres," said Honeywell evenly. "Somebody shoved tyres over their heads and chests before setting fire to them."

Mass screwed up his face in horror. "What? Why?"

Honeywell glanced around the fields as though he suddenly feared being ambushed. Once he settled, he shook his head and said, "There was a South African gang in London that used to execute their rivals this way. They call it necklacing. You shove a tyre soaked in petrol over a person's shoulders to incapacitate them and then set light to it. It's brutal. It's sadistic. Christ, even now, we're still finding reasons to kill ourselves. There must be a dozen bodies in this pile."

"I don't believe it," said Mass, shaking his head and wondering if he needed to bend over and be sick. The smell horrified him most. It reminded him of freshly cooked chickens at the supermarket rotisserie – a smell that once made his mouth water. "People wouldn't turn on each other like this. Not now. Not after everything."

Honeywell shrugged and turned away, shaking his head in disgust.

Tox grunted and got Mass's attention with his thick Scouse accent. "Boss, summin's moving over there. You want me to kill it?"

"What? No!" Mass jolted and hurried away from the pyre, wincing as his boot crunched on a charred bone. There was indeed movement ahead, partially obscured by the long grass. A soft moan came from the same spot, so subtle it could've been the wind.

Honeywell barked a warning. "Mass, be careful."

Mass waved a hand at him to be quiet. He had his Uzi at the ready, a weapon he'd found while searching the office of a Portsmouth strip joint. (He'd also found a shitload of blow but had left it right where it was. Growing up on the streets gave him a natural wariness of taking drugs that weren't his). It soon became obvious that the movement was coming from a person crawling in the grass. Mass lowered his weapon and rushed to help.

Honeywell shouted again. "Mass, get back!"

Mass skidded to a halt, horrified by what he saw. The woman's face was so utterly charred on her left side that her eye had melted inside its socket. The burns covered her neck and spread across her shoulder and arm. Only half a tyre encased her, and when Mass searched the grass, he spotted the other half lying nearby. It had split apart, leaving the woman only half-burned to death. How long had she been like this? The pyre was cool. The fire had ceased burning at least twelve hours ago.

"H-Help me…" the woman moaned, her voice raspy and ruined.

Mass knelt beside her, the stench of her seared flesh making his eyes burn. "Who did this to you? Tell me and I'll make them pay."

"Deserved it…" Mass shook his head, but the woman hadn't finished. "He said we deserved it."

"No one deserves *this*. Who did this to you? Tell me!"

"The… The Reclamation."

Mass frowned, wondering if he'd heard her correctly. "I-I don't understand. Who did this to you? Where can I find him?"

"H-Help me."

"I will, but I need to know what happened."

"Help me... *please*."

Honeywell spoke. "You can't do anything for her, Mass. She's suffering. It's a miracle she made it this long."

Mass waved him off. "Just a minute, Rich!" He looked back at the injured woman. "I can only help if you tell me what happened."

The woman reached out weakly for Mass's Uzi. For a moment, he thought she was trying to take it, but then her arm flopped back into the grass. "*P-Please*."

Mass shook his head. He needed to know what monster had killed these people. Mankind was at war with a colossal enemy and needed every soul. If someone was out there killing people... It was more unforgivable than ever.

"Just try to concentrate," said Mass. "I need you to tell me—"

Honeywell took a step forward, levelled his shotgun, and blew the woman's head open. Then he glared at Mass and shook his head. "Enough!"

"What the fuck are you doing?"

"There's sufficient suffering in the world without letting it linger. She needed you to help her and you refused."

"I didn't refuse, you sodding idiot. I was trying to help her."

"Well, you were failing. I'm sorry if you don't see that."

Mass wiped the woman's blood from his face and stomped away. He would get the person responsible for this, and Honeywell wouldn't be able to put a stop to the suffering that followed.

---

"What the...? Dog shit! You have got to be dicking me?" Smithy lifted his foot and grimaced as the stench slid inside his nostrils. He'd survived the end of the world, but dog shit was still the worst.

*What did this dog eat? A goddamn burrito!*

In a temper, Smithy wiped his tatty Reebok against the kerb. He took it personally. Not much happened during a typical day, so something like this was enough to ruin his mood all week. The day he stood in dog shit would forever occupy a space in his mind beside 'that day he cut his lip trying to drink out of a broken beer bottle' or 'that day he sprained his ankle trying to climb a roof'. The good days included such things as 'found an entire box of *Peperami*' and 'found a porno mag under a bed'. There were far fewer good days than bad.

The demons had never showed interest in stray dogs – only people – which was why packs of them now roamed the landscape like starving hooligans. In the early days of the apocalypse any breed was a rarity, but it was clear now that the hounds had only been hiding until starvation left them with no choice but to re-emerge. Nowadays, they rooted through bins and dug their way through empty kitchens as if the world was theirs. Now and then, one would take a nip at Smithy, but he was always happy to reply with his ice hockey stick. He'd taken it, along with his once-white Reeboks, from a sports shop many months ago.

Smithy's tummy rumbled. While trainers and hockey sticks were easy to find, food was getting scarce. Most of it was rotten or spoiled. He was rapidly losing weight, but luckily he'd been three stone too heavy to start with. He was far from skinny, but hunger was a growing concern. Starvation, for the first time in his life, was a possible reality.

*God, deliver me a kebab with hot sauce and jalapeños, and a bottle of Lucozade to wash it down.*

He didn't know the name of the town he was in – it was easy to wander these days without paying much attention – but it was just like most others. A row of shops lay ahead and formed the high street, but they all had smashed-in windows. Torn-up bodies littered the pavements, along with boisterous weeds and fading litter. During the summer, the bodies would've hummed with flies and stink, but the recent winter had frozen their rotting flesh and sent the flies and the smells away. Now the corpses were stale and greasy like oily cardboard. Smithy wore a scarf across his face most of the time, but he didn't know for sure if the bodies were pestilent. Eventually, he supposed, they would become harmless bone and dust.

If only he could find some living people. Not the odd stranger here and there, but a town full of hardy survivors with cool nicknames like 'Dutch' or 'Ryker'. He constantly envisaged rounding the next bend and finding a working farm with armed soldiers on the walls and a tank guarding the heavily fortified entrance. Surely some part of civilisation had survived.

*The bloody strays have managed it! I can still smell shit on my Reeboks.*

Eight months had passed since the gates first opened, but it seemed like a decade. Smithy knew it had been less than a year because of the gold Seiko around his wrist – an eighteenth birthday present from his old man. It had both the time and the date, and it was the only thing he owned of any importance. Keeping the calendar alive seemed important.

Eight months.

*Eight months since I watched a footie match. Eight months since I had a Sunday roast.*

*Eight months since I had a sodding shag.*

*How much longer can I do this?*

Loneliness had never been an issue in Smithy's former life. He'd been a qualified web designer with his own fledgling business and two younger brothers. He was popular – the life of the party – and while he'd had no girlfriend when the gates had opened, a long list of conquests filled his past. Life had been good. Not amazing, but good. Now he was a ghost haunting a dead world, digging through trash with *stray dogs*.

At the last count, Smithy had killed fourteen demons. In the early months of the apocalypse, the monsters had travelled in packs, but a while ago things had changed. Now they wandered in dazed stupors, seeming not to know where they were or what they were doing. Some didn't even attack when they saw you – they just mumbled and fidgeted like lost children. On the odd occasions when he couldn't avoid a fight, his advantage came from the fact that demons rarely thought to arm themselves. It was simple to take them out with a claw hammer or the sharpened butt-end of his ice hockey stick. There was something sad about putting them down, almost like he was giving them mercy.

Christ, he was lonely. To have a companion would be great, but whenever he found other survivors, they were half-starving and mad. Just a few days ago, he'd come across a skinny woman chewing on a tree branch. Perhaps she thought the bark would give her sustenance. She hadn't spotted Smithy, so he'd snuck away without saying hello. He needed a survival buddy, not a burden. He could barely feed *himself*.

But he hadn't been able to stop thinking about that woman since. She'd survived as long as he had, so perhaps she knew a thing or two. Maybe he should have said hello.

*Yeah, right. We could have gone halfsies on some bark. Sorry, but I'll pass. Give me a Big Mac any day.*

*Christ, I'll never get to eat another Big Mac. Not even the gherkin. I'd even take a Filet-O-Fish at this point.*

Smithy felt close to tears. The previous him would have been embarrassed, but when you lived each day in complete solitude, it actually helped to have a cry. It was cathartic. The lads weren't there to laugh at him, so what was the harm? No sobs escaped him then though, only a voiceless trickle of tears. The chilly nip at his cheeks was rousing. Emotion was the only thing that reminded him he was still human in a world full of monsters, beasts and corpses.

When he stepped in another slopping pile of dog shit, his tears turned to curses. "Oh, you have got to be joking me? My *Dog's Trust* membership is hereby revoked. Jeez, it smells like day-old curry. That dog needs a vet."

Disgusted, Smithy started wiping his stinking Reebok against the kerb again, when he heard a shuffling sound to his right. It was a surprise to see a demon standing right there in the doorway of *a charity shop*, and at first he didn't even realise it was one. Only the blistered flesh of its cheeks showed it was *undead* – or whatever.

Smithy gripped his hockey stick in both hands and rushed at the demon, but he skidded to a stop when it pointed a finger at him and growled. "You come near me with that, blud, and I'll make you eat it, you get me?"

Smithy frowned. He'd heard demons talk before, in varying degrees of fluency, but none so clear as this. "W-Who are you?"

"I'm Frankie Walker, innit? I'm looking for my little bro. You seen 'im?"

"I, um..." Smithy cleared his throat. "What's his name?"

"Davey. Blonde, short, nothing impressive, but he's my blood. I need to find him, you get me?"

"Yeah, I, um, get you. Sorry, I haven't seen anyone. Is he... Is he dead like you?"

The demon – or was it a zombie? – shrugged awkwardly. One of his shoulders seemed to pop in and out of place. "Dunno, blud. Waited for him in the other place, but he never came. Don't remember how I ended up there, but Davey wouldn't turn his back on me. He's my little bro, innit?"

Smithy swallowed a lump in his throat. This sudden, unexpected conversation had left him off-balance. "Oh, um, well, maybe he didn't end up in Hell then. That's good, right?"

The demon suddenly changed. His oily face contorted and his bony hands bunched into fists. A knuckle broke through the skin. "The fuck you on about? I weren't in Hell, was I! Why would I be in Hell? Was just some other place."

Smithy gripped his hockey stick and looked left and right, wary of more demons appearing from shopfronts and alleyways. "Easy! I don't know where you've sodding been, do I? Was just making conversation. But you are, you know, dead or whatever?"

The demon stopped being angry and sighed. "I dunno, mate. It's a proper head fuck. I remember hanging with my crew, smoking bud and chillin' like normal. I remember being banged up in the nick for a while too. Other than that though... It's all blurry. There ain't no memories of how I went from my old life to... *this.*" He motioned to his body, rotting away beneath a black T-shirt and jeans. "You asked me if I'm dead, but it don't feel like it. I'm still me, yeah, but it's weird. Like I'm wearing my body instead of it actually being part of me. And there's this tugging... like I'm supposed to be somewhere else."

Smithy lowered his hockey stick and relaxed. This demon – as with all demons – was obviously dangerous, but it wasn't a mindless monster like most of the rest. "I'm sorry, man. That sounds horrible. Did you, did you come through one of those gates?"

The demon ran a hand over its moulting scalp and coughed. The sound was like wasps escaping a drainpipe. "Last I remember is waking up in a pile of corpses. There were these soldiers putting bullets in anything that moved, so I got up and did one. Trust me, I'm gunna go back one day and take 'em all out. Fucking murderers. You reckon they killed Davey? He might have been with me in Portsmouth. If they hurt him…"

Smithy raised an eyebrow. "You were in Portsmouth? There were soldiers there?"

The demon kicked at the ground with a pair of heavy tan work boots. "Pussies with guns, innit? I'd like to see how hard they are without 'em."

"But you were in Portsmouth, right?"

"Yeah, blud. There were signs that said Portsmouth everywhere, innit? The pile of corpses I woke up in was by the sea. There were boats. Dunno where I am now though. Lost track a while back."

Smithy chewed his lip and lost himself for a moment. So there were still soldiers around? Still some remnant of humanity? Was Portsmouth a safe place? The type of place he had been dreaming of finding?

"You need to help me find my little bro."

Smithy flinched as he realised the demon had walked right up to him, close enough that the odour was dizzying. The stench was worse than the dog shit.

Smithy took a step back. "I, um, I have to get going. You'll find your brother, though, I'm sure."

"Got better things to do, 'ave ya?" The demon waved a rotting arm, indicating the ruined town around them. A mud-caked border collie slunk out from behind a tipped-over wheelie bin and appeared to watch them for a while before heading into an alleyway next to Argos.

Smithy raised his hockey stick but was startled when Frankie lashed out and snapped it in two. Both pieces clunked against the pavement. The demon was strong. Angry. "Whoa, what the hell, man?"

The demon was trembling with rage, but it stayed rooted to the spot, almost like it was trying to calm itself down. After a few moments passed, it put its hands up. "Look, I'm sorry. My temper is… It's a little up and down right now. I just need to find my little bro. Davey needs me. Please, man, can you help me? I don't know where to start."

Smithy nodded – partly because he was afraid to tell this thing no, but partly because he felt sorry for it. "It's Frankie, right?"

"Yeah, blud. What's your name?" The demon offered a hand. Mindful not to show his revulsion, Smithy reached out and took it. Oily skin soaked his palm.

"I'm Smithy."

"Good to meet you, Smithy. You seem like a good bloke, innit? You'll help me, yeah?"

Smithy gave a thin-lipped smile, wishing he'd chosen to make friends with the woman chewing on bark and not this shambling corpse. Nothing about this seemed like a good idea, but he had to admit it was nice having company. "Yeah," he said, "looks like I'll be helping you, Frankie. Let's go find your brother."

---

Maddy paced her office, unable to do anything but wait. She knew that at any moment someone would barge in and announce the worst news – that some stuffy old general, once probably weeks away from retirement, had arrived. While Wickstaff might not have taken command conventionally, Portsmouth was hers. She had fought for it. She had won it. The spoils of war belonged to the victor. Maddy feared for her place in the world if it wasn't by Wickstaff's side.

From what Maddy had heard, General Thomas had helped liberate a large chunk of the Middle East and Eastern Europe, so he was someone to be respected. That didn't mean he could just waltz into Portsmouth at a moment's notice though. Rationally, Maddy knew Thomas was coming home to help. After securing the Middle East – and the stability of the new German Confederation – Thomas was clearly turning his focus to where it would matter most. Perhaps he should be received as a hero for that.

And not as an unwanted guest.

Wickstaff had reclaimed less than ten per cent of the United Kingdom, but people still hailed her as the great saviour. It was good PR, but built on sand – Wickstaff had confided as much. One more combined, focused assault by the demons would topple Portsmouth, and only luck had seen it prevail this long. Most of their larger munitions were spent, and a majority of Portsmouth's professional soldiers had died in the Great Battle. Luck had followed luck, however, and the demons had scattered and become confused after Portsmouth defeated the fallen angels. But if they found a new leader to guide them, war would reignite.

Maddy yelped as her office door flew open and Diane burst into the room. She gawped at Maddy with wide, excited eyes. "You told me to come get you as soon as he arrived."

Maddy nodded, willing her stomach not to lurch into her throat. Wickstaff had said it would give the wrong impression to meet General Thomas at the docks herself, so she had handed the duty of greeting him to Maddy. The stuffy old relic would have to wait before being brought to Wickstaff at her convenience. They couldn't treat him like a VIP in front of the troops until they understood his intentions.

*He probably won't like it.*

Maddy had survived a demonic war and worked her way into becoming a general's aide-de-camp, but interpersonal conflict made her fall to pieces. It was why she had lost almost every argument when she'd been married. She would usually give in rather than continue fighting. The thought of getting in the middle of two manoeuvring generals was making her nauseous.

But Wickstaff was relying on her.

"Thank you, Diane," said Maddy. "Which berth did General Thomas sail into?"

Diane shook her head grimly. "All of them."

Deciding not to ask questions and instead just get the ball rolling, Maddy hurried out of her office inside the port authority building and exited onto the docks. What she saw took her breath away. General Thomas had not arrived by ship. He had arrived by *fleet*. Twenty warships filled the horizon alongside dozens of smaller craft, twice the number of Portsmouth's own navy. Several vessels had passed through the blockade and now sat at the quays. All flew the Union Jack proudly. In contrast, Portsmouth no longer flew flags. National pride seemed outdated after what had happened during the last year. They were no longer tribes from across the world – they were the living united against the damned. Apparently, not so for General Thomas and his forces.

It was easy enough to spot the general. The uniformed old man stood on the dock with two dozen well-presented soldiers milling around him. Again, in stark contrast to Portsmouth's forces, who wore whatever clothing wasn't ripped or covered in blood. Despite the differences, Portsmouth was unimpressed. The guards conducted their duties with only a cursory glance at the newcomers. Many held weapons at the ready as they stood at their posts, but others merely gazed at the massive fleet that had suddenly arrived on their doorstep.

Maddy straightened up her shoulders and marched across the tarmac. General Thomas acted as though he didn't see her, right until she was nearly standing on his shoes. Then, suddenly, he feigned surprise, raising both of his fuzzy grey eyebrows at her. "Oh, are you finally here to receive me? I've been standing in this cold for twenty minutes."

Maddy forced a smile, and she noticed that the day was not chilly, but mild bordering on warm. The sun was high in the sky. "I'm sorry, General. I just got word of your arrival."

General Thomas lifted his nose and sniffed. "I'm assuming you're *not* General Wickstaff, but forgive me for not knowing how to address you, you're not wearing your uniform."

Maddy chuckled. "Oh, no, I'm not a soldier. My name is Maddy. I'm General Wickstaff's aide."

"Are you telling me a civilian greets me? What kind of insult is this?"

"What? No, it's just... I'm not quite sure what you..."

The old man stomped one of his large feet and folded his narrow arms across his shallow chest. "I come here to meet a fellow officer and they can't even be bothered to come and greet me themselves."

Suddenly there was the sound of running footsteps and Commander Tosco came hurrying across the tarmac. "General Thomas, sir, I do apologise. I was conducting a briefing with the junior officers and it overran. You made good time." He snapped off a crisp salute. "I am Commander Tosco, General Wickstaff sent me to greet you. The tardiness is entirely my error." He looked at Maddy and gave her a barely detectable nod. Had he overheard the frosty exchange and rushed to help? Or was he politicking, something he had a reputation for? He'd taken his current command from his dead superior, Commander Granger. The man's daughter had become his ward.

General Thomas squinted at Tosco and curled his furry upper lip with a tut. "You're an American?"

"I am indeed, sir. United States Coast Guard, as it happens, but Portsmouth is my new home. I fought here alongside some of the bravest men and women I've ever met."

"Really, well, my business is with Wickstaff."

"*General* Wickstaff," corrected Maddy.

General Thomas bristled and kept his disdain barely disguised. Tosco interjected once more. "Shall we go indoors, General? We have tea, coffee, whatever suits."

The general turned away from Maddy, trying to dismiss her in favour of Tosco, but she was Wickstaff's representative and would not be ignored. A poor start did not guarantee a poor conclusion. She moved to the front of the group as it headed towards the port authority building. "Yes, please come with me, gentlemen," she said, back in control of her nerves. "I'll have General Wickstaff informed of your arrival."

Tosco moved up beside her and whispered. "You're pissing this guy off."

She shrugged. "Who gives a shit? No one invited him here. Nobody has even met him before, but he's waltzing around here like he's the king of bloody England."

"He's the head of the British Army."

"Well, this place doesn't belong to the British Army. I'm a civilian. You're US Coast Guard."

"Wickstaff is British Army. If she doesn't respect that, she undermines her own right to lead. General Thomas is her superior."

Maddy scowled. "Her *equal. And she leads because she earned it, not because of whatever rank the Queen once gave her.*"

Tosco glared at her. He opened the door to the port authority building and gave a friendly smile to General Thomas and his entourage. "Please, gentleman, make yourselves at home."

"Thank you, Commander," said General Thomas, moving past Maddy without a glance.

Diane was in the reception area and made herself busy by fetching drinks for everyone. Maddy cornered her in the small back office behind the front desk. "This guy is a complete knob. He's even worse than I'd feared."

Diane pulled a face. "Are you serious? What did he do?"

Maddy sighed, leaning back against the wall and folding her arms. "I don't think he likes the way we do things here."

"Then fuck him. I'll take him out myself if he gives us any trouble."

Maddy cackled and had to cover her mouth as she caught General Thomas glaring at her from across the reception. Not wanting to be seen wasting time, she patted Diane on the back and headed down the hall to Wickstaff's office. She knocked and was summoned.

The general stood behind her desk anxiously. She breathed a little heavily. "I take it General Thomas has arrived? If the vast fleet surrounding my dock is any indication."

"He's waiting in reception. Would you like me to ask him to wait?"

"No, no, send him in, but first, could you tell me what kind of man he is? Anything I should know?"

Maddy pursed her lips a moment before talking, then said, "Well, he'll be pleased to see you're wearing a uniform. Probably less pleased you're a woman."

Wickstaff rolled her eyes. "Send the dinosaur in."

Maddy chuckled and exited the room. Back in reception, she summoned General Thomas. "General Wickstaff will see you now, sir."

"Splendid." He snapped his fingers at his men, who began to follow him through reception.

Maddy objected. "Excuse me, sir, but your guard will have to remain here. General Wickstaff's office is right at the end of the corridor, but it's not big enough to host a party. Also, I notice your men are armed. We don't typically allow weapons inside the administrative areas. There are civilians working here."

General Thomas sniffed irritably, but he eventually gave a nod to his men to have them stand down. He did, however, summon one man forward. "My colonel shall attend. He is to be afforded the respect of a fellow senior officer."

Maddy picked her battles and agreed. To her surprise, the colonel stepped forward and offered a hand. He wasn't young, but nor did he look old enough to be a colonel. He had a gruffness that reminded Maddy more of the sergeants on base than the officers. "Colonel Tony Cross," he said. "Pleased to meet you, Maddy. You seem a laid-back bunch around here, and that's no criticism."

"Yes, well, we've been through a lot here. We're like one big family. Ten thousand strong."

"And here's me thinking I grew up with a big family."

Maddy smiled.

General Thomas grunted. "Shall we?"

"Yes, of course." Maddy led the two men to General Wickstaff's office and knocked on the door.

"Enter."

Maddy held the door open while General Thomas and Colonel Cross entered. Maddy announced both men and turned to leave, but Wickstaff bid her to stay. It was unexpected. She'd been looking forward to escaping this awkward encounter, but then she realised Wickstaff deserved moral support from a friendly face. She took a position in the corner of the room, pulled out the notepad and pencil she used daily, and prepared to listen.

General Thomas and Colonel Cross took seats opposite Wickstaff. Despite her earlier anxiety, Wickstaff sat straight-backed and firm-shouldered in her leather-backed chair. Her chin was raised, her expression impassive, even as she welcomed the two fellow officers to Portsmouth. "It's good to see fellow survivors of the war. How was your journey home, General Thomas?"

General Thomas folded his hands together in his lap and cleared his throat. "Quiet, considering the amount of bloodshed the last year has brought. The enemy are still everywhere, I'm sure you're aware, but we've finally got the buggers on the run. We're fortifying towns and cities all over the continent and eradicating the bastards systematically. It's got easier, as of late."

Wickstaff nodded. "The demons seem to have lost direction, haven't they? We've experienced that here also."

"Demons? Is that what you people call them?"

Wickstaff remained impassive. "What would you call them?"

"Abominations, but ascribing them superstitious names like 'demon' or 'monster' won't do much for morale."

"I find realism is a great tonic for morale, General. Portsmouth's warriors understand very well the threat they face, and it is not for me to pull the wool over their eyes. Nor is it your place to come into my office and tell me how to do things."

"That's where you're wrong, Major Wickstaff. You have not received an official commission to your rank of general. You are still, and only, a major. What you have done here is remarkable. You were right to take command as the most senior active officer at hand, but I'm afraid I shall now have to relieve you."

Wickstaff allowed a smirk to spread across her lips. "And there it is. Things don't change, do they? Arrogant old men will forever think they have the right to rule the world. I'm sorry, General Thomas, but you don't belong here. If it's a fiefdom you're after, you can sod off back east."

General Thomas leant forward, meeting Wickstaff's unyielding stare. "I seek no fiefdom, nor insolence from a subordinate. I am here to reclaim our country. As head of the British Army, it is my duty."

"The world has changed, General Thomas."

"And I intend to change it back."

Wickstaff smirked and flopped back in her seat petulantly. Thomas was growing red in the cheeks. Colonel Cross placed his hand on the desk with a mild *slap* and announced his intention to speak. "General Wickstaff, might I ask you a question?"

Wickstaff narrowed her eyes at him, then nodded.

"What is the most important thing to you?"

"Humanity's survival."

Cross nodded and gave a brief smile. "Mine too. I've seen more people die this last year than I ever thought possible, but I've also seen ordinary men and women do extraordinary things to survive. General Thomas and I have come here with fifteen thousand troops and several thousand tonnes of hardware. You might be well within your rights to send us away – this is your operation – but we would then set up somewhere else along the coast. Wouldn't it be better to welcome us with open arms and add our forces together?

We would have a real chance of reclaiming our homeland. Not just the South, but the entire United Kingdom. If you object to that just because you don't get to be in charge, then I would ask whether it's *you* who is interested in fiefdoms."

Maddy gasped. Out of pure offence, she opened her mouth to argue, but Wickstaff gave her a look telling her to stay out of it, then turned back to Colonel Cross with an amused grin on her face. "If you consider overall command to be such an insignificant factor, Colonel, then I might suggest there's little harm in General Thomas stepping down. Surely he's earned his retirement."

General Thomas spluttered. "That will not happen. In fact—"

"You're right," said Colonel Cross, cutting off his superior. "General Thomas stepping down *is* an option, but it wouldn't work."

Wickstaff leant back in her chair, causing it to creak. "And why is that?"

"Because the fifteen thousand men under General Thomas's command still consider themselves part of the British Army. They respect the chain of command and the legitimacy of rank. It's clear, however, that the forces of Portsmouth are, to put it kindly, less professional."

"Each of my men is worth ten of yours."

Cross nodded, brooking no argument. His face was such a mix of scars and sun-beaten skin that it was hard to get a read on what he was thinking. It was only when he smiled that he gave any indication. "In bravery and ability, your men might be without equal, but that's not the point I'm trying to make. My point is that General Thomas's men will not follow someone they deem to be illegitimately in command. They respect the rank not the man. Your people are different though. They don't respect rank, they respect *you, General Wickstaff*. They will act as you tell them to."

Maddy found herself nodding, for it was true. Whether Wickstaff was officially a general or not, people wanted to follow her. They trusted her.

Wickstaff rolled her eyes. "We respect each other and what we've been through. The people here have fought and died to protect what we have. Rank is far less relevant nowadays."

Colonel Cross nodded as if he understood. Maddy assumed the

man probably had stories of his own he could tell. Each scar on his face and neck likely had its own punchline.

"Step down," said Cross softly, "and the people here will be safer. They'll have another fifteen thousand fully armed soldiers protecting them and enough weaponry to blow up the moon. Your civilians can go back to being civilians. Your injured can rest. No one is asking you to go away, General Wickstaff, only to relinquish the role of senior commander. You'd still outrank me." He smiled, but the joke didn't land. Wickstaff did nothing but raise a thin tawny eyebrow at him.

"Colonel Cross is correct," said General Thomas, less bristly now. Perhaps he'd realised Colonel Cross was getting somewhere with his softer approach. "I shall promote you legitimately to *brigadier* and you shall be my second in command. You'll have authority over even more men and resources than before and I intend to rely on you heavily. Understand, however, that I am the senior officer in the British Army. I have my own list of victories and reasons to be respected. Accept my command, and we'll wipe the floor with the enemy. Refuse it, and we'll end up stepping on each other's toes, two splintered forces fighting over the same spoils. If the demon's current predicament proves anything, it's that an army fights better with a strong, focused chain of command."

Wickstaff chuckled. "I thought you disliked the word 'demon'."

General Thomas cracked a smile. He leant back in his chair and appeared to relax. His wide, bony shoulders lowered. "Well, I suppose I can accept a few things you do around here." He ran a hand over his short grey hair and let out a sigh. "Look, perhaps I came on a little strong initially."

"A tad," said Wickstaff.

"I apologise. Unfortunately, it's become somewhat of a habit. Living in the desert with officers from a dozen nations, all trying to be top dog, all trying to win a never-ending pissing contest for their respective courts, can be rather stressful, to say the least. There's a reason Germany has control of most of Europe, and it's because they pissed on everything first. I came here to ensure that our homeland remains in our possession by fighting whoever may try to take it."

From the corner of the room, Maddy tried to make out the man's sincerity. She hated to admit it, but he seemed earnest.

"Okay, look," said Wickstaff, placing her palms together and leaning over her desk. "If I were to be honest, being in charge of the lives of so many people is not as fun as it sounds. If someone wants to come along and share that burden with me, then I'm not instinctively opposed to the idea. But understand this, gentleman, if you want my fealty, you shall respect the men and women of Portsmouth as if they were your own – British Army or not. We are fighting for mutual survival here and no man is lesser when the enemy is at the gates trying to exterminate us as a species. I won't stand for it if you stamp your boots all over this place and disrupt people's lives. They've been through too much already."

Colonel Cross nodded eagerly, like a salesman who sensed a done deal. "I have no doubt General Thomas will be happy to hail your people as the heroes they are. We need every fighting man we can get. There's no reason for there to be an 'us and them' mentality. We are fellow countrymen."

"And women," said Wickstaff, raising an eyebrow and giving Maddy a quick smirk.

Colonel Cross chuckled and gave a smile of genuine warmth. "Of course."

Maddy instinctively liked Colonel Cross, and she would have preferred it to be him who was intending to take command. He spoke softly and respectfully, and underneath his considered words was an uncouth, working-class accent that suggested all this politicking was a terrible bore. He was doing his best to be a senior officer but hadn't been born to it. Like the people of Portsmouth, he'd stepped up in a world that had suddenly demanded so much from ordinary people. What she absolutely hated, however, was the fact that his words were getting through to Wickstaff. Was she actually considering stepping down?

*Please don't.*

Wickstaff gave Colonel Cross a swift nod then looked at General Thomas. "Is that right? Can this transition of power be smooth and painless? I'm not so sure."

General Thomas seemed to regain some of his pissyness, but after he let out a long sigh, he nodded. "If I can count on your support, Major Wickstaff, then I promise we shall move forward in as frictionless a manner as possible."

For a second, Maddy thought Wickstaff might react to the barb fired her way – being addressed as *Major* – but she remained silent. Slowly, she rose from her chair and leant over her desk. She glared at the two officers for a few moments before snapping off a leisurely salute and saying, "This is your new office, General Thomas. You're welcome to it."

General Thomas stood up and saluted back to her. "Thank you, *Brigadier* Wickstaff."

Maddy swallowed a lump in her throat.

What the hell had just happened?

## CHAPTER THREE

SMITHY WAS STILL SOMEWHAT bemused that he was attempting to reunite a demon with its family, but as much as it worried him, it also gave him a twinge of hope. When the demons first arrived, they'd been intent on destroying everything in their path – Smithy still remembered the streams of blood running through gutters and the screams that filled the night – but now he was travelling with a demon that not only *didn't* want to kill him, but could hold a conversation.

"So, um, d'you have any idea where your brother might be?"

"Wish I knew, blud. Maybe he's still at home taking care of the bitch."

"Who's that?"

"My crackhead mother."

Smithy winced. "Yikes. That's harsh."

Frankie shrugged, clomping along in his heavy boots as if he didn't have a care in the world. "She's a train wreck, mate. Had to raise Davey on my own, innit, but he can't bring himself to kick her scrawny ass out of the house. He's a sweet kid, but too weak. That's why I need to take care of him."

"Okay, so where's home? We should look there."

"I... I'm not sure. It'll come to me, though. I just need to get my head together and that."

Smithy kicked a loose stone on the pavement and sent it skimming into some bins. It was a careless thing to do – the noise could attract danger – but walking with a demon made him bold, like he had an 'in' with a rival gang. Surely he was safe now that he was friends with 'one of their own'.

"So," said Frankie, his voice suddenly thick with phlegm, or some other decaying liquid. "What's your story?"

Smithy shrugged. "Don't have one. Not no more. Only reason I survived was 'cos I lived in a flat above a newsagent. The staff stopped coming in to open up eventually, so I found myself with access to shelves full of food and bottled water, and a steel shutter protecting the entrance. Eventually the food ran out and I had to leave, but I had it better than most for a while. Been surviving on the road about six months now."

Frankie raised a patchy brown eyebrow. "You must be a proper gangster to have kept your shit together through all this. Everyone's dead, yeah? I've seen bodies all over the place, innit?"

"Well, yeah, everyone is dead. Don't you remember what happened?"

"Told you, I don't remember much of anything. This is, like, the end of the world or something, yeah?"

Smithy couldn't believe Frankie didn't know. Had he not torn people apart with the other demons? Surely he came through a gate. "It started when these strange gates appeared," Smithy explained. "They were everywhere, like, in every country. Hell, almost in every dicking town. When they opened up, monsters came through and attacked everyone. They hit everywhere at once, massacring people at work, killing kids at schools..." Smithy closed his eyes tightly as he pictured it, wishing it was only a dream. "Before we knew what was happening, it was over. Every single person I knew got ripped to pieces, and there was barely anyone left."

Frankie fell silent, his pallid brow wrinkling in contemplation. Smithy left the demon to digest what he'd just learned. It really did seem like he hadn't known.

The road they were travelling was empty, but ahead lay a single-storey building. A row of motorcycles were parked outside – the Hell's Angels kind with big silver handlebars – and once they got close enough, Smithy spotted a Harley-Davidson sign hanging in the front window.

*I would've looked great on a Harley. Just another thing I'll never experience.*

When Smithy had first ventured out of the newsagents, it had terrified him to be out in the open. He'd seen things through his bedroom window that he could never unsee, and he fully expected to die the moment he hit the streets. Fear had caused him to run for his car, where he intended to make for the main roads, but he had never made it past the first bend. Snarled traffic blocked every thoroughfare. The roads were impossible to navigate by car.

*But on a motorbike, perhaps...*

"This place looks untouched," said Smithy, his eyes wide with surprise. It was rare you found a place still locked up and secure. "You good to check it out?"

Frankie frowned. "Why? It's just a motorbike shop."

"There could be food."

"I'm not hungry," said Frankie. "Not even sure I need food any more."

Smithy chuckled. "Well, forgive me, but I still need to eat. I'm bloody starving."

"We'll look for food after we find Davey."

"You're kidding, right? We don't know how long it'll take to find him. I need food now."

Frankie turned on him, splintered teeth grinding in a foul snarl. "We're not stopping, you get me? Once we find Davey, you can stuff your ugly face. Till then, we keep looking."

"You don't even know where to start! I can't just wait for you to—"

Frankie lashed out and caught Smithy in the face, causing him to double over and clutch his cheek. His fingers came away bloody. "The fuck, man?"

Frankie pointed a bony, fleshless finger at him. "I'll bury you if we don't find my brother by the end of the day. I'll stamp your skull into the pavement and see what comes out. Don't fuck with Frankie fucking Walker, blud, because it'll be the last thing you ever do. You fucking get me?"

Smithy instinctively went to defend himself, but he realised his hands were empty, his hockey stick now in shards somewhere back the way they had come. He wasn't certain he could take this demon on with just his bare hands, and in fact he was afraid to try. Frankie was volatile.

Smithy straightened, still clutching his bloody cheek, but trying to act like it was no bother. "Okay, man, cool. Let's just move on then. I'm sure Davey is nearby."

Frankie's scowl faded like a dying match, and he reached out, which made Smithy flinch, but he only patted him on the back. "You're a sound bloke, Smithy. I might have to keep you around."

Smithy gave a thin-lipped smile. "Sounds good."

"Now, let's go find my little bro. Like I said, I want to find him by tonight or I'm gunna lose my temper."

Smithy walked behind the demon with his fists clenched and his jaw set. First chance he got, he was making a run for it.

*Fuck Frankie Walker and his goddamn temper.*

---

Mass knew he should rejoin the line, but he was too angry. Instead, he walked alone in front of the group that Honeywell had ordered into a column. The pile of burnt bodies lay half a mile behind them now, and the men rose out of the valley towards the treeline.

Mass pulled up into a crouch beside the trees. As much as he needed space, he wasn't dumb enough to wander into the woods without thought. The trees could hide a hundred men.

Honeywell halted everyone and joined Mass in a crouch. "We need to exercise caution."

"Don't you think I know that? If you'd let me question that woman longer, we might have had some idea about what we're facing."

Honeywell sighed. "She wouldn't have told you anything."

"She might have."

"No."

"Okay, fine, maybe not, but it's screwed up. It's totally screwed up, Rich. We've been out here for months and we ain't ever come across something like that pile of bodies. It's... It's sick."

"You can't let it affect you, Mass. How many people are alive because of you? Focus on the good we're doing, not the bad that still exists."

Mass rocked forward and put his hands into the long grass, letting his head drop. "I can't! It's in my frigging head. All of it, not just today but every second of this screwed-up nightmare. I've had nine months of this shit. I... I can't keep doing this."

"How old are you, Mass? I don't think I've ever asked."

Mass frowned, wondering where Honeywell planned on taking the conversation. "I'm not sure if I've had a birthday. Let's say twenty-two."

"You're a boy."

"I'm in charge, you fucker!"

Honeywell chuckled. He picked up a twig from the ground and rolled it between his fingers. "And you deserve to be in charge, Mass, truly. You're as tough as men come, and your courage inspires the men, but that doesn't mean you're not a boy. Trust me, when you reach my age, you can spread things out. You don't have to feel everything all at once. If you did, I would have put this shotgun in my mouth a long time ago."

"What's your point, Rich?"

"That it'll get better. Bottle up whatever you're feeling and put it aside for now. Dip into it a little each day until it's all gone, but don't swig the entire bottle in one go. You need to be the grown-up here, not just the leader."

"I'd have to be *really* grown-up to be as old as you, you old bastard."

"That's true, so learn from my wisdom." He patted Mass on his back, leaner these days rather than bulked out. Gym memberships were scarce in the apocalypse. "You're a good lad. Don't let this world grind you down."

Mass nodded. He knew he was being emotional but couldn't help it. He'd reached a point where he just couldn't absorb any more wretchedness. "Just give me a minute, Rich," he said, "and I'll get my shit together, okay?"

Honeywell nodded and moved away, but he quickly dropped onto his belly when a bang sounded in the distance. Everybody went prone, shuffling around to face back the way they'd come.

The bright sun made the flare difficult to see, but they heard it hiss into the sky.

"It's Gross and Tusk," Tox yelled from on his belly.

Mass leapt up and started back down the grassy valley. "They're signalling for help. Come on!"

Honeywell stood and bellowed with his police sergeant's voice. "All right, double-time. Gross and Tusk have their arses stuck in a bucket and we need to pull them out."

The men sprinted, but experience kept them together in a line. Each held their shotguns at the ready, but their firearms would be ineffective until they got close enough to see a threat. Only Tox had a rifle accurate beyond a hundred yards. He'd been an army cadet as a kid, making him the only one with a decent, practised aim.

Mass cursed himself for not leaving Gross and Tusk with more men. They'd been doing this for months now and things had become routine. Every day, they would enter a new zone and clear out any demons before setting out in a line and sweeping a grid until they had the whole area secured. Things had got too easy. The threats had become minimal. Still, no need to panic yet. Gross and Tusk were warriors not children.

The line of men raced through the valley and then started uphill. They were machines, functioning on adrenaline and bloodshed. Mass knew of no reason for Gross to fire a flare other than encountering an enemy. Best-case scenario, he'd spotted a pack of demons that were yet to spot him. Worse-case scenario, he'd been attacked and killed. Neither possibility made absolute sense. Why hadn't he fired?

The four tents the group had set up in the field lay ahead, still erected. No one had tampered with them or tried to take them down. No threat presented itself, and when they neared the gravel car park, things began to look more and more like a worst-case scenario. The LMG was still in place on top of the brick building, but there was no sign of Tusk or Gross. Where the hell were they?

The line spread out, making itself a harder target in case an enemy suddenly appeared. Honeywell moved up beside Mass. "This doesn't feel right."

"There was no gunfire," said Mass. "How could they not have got off a single shot?"

Honeywell gave hand signals to the line *to engage cautiously*. They moved forward, spreading out even more and crouching as they went. They tucked their shotguns against their shoulders. Tox sighted through his hunting rifle. Still no enemy appeared, and his footsteps in the grass were the only sound Mass heard. The brick toilet block was the only thing he could see.

The line reached the fence and Mass opened the gate. He scrambled through and scanned left and right with his Uzi. The lorry and BMW were still parked where they'd left them.

*Gross? Tusk? I'll kick your bloody arses if this ends up being a false alarm.*

*Please, let this be a false alarm.*

Honeywell and the other men moved into the car park behind Mass. Their footsteps hit the gravel and raised a crunching cacophony.

"Where the hell is he?" Tox sounded irritable and tense, making his Scouse accent even thicker. "He's vanished off the face of the Earth."

"Shall I check the toilets?" asked Addy, aiming her shotgun at the dark opening of the doorway.

Mass thought for a second, then nodded. "Do it."

Addy moved up beside the doorway and took a moment to listen for movement. Then she turned on the ball of her foot and slipped inside. The men outside waited nervously, and when she came back out, they breathed a sigh of relief. "No one in there," she told them, "except for an old shite in one of the bowls."

Tox alerted everyone by kicking the lorry's rear bumper. "Damn it!"

Mass marched over, his heart beginning to pound. This was all wrong. "What is it?"

Tox pointed to the rear of the lorry. The shutter was still raised from when they'd first set up, but the supplies were all gone. Stolen. A week's worth of food and water. Weapons too.

Mass kicked up a mound of gravel and sent it scattering against the lorry's chassis. "Someone is picking a fight with us."

"They must have taken Gross and Tusk," said Addy. She started bunching her ponytail tighter as if getting ready for action. When she lost her temper, she was the fiercest warrior on the team.

Mass felt his mouth grow dry. "If Gross had time to light a flare, he would have had time to fire a shot. I don't understand it."

Honeywell cursed and redirected their attention once again. The lorry's front tyre had been torn to shreds. "Someone was here and we missed it."

Mass turned and looked at the X5. Its front tyres were also hacked to pieces. This was the work of cowards, people who stole and ran.

Addy raised her shotgun and searched for a target. "Someone wants to make sure we don't follow them."

"There's no blood," said London, the unit's oldest member after Honeywell.

"We need to find them," said Mass.

London nodded. "Too right. Gross owes me half a bottle of whisky."

Addy showed her teeth. "We aren't going to let this stand. We're going after these jokers, right?"

"What if it's the guys who burned all those people in the field?" said Tox.

"Then we'll make them pay for it all," said Mass. "Let's move."

---

A hospital lay ahead, which was a bad sign. While the demons had attacked everywhere, devastating entire cities overnight, some hospitals had held out for a while, treating the wounded as they staggered inside. It didn't take long for the demons to push through the last lines of defence though, and so the surviving hospitals had become deathtraps full of labyrinthine corridors and cramped wards. Whenever Smithy encountered a hospital, he found nothing but bodies.

"We should move away from here," he told Frankie. The demon had been silent for over an hour now, and it seemed like he was constantly thinking. What was his deal? Did his brother, Davey, even exist?

Frankie broke from his thoughts and shook his head. "No, my

brother could be inside. I... I remember a hospital. Something happened at a hospital. I can see Davey in a room with a bed."

"But they're nothing but disease pits. Only thing we'll find inside is the dead, I promise you."

"We're checking it out, blud!" Frankie started to snarl, as much animal as human.

*A demon. Don't forget he's a demon.*

"I'll wait for you out here," said Smithy, deciding it was worth a shot.

Frankie growled, and one of his teeth plopped out of his mouth and hit the pavement with a soft *clink*. He didn't seem to notice. "I don't want to get nasty, so do what you're told, yeah?"

Smithy considered taking his chances in a fight. He'd killed plenty of demons before, so what made this one any different? Other than being coherent and insane at the same time, Frankie was just another meat sack spat out of a gate.

*Better to wait. Eventually, he'll turn his back long enough for me to ditch his rotting ass. Frankie might be dead, but he's still a dangerous thug.*

"Okay, Frankie. I'm with you. Let's make it quick though."

Frankie grinned and slapped Smithy on the back. It left him feeling wet, and he didn't want to think about what had been left on his shirt.

The hospital's large glass entryway had been jammed open by an overturned trolley bed. A desiccated corpse was sprawled on the pavement beside it with a massive hole where its stomach should have been.

Frankie snorted in amusement. "This guy got messed up, yo. Look, you can see the spine."

Smithy had seen so many bodies it barely affected him any more, but he still didn't find it humorous. The only comforting thing was that the body was dry. While it was probably superstition, he considered dry things less plague-infested than moist things. He stepped around the trolley bed and hopped over the corpse.

The stench inside the hospital's gloomy waiting area was a mixture of damp towels and cat urine, unpleasant but bearable. It was a smell that made you gradually nauseous rather than one that sent you immediately into convulsions. It was as good as things got these days.

"I don't think we'll find your brother here," said Smithy, wary of Frankie's anger. "Don't you agree?"

Frankie didn't get angry. He seemed disappointed. "Davey, where are you, bro? I'm right here."

"We'll find him," said Smithy, not actually giving a shit. "We'll just keep looking."

Frankie glanced at him. His eyes were wet, but no tears fell because his eyelids were a goopy mess. It seemed like he might have been crying otherwise. A demon. Crying.

Smithy felt bad for a moment. Maybe Frankie couldn't help being a violent sociopath. Perhaps it was part of his undead condition. Frankie Walker might have been a saint in a previous life.

*Yeah, I don't see it. He already mentioned his love of 'smoking bud and chillin'. Although, right now, that sounds like a pretty good way to live.*

"You mind if we take a quick butcher's?" asked Frankie, almost pitifully. "I just have to be sure. There's something about a hospital..." He batted at his own head. "Damn it, it's right in there. Just can't get at it."

"Okay," said Smithy. "Let's look."

The deeper they got into this dark and hazardous place, the better chance he would have to do a runner and lose Frankie altogether.

They cut a path through the carpet of dust covering the tiles and headed into a narrow corridor that might have been a staff area. Clipboards and folders littered the floor and Smithy had to kick aside a bundle of bloodstained bandages to get past. Several bodies littered the various offices and cubicles, as well as an unexpected pair of demon corpses, emaciated and vile. Somebody had fought back.

*Good on them.*

"I used to hate these places, even before they were full of dead bodies," said Smithy as he searched a desk for anything he could eat. His stomach rumbled despite the dead bodies. A paperback book caught his attention and he considered swiping it for a moment – the only entertainment there was nowadays – but then he saw the naked lovers embracing on the cover and decided against it. He tossed the tawdry novel to the tiles and kicked it away with distaste.

*Not quite that desperate yet. Although, it's a tragedy that there's a billion hours of porn on the internet and no way of watching it. God, I'd love me some proper filth right about now. Even some nasty old pegging would do it.*

Frankie grunted. "I hate hospitals too. Mum used to get carted off in an ambulance at least twice a year. She would drink too much Special Brew or snort some blow, then fall down the stairs and crack her stupid head off the floor. One time, she got fucking pneumonia and was in for two weeks. I had to feed Davey with no money and get him off to school every morning. I was fourteen. No, wait, I think I might have been younger."

"That sucks. Man, I mean, that *really* sucks. Davey was lucky to have a brother like you."

Frankie made a face that might have been intended to resemble a smile but was more a grimace. "I tried my best, you know?"

Smithy nodded. Frankie's story made him miss his own family. His mum and dad had been good to him, and both his brothers were older and protective. Responsibility hadn't entered Smithy's life until at least his twenties, and by then he was a happy, well-adjusted individual. Of all the things he missed, family dinners around the table on a Sunday afternoon took top spot.

*Ah, Mum's gravy, and cheesy mashed potato. A nip of brandy once we're done.*

Frankie turned and shoved a door at the end of the narrow corridor. On the other side was a wider area that might once have been a ward. Now it was a mass of beds, wheelchairs, and snarled medical equipment. Bodies lay everywhere. Blood stained the walls in several places.

Frankie took a step inside but then paused. In fact, it wasn't so much that he paused but that some invisible force had struck him. Smithy went to join the demon but stopped a few feet short when he remembered how volatile his companion was. "W-What is it, Frankie?"

"I... I remember."

"Your brother? You remember what happened at the hospital?"

"I had a gun. I... bought a gun with me to the hospital."

"A gun? Why?"

"There was this guy, this piece of shit who reminded me of..." Frankie trembled on the spot like an electrical current was passing through him. His voice had started out in a mutter, but it grew angrier now. "I came to the hospital because I was looking out for my brother, but... he shot me."

Smithy struggled to understand. "The man? The man who hurt Davey shot you?"

"No... No, it was Davey who shot me. My little bro shot me. My. Little. Brother. Fucking. Shot. Me." Frankie started raging. "I'm dead because of that little shit! After all I did for him. He-He fucking shot me. He killed me. Davey killed me. What the fuck!"

Smithy started backing away. Frankie bellowed so furiously that the door frame rattled. If he got any angrier, his rotting flesh might erupt and spill his insides on the floor.

*This is my chance to sod off. He's distracted.*

Smithy turned slowly and made for the exit. In the dark, he bumped against the wall of the narrow corridor and staggered. He had been about to curse but bit down on his lip and stopped himself. Behind him, Frankie continued to bellow almost incoherently.

*Good riddance, you crazy motherf—*

Smithy's ankle turned and his leg flew awkwardly out to the side. He crumpled to the tiles with a painful thud and nearly yelled out in agony. It was a miracle he stayed quiet, opening his mouth and miming a scream instead of actually letting one go. He clenched both fists and breathed through the pain. The erotic novel lay on the floor beside him. He'd trodden on it in the dark and sprained his ankle.

*Bloody filth.*

Frankie still faced into the ward, still yelling about his brother and some guy who had apparently wronged him. His anger was fading though. Smithy had to get up and get out of there. Gritting his teeth against the pain, he climbed onto one leg and limped as quickly as he could for the door. The two dead demons were in his way and he had to hop over them, but then he reached the door and yanked it open. The cat-piss stench of the waiting area hit him again, but it might as well have been fresh air. This whole thing with Frankie had been heading in a bad direction, and it was a relief to finally turn his back on the demon. He felt sorry for Frankie, the dude was clearly crazy, but it wasn't Smithy's issue at the end of the day.

"See you in the next life," Smithy muttered as he hobbled out into the waiting area.

"Where you going, blud? You ain't running out on me, are you?"

Smithy froze, but then he fell forward as an elbow struck the small of his back. Having been balanced on one leg, he went sprawling onto his side, quickly disorientated by the darkness and dust spiralling around his head. Frankie was a shadow in the doorway behind him, and for a moment he remained completely still – not a living thing but a watchful wraith. Smithy started to inch away, hoping the demon would stay where it was, but Frankie leapt out of the gloom. His face was a mask of hanging flesh and bloody blisters. He bared his teeth and all but his fangs tumbled out from behind his swollen lips, falling soundlessly into the dust on the floor. "Nobody makes a mug of Frankie Walker," he growled. "Night night, Smithy."

Smithy tried to get up, but before he even got close, a heavy tan boot struck his jaw and turned off the lights.

# CHAPTER FOUR

"We head back the way we came," said Mass. "It's the only place they could've gone."

"I don't like it," said Honeywell. "We shouldn't react without thinking. Let's just take a moment to—"

Mass growled at him. "Gross and Tusk are our boys. Once we find the people behind this, we're going to crush them like fucking insects."

"Calm down."

"How can you say that, Rich? You lost your whole family trying to protect what we have. Now someone is threatening us and you don't want to hit back?"

"Of course I do! Sometimes, all I want to do is snap our enemies in two with my bare hands, to tear them apart with my jaws. Then I remind myself that I'm not an animal. I'm a father and a husband, and I'm fighting for future wives and children. This is bigger than our personal losses, Mass. We need to think this through."

Mass ignored his sergeant's pleas. "Let's move out."

The group hurried down the road, trying to spread out but hemmed in by hedges on either side. Mass raced ahead by himself, legs hollowed out by his anger. Gross and Tusk were good lads. Gross, in particular, had a talent that kept them all entertained. At night, whenever they made camp, Gross would sing old pop songs from before things had turned to shit. His impersonations of certain male singers were spot on – particularly his Tom Jones medley, made even more impressive because he was a diminutive Geordie and not a barrel-chested Welshman. Mass suspected he and Addy were an item, and the look on her face since he'd been taken made it clearer. She was furious, but also distraught.

They had to get Gross and Tusk back.

They passed by a road sign with the bottom panel missing then took a knee at Mass's command. The kidnappers could've gone in several directions, but an agonised scream alerted to them to an A-road heading north.

"Is that Gross?" Addy had already started off in that direction.

Mass threw an arm out and waved the others forward. "Move!"

"Wait," said Honeywell. "This could be an ambush. Think!"

The screaming continued. It was unclear whether it was Gross or Tusk. "Eyes open," said Mass, "and stay down."

Tox raised his hunting rifle and barked a warning to the others. "Heads up."

A young red headed woman hurried towards them, clearly distraught. When she saw their guns pointing at her, she put her hands in the air and begged for help.

"She's hurt," said Mass, seeing blood on the woman's blouse.

Honeywell raised a suspicious eyebrow. "Is she?"

The woman stumbled towards them. She appeared alone, and was apparently unarmed, but she was also a survivor of the apocalypse. They couldn't take her lightly.

Mass turned to his men. "Take cover. I'll meet her."

Honeywell and the others filtered to the side of the road and went prone while Mass marched down the road to meet this mystery woman. Fifty metres lay between them, but he closed thirty of them himself by jogging, then stopped to allow the woman to walk the rest of the way. There were no buildings nearby. No hills or blind corners. It didn't seem like an ambush.

"They hit him," said the woman, a blubbering mess. "They ran him over."

Mass studied the woman. The blood on her blouse might not have been hers as she had no visible wounds. "Who did?"

"The people on the bus. They ran over Bobby. Please, I need you to help him. He's hurt so bad."

Mass stared down the road. The screaming had stopped. A bad sign if someone truly was hurt.

"Please, you need to come with me. You need to—"

Mass grabbed the back of the woman's head and threw her to the ground, then pointed his Uzi right in her startled face. She had reddish-brown freckles matching the colour of her hair. "Where are your people? What game are you playing?"

"W-What? I don't know what you're talking about. Please, I just need your help."

"I don't like liars, so say goodnight."

The woman screamed, utterly terrified.

Mass removed his Uzi from her face and let her get up.

"P-Please don't kill me!"

"I'm not going to. Take me to Bobby."

The woman scurried away, afraid but still wanting his help. "This way. Bobby's just down the road."

Mass watched the hedges on either side as he followed the woman. Again, he saw no one hiding or any obvious signs of an ambush. When he spotted the man lying in the road ahead, he grew confident the woman was telling the truth. Someone was hurt. He caught up and walked beside her. "You say Bobby was hit by a bus?"

"Yes. A white coach full of people. It had writing on the side."

"Did you see anyone being kept on board against their will?"

"I'm sorry. It was moving too fast."

Mass grunted and hurried to the man lying at the side of the road. The blood had come from him. His head was bleeding and his right leg bent almost sideways. He might've had more injuries, but he wore a thick duffle coat that made it hard to tell. Mass hissed through his teeth. "This is bad."

Tears filled the woman's eyes, and she nodded to show she understood her friend was dying.

"Who is this man to you?"

"My husband."

Mass winced. The pressure to help the man increased. "We

have doctors back at Portsmouth, but our vehicles are damaged. Do you know anywhere we can get a car?"

The woman shook her head. "There's a farm nearby. We were searching it for food. I think, maybe, there were a couple of tractors there. If they work, you could use one to carry Bobby." She sounded hopeful.

"Okay, if we can find transport at the farm, I'll have my guys drive you and Bobby to Portsmouth."

"Thank you. Thank you so much."

"Don't mention it. I must ask you more questions about that bus though. Our friends might have been on board." He moved away from the woman and waved a hand to the others still taking cover fifty metres away. Honeywell emerged from the bushes and started bringing the line cautiously forward.

The injured man's head wound was severe, blood pouring out onto the road. His leg was also a gory mess, with a snapped shinbone poking through the flesh. How on earth were they supposed to move him, let alone help him?

Honeywell arrived before the others. "Is there anything I can do?"

Mass shook his head. "This is Bobby. We need to get him to Portsmouth."

"How?"

Mass looked at the trembling woman. "What's your name, love?"

"Gemma."

Mass looked back to Honeywell. "Gemma says there's a farm with some tractors nearby. If we can get one of them running, a couple of us can head back to base and take Bobby to the docs."

Honeywell sighed. "I don't like this, Mass. Too much is happening all at once."

Mass had a bad feeling too, but Bobby needed help. "Tox? Take two guys and head with Gemma to this farm. Get back as quickly as you can, understand?"

Tox shouldered his rifle and nodded. "I'll see if there's a trailer we can hitch to the back. We can move him that way."

Mass nodded. "Good thinking."

Tox took two guys as commanded and hurried away with

Gemma. Mass returned to attending Bobby, patting him down for injuries, but he realised he had no idea what he was doing. "Rich? I think you need to take this. He's hurt bad."

Honeywell was their unofficial medic because of him having received extensive first aid and trauma management training during his decades as a police officer. "Okay, give me some space with him. I'll see what I can do."

Mass moved out of the way. The others huddled nearby, scanning the road for threats. Addy stood on her own, staring into the distance. Bobby moaned and seemed to regain a modicum of consciousness. Blood burbled from between his lips and cascaded down his chin. The gore was making Mass lightheaded, so he moved away to get some air, joining Addy over by the hedges. "You okay?" he asked.

"I need a cigarette."

"Thought you'd quit."

"Not by choice. Seems like everybody's first idea when Armageddon hit was to stockpile all the fags. I'm okay, I'm just—"

"Worried about Gross. Me too. We have a lead though. A bus hit Bobby. It has to belong to the group that took Gross. We'll find him."

"We're seeing each other," said Addy. Her expression remained the same, but she looked him in the eye briefly. "We've been meaning to tell you, but... I don't know, I suppose it scared us. Saying it out loud would make it real, and real things don't last in this world any more. Things have a habit of turning bad."

"I know you two are together, Addy. No big deal. And real things *can* still last. That's what we're fighting for."

She nodded to Bobby, still moaning in pain. "Is there any chance we can even help this poor sod?"

"Gemma is his wife, so we're going to try. Let's give them a long and happy marriage."

Addy smiled glumly. "That would be nice."

"G'away!" Mass turned to see the injured man trying to move, swiping at Honeywell and slurring. "G'way fra'me."

"Calm down," said Honeywell. "I'm trying to remove your coat. You're hurt, but you're going to be okay. Just let me help you."

"No! No, g-get away fra'me! G'way!"

Addy and Mass shared a look of concern. Mass took a step forward to help, but froze when Bobby's duffle coat fell open and revealed something underneath. Pipes and wires.

Mass's stomach hit his shoes. "Shit, it's a b—"

The air thudded and a blinding light tore the world apart. A gale erupted, a blast so fierce it lifted Mass off his feet and threw him backwards. For a stretched-out second, he was weightless. Then his skull hit the road and his vision whirled. A high-pitched whining filled his ears.

*I can't move. I can't move.*

He lay there, terrified, sure that this was the end. His broken body would remain there on this road, rotting in the sun and pecked apart by birds.

*Seconds passed by like hours.*

Addy appeared in the narrow portal of his blurred vision. Blood coated her face, and what looked like a nail jutted out of her cheek. She grabbed Mass by the shoulders and shook him. Her mouth moved, but he heard nothing besides that endless high-pitched whining. He turned his head and saw Honeywell. The police sergeant lay on his side, half of his face shorn away by the blast, his eyes bloodshot and still. Dead eyes.

*No.*

*Rich... No...*

Addy shook him again and his ears popped. Sound came rushing back, but too much of it. Addy yelling. Someone screaming. Birds squawking. Beneath it all was the gentle hiss of the wind. It overwhelmed him and made him want to vomit. He felt his foot move and almost cried with relief. Slowly, more of him came back to life.

"Mass, get the hell up." Addy continued pulling at his shoulders. "Get up!"

He got to his feet but stumbled drunkenly. Everywhere he turned, he found death. Honeywell had caught the worst of it as he'd been leaning over Bobby. Both of their bodies were now in pieces, blood gushing from dozens of different wounds. From the state of Honeywell's face, he must have died in an instant.

*No last words, not even any last thoughts. Just gone. Fucking gone.*

The men nearest had caught the blast too, and crude nails and bits of steel riddled their bodies. Jugulars spurted and legs kicked, but they were beyond helping. Only those furthest away were still conscious. Bride and London were alive but injured. Bride, in particular, had a long nail buried deep in his left biceps and another one right in the side of his skull. He moaned quietly, like he was singing a lullaby only to himself. London moaned louder, torn up in a handful of places and in obvious pain. His worst injury was to his left hand, which dripped blood into his lap like an open tap. Then there was Mass and Addy. If he hadn't gone to check on her... If he hadn't asked Honeywell to take over...

*I killed him.*
*No. That bitch did.*

"This was all a set-up," said Mass. "Gemma set us up."

Addy grabbed him and yelled into his face. "Tox and the others went with her to that farm."

Mass searched for his Uzi but couldn't find it, no matter how hard he tried. Had he dropped it into the thick hedges when he'd been lifted from the ground? Honeywell's shotgun lay next to his body, so he picked it up and checked it was loaded. It was. Now it was his shotgun and he intended to use it. "The plan was for us all to die, and if Honeywell hadn't been shielding Bobby, we would have. That means they won't be expecting it when we arrive at that farm and start cutting them down at the knees."

Addy grinned maliciously. She had somehow kept hold of her shotgun, and she looked eager to unload on something. The nail still poked out of her cheek and made her look demonic. He wondered if she even knew it was there.

London dragged himself up and wobbled on his feet. "I-I don't understand what happened."

"We got fucked," said Mass, "but not hard enough to keep us down. We need to move. Help Bride get to his feet."

Mass stared down the road, wondering how far this farm was – or if it even if existed. Were Tox and the others still alive, or had Gemma detonated another bomb strapped to her torso? Were these people all suicide bombers?

*No, Bobby tried to warn us. He was a victim.*
*But a victim of who?*

London cleared his throat. "Boss, Bride can't get to his feet."

"Why not?"

There were tears in London's eyes as he spoke. "Because Bride is dead."

Bride had slumped forward like a sleeping Buddha. The nail in his skull had finally done its job. Another man dead. Killed by a stranger for no reason. A human being, not a demon.

Mankind hadn't lost its talent for murder.

---

Maddy helped Wickstaff move into an office beside the *Mary Rose* Ship Hall. The touristy area of the docks around the half-ruined HMS *Victory*, battered during the battle with Lord Amon and his forces, was quieter than the warehouse section, where people lived, worked, and trained. Maddy wondered if Wickstaff was glad to move away from the hustle and bustle. Since stepping down as general that very afternoon, the woman had gained a spring in her step. She seemed lighter.

*It's fair enough if she wants to take a step back. She's done enough. More than anyone. I just thought she would have put up more of a fight.*

Maddy shouldered the door to the office and struggled inside with a cardboard box full of papers. "This is the last of it, ma'am."

Wickstaff waved a hand to the chair next to her desk. "Sit down, woman. Take a load off."

Maddy dumped the box on the desk and tittered. "Oh, erm, thank you."

"Coffee?"

"I'd love one."

"You know, eventually, we'll run out of the stuff. Where are the beans grown? South America? Tea from India and China? I'm no horticulturist, but I don't think any of it's local."

"I suppose we'll run out of a lot of things soon."

Wickstaff turned with a steaming mug of coffee and handed it to Maddy. "As long as we don't run out of people we'll consider it a victory."

Maddy sipped the coffee and enjoyed it immensely. There were so few luxuries in the world nowadays that each one was exquisite. Last week, one of the scavenger teams had brought back a haul including several hundred tiny boxes of raisins. She'd never tasted anything so good.

Wickstaff sat in the chair behind her new – much smaller – desk and took a sip from her own mug. She smacked her lips. "Ah, that's the stuff. When was the last time I got to put my feet up?"

"About nine months ago, ma'am, I would imagine."

"Long enough to create a baby."

Maddy studied the woman, trying to see the cracks, but there seemed to be none. "General, are you—"

"Brigadier."

"Yes, erm, are you happy, Brigadier Wickstaff? Are you happy that General Thomas relieved you of your command within an hour of arriving?"

Wickstaff sighed, a sliver of irritation in her dark-brown eyes. "I seem to recall demoting myself voluntarily. If I had wished to fight the situation, I would have."

"Why didn't you? This place is all down to you."

"Portsmouth is down to me, is it? The place has been around far longer than you and me. We all have a stake in this place."

Maddy nodded. "And you gave yours up."

"Maddy!" Wickstaff put down her coffee and leant forward over her desk. "I gave up nothing! If I'd resisted General Thomas, what would have happened? Bloodshed, that we would have been on the worst end of."

"How can you say that? We fought the demons – an entire army of them. We took down a fallen angel."

"Yes, and it left us battered and broken. If General Thomas ordered his people to fire on us, it would cost lives – the lives of people who have fought and earned the right to live. There was no option for me but to step down."

"It doesn't seem right."

"It's not, but let me tell you something, Maddy. A sound leader does not react, she plans. She waits. General Thomas is an old man. There are no other generals here – Brigadiers either. In fact, it seems a little silly having such lofty ranks when there're only a handful of officers to manage. I imagine General Thomas picked my new role for its connotations as much as its prestige. Brigadier is the final rank one can attain without interfering with the big boys and their power games."

"You took it so easily," said Maddy. "That old fart came in to humiliate you, yet somehow you made it seem like you were happy to step aside."

Wickstaff huffed. "I won't give a man like that the satisfaction of seeing a woman beg. You're getting het up for no reason, Maddy. General Thomas will fulfil what he feels is his rightful duty and then I shall step up to lead once more. In the meantime, we have fifteen thousand fresh troops and a great deal more supplies. The safety of the people of Portsmouth is my paramount concern, and if I had resisted General Thomas, it would have been in jeopardy. His people will never agree to take my command, but two years down the line, I shall take the mantle of general legitimately and move forward with a unified force. I have no problem playing the long game if it means more people live."

"So what are you going to do in the meantime?"

"My job. The life of a brigadier isn't all sunshine and crumpets, you know? I shall be busy enough, don't you worry – and yet not quite *so* busy. It will be nice to share the worry for a change. Let General Thomas and Colonel Cross make the life and death decisions around here for a while. To tell you the truth, I'm not sure how much longer I could have held things together. I'm not made of iron."

"What do you think about Colonel Cross?" Maddy realised she had asked the question somewhat randomly.

Wickstaff went to answer, but then her words stopped and a smirk settled on her lips.

Maddy felt herself blush. "What?"

"I might ask what *you* think about Colonel Cross."

"I asked you first."

"Hmm, well, he's a little too weather-beaten for me. I like a clean-cut, soft-skinned man. I'm surrounded by tough men all day, so give me a gentleman to warm my bed. I will say, though, that Colonel Cross seems a competent and temperate man. With any luck, his influence on his superior will be great."

Maddy nodded. She wholeheartedly agreed. "He managed to

convince Thomas to step down his aggression towards you. He sought compromise."

"I think Colonel Cross saw conflict and sought to quell it. He knew I would step down one way or another, but he made sure I could do it with my dignity intact. A clever man. Cleverer than you would think by the look of him. I doubt he was always an officer."

That was exactly what Maddy assumed. Cross was a good man with good instincts. Perhaps things wouldn't be so bad with him around. "I would still like to remain your aide, ma'am, if that's okay?"

"I wouldn't hear of anything else. Stick with me, Maddy, and we girls shall prosper. Especially now the assassins will be targeting General Thomas instead of me. Things will work out just fine."

A knock at the door, and Diane entered in a flap. "General Wickstaff, you need to come right away."

Wickstaff groaned. "What is it?"

"The men are fighting."

Wickstaff looked at Maddy and blew air out of her cheeks. "I just wanted one evening. Is that too much to ask?"

Maddy got up and waited for the general – for the *brigadier* – to join her.

*Gonna take a while to get the hang of that.*

Wickstaff sipped half her coffee, and then the three women hurried to the docks, heading for the shipping containers where Diane said the hostilities were occurring. It didn't take long for them to hear the cavemen yells of fighting men.

General Thomas arrived at the same time they did. His eyes narrowed as he surveyed the scene. Several men were involved in a punch-up, and it was clear to see the make-up of the two sides. General Thomas's uniformed soldiers were throwing punches at Portsmouth's scruffy militia. The uniformed soldiers were coming off worse. A young guardsman Maddy knew, named Tom, had just knocked a corporal on his arse. The corporal's buddy then rushed in for revenge, but another of Portsmouth's guardsmen threw himself into an almighty tackle and knocked the soldier for a loop. Then things descended into an all-out brawl.

"What flavour of shit is this?" Wickstaff bellowed, immediately bringing a halt to the melee. She marched up to face the men, her face reddening. The force of her shout made the hairs on the back of Maddy's neck stand up. Portsmouth's men stood to attention and saluted.

"General Wickstaff," said Tom. "I'm sorry. These men were ordering us to leave our posts."

Wickstaff glanced at the corporal, still down on his ass. "Why is that?"

"Because I ordered it," said General Thomas. "I want professional soldiers keeping watch over Portsmouth."

"These civilians have kept this place safe for the best part of a year."

"It's in ruins."

"Exactly," said Wickstaff. "Without these men, it would have been wiped completely off the face of the Earth. Be thankful you have come home to ruins."

"Nonetheless, I shall be organising new shift duties."

"That's fine, but do you really think it needs to happen on the very day you arrive here? What happened to smooth and painless?"

"General, we didn't start the fight," said Tom. "They were talking shit to us like we were a bunch of kids. We're every bit the soldiers they are."

The corporal got up and snickered. "Not even close."

Wickstaff eyeballed the man. "Well, this civilian just knocked you on your arse, boy, so perhaps you should reconsider what you think you know about ordinary people."

Tom spoke again. "General, we never wanted this to—"

"Brigadier," General Thomas barked. "You are addressing a brigadier, not a general."

Tom frowned, clearly confused. Wickstaff gave a slight nod to assure him. "It's okay, lad. A few changes are coming, but it's all for the good."

General Thomas began tapping his foot, a bottle rocket ready to launch. "Brigadier Wickstaff, why are you allowing men to address you as 'General'?"

"Because I assumed it would be more efficient to inform the entire base tomorrow morning after I've had my first night's sleep in nine months. Unless you would like me to correct them all, one by one, until they learn."

"Do not test me, Brigadier. I've already made my peace with the condition of this place, but things change right now. Relieve the civilians from their duties and allow my men to replace them."

Wickstaff gave Maddy a sideways glance, but Maddy had no idea what it was meant to convey. Nor did she know what would happen next. Thomas was completely out of order. He couldn't get away with this.

Wickstaff stood in silence for a moment, breathing in and out slowly. She turned to the guardsmen, Tom. "Remove all guards from their posts and give them the night off. Assemble in Dining Room Two at twenty one hundred. I have seventeen bottles of red wine I've been collecting and they'll be waiting for you all."

Tom was shocked for a moment, but then a modest grin took over his lips. Not only did he unexpectedly have the night off, but he could spend it getting pissed – a rarity nowadays as there were more people in Portsmouth than alcohol.

Tom ran off to give the orders, but Maddy didn't feel relieved by the tension breaking. She'd just witnessed Wickstaff lose even more power. Uniformed strangers would now guard Portsmouth – troublemakers who looked down on the people whose home this was. Did Wickstaff understand that? She had just bowed to General Thomas in front of her own people. Humiliation.

General Thomas glared at Wickstaff. Wickstaff glared back. "This isn't the way to do things, General," she said evenly. "You said your people would respect my people."

"They aren't your people any more."

"That's where you're dead wrong, and if you treat them like second-class citizens, they'll never be your people. I am on board with the transition of power, but this is not the way."

General Thomas gritted his teeth for a moment – resembling a snarling ferret – but then he let out a sigh. "They never make it easy on you, do they?"

Wickstaff frowned. "Who?"

"Who d'you bloody well think? The men! Treat them like adults and they behave like children. I agree, Brigadier Wickstaff, this isn't the way to do things. You mentioned red wine. You don't happen to have any brandy, do you?"

Wickstaff was visibly confused, and so was Maddy, yet it was she who spoke. "Um, we have several bottles in Storeroom Three, sir. I could get a bottle if you'd like?"

General Thomas glanced at Wickstaff and raised a fuzzy grey eyebrow. "Any imminent threats you're aware of?"

She shook her head. "No significant demon gatherings for thirty miles at least."

General Thomas grinned at Maddy. "Better make it three, sweetheart. I'd like to share a drink with you both."

"I don't usually drink with men I dislike," said Wickstaff, "but I suppose it's a different world we're living in. I'll bring the crisps."

General Thomas chuckled and walked away. "Excellent. I'll be in your old office, Brigadier."

---

Smithy was tied up, his hands bound with bandages. A thick, corded wire – taken from some machine back inside the hospital – encircled his thighs. He could still walk, but he did so like a penguin with a boil on its ass. His sprained ankle wasn't making things any easier.

Frankie growled at him. "Keep moving."

"It's about to get dark!" Smithy groaned. His nose was throbbing and dried blood irritated his nostrils.

*How the hell did my day end like this? This morning, I thought dog shit was the worst of my problems. Now a demon has taken me prisoner.*

"So what?" asked Frankie. "Are you afraid of the dark?"

"No, but I'll need to make camp and sleep. I think you keep forgetting I'm alive. If you appreciated that a little more, I wouldn't have tried to ditch your ass."

"Try it again and I'll beat the shit out of you."

Smithy rolled his eyes. "Nice. So, are we still looking for your brother?"

"No! I ever see that traitor again, I'll kill him."

"Because he shot you?"

"Yeah."

*Can't blame him. Sounds like he was the brother with the brains.*

"What do you want with *me* then? Let me go."

"You're my pet now. My little bitch to play with whenever I like. And you know what happens to bitches, don't you?"

Smithy rolled his eyes. "Just be cool, okay? We can still be mates."

Frankie whacked him in the back of the head. "Nah, I don't want to be mates with a pussy that legs it as soon as I turn my back."

Smithy growled, the pain angering him. "Just cool it!"

Frankie hit him again, then grabbed Smithy by the hair on the back of his head and snarled. "I'll show you what happens to bitches." He dragged Smithy across the street to an abandoned Nissan and shoved him forward over the bonnet. Smithy's eyes went wide as slimy hands started to tug down his trousers and boxer shorts. Seriously, this wasn't actually happening, was it?

*No way, Pedro.*

Smithy struggled, but Frankie was heavy. His hands had already got his trousers around his knees, and he was stooping to get them lower. That was when Smithy got his chance. He threw back an elbow and connected with Frankie's face. There was a sickening *crunch* and Frankie staggered backwards. Smithy fumbled with his trousers, struggling to get them back up with his hands tied. "The hell is wrong with you, man? First you want me to be your mate, then you want to make me your girlfriend. You got some real serious issues, you know that?"

Frankie grinned through the congealed blood slopping out of his nose in chunks. "Hey, I'm a demon, right? Might as well have some fun with it."

Frankie lunged at Smithy, but Smithy hopped his butt up onto the Nissan's bonnet and kicked out his legs. He caught Frankie in the ribs and cracked bone. As strong as the demon was, his body was barely holding together.

Frankie slumped to one side, staggering as his chest caved in on itself. Smithy took advantage of the opening and charged. Like an angry penguin, he hopped at the demon and shouldered it to the ground, buying himself time. He tried to run, achieving only a panicked waddle, and made for some distant woods behind a row of posh houses. With any luck, he could lose Frankie in the trees, but he wasn't going to make it with his legs tied together. He had to risk stopping to untie himself or he would have no chance of getting away. He yanked at the wire wrapped around his thighs. "Come on, come on."

To his delight, the wire came away easily once he got his fingers underneath. He didn't untie the knot, but he shuffled the wire towards his knees until it slackened and fell to his ankles. Then he worked on the bandages around his hands, but Frankie was getting back to his feet. There was no time. It was time to run.

"I'm gunna mess you up, bitch!" Frankie bellowed as Smithy broke into a hobbling sprint. His legs were already tired after all the hopping – and his left ankle was stiff and numb – but his absolute terror did enough to stoke his fire. As planned, he headed for the trees behind a row of large double-fronted houses.

Frankie pursued, but the demon's body was in poor shape. While he might have been strong, he was clumsy, and it led to a meandering run that caused him to stop constantly to reorientate.

Smithy moved through a gap between two of the houses but was barred by a narrow section of fence. The panels were tall, and he wasn't sure he could scale them, but then he noticed they were slid inside concrete frames. He might be able to grab hold of one of the wooden panels and heave it upwards. Grabbing the nearest panel, he hoisted it with his knees. It lifted easily, but the hard part was getting under it without it coming back down like a guillotine. Smithy lifted the panel above his chest.

Frankie barrelled into him and they went tumbling through the gap into the garden. "Got you, bitch. You ain't running nowhere."

Smithy kicked and caught Frankie in the face. "I'll kill you, you demon piece of shit."

"You're a dead man."

"No, that's literally you!"

Smithy punched Frankie in the ribs, trying to cave in more of his chest. He failed and his fist came away sticky. The split-second of revulsion allowed Frankie to recover and headbutt Smithy on the collarbone. The pain was sharp and intense and Smithy rolled aside in agony. He clambered to his feet and hobbled away. The fence at the back of the garden was broken, two entire panels lying flat against the grass. An escape route, and he rushed for it. He made it through the gap and entered the woods beyond. "Eat my shit, wanker!" he shouted triumphantly.

Dusk had arrived and given way to night, which made sprinting through the trees a perilous activity. Branches whipped at Smithy's face, and he stumbled every other step. If he wasn't careful, he would end up turning his sprained ankle into a broken one.

Frankie entered the woods behind him, cackling like a madman. "Looks like we got ourselves a *Blair Witch* situation in here. I'm coming to get you, bitch."

"That movie was like twenty years ago, idiot!" Smithy was so angry he wanted to keep shouting insults, but it would only alert the demon to his location. Enough trees lay between them that he had a real chance of losing Frankie.

"Where you at, bitch?"

Smithy zigzagged and dodged, hoping to loop around and exit the woods on the side they'd entered. With any luck, Frankie would keep moving deeper in the opposite direction.

*Go toy with someone else, you sadistic fu—*

Smithy's head whipped back as he ran into a branch hanging just above his forehead. The momentum of his legs continued, and he ended up on his back. He groaned and rolled onto his hands and knees, trying to get back up. When he touched his hairline, he could feel a lump already forming. "Who put that bloody tree there?"

Frankie was still calling for him, but his voice was far away. There was still a chance to escape, so long as he didn't knock himself unconscious.

*Just get up and keep running.*

Smithy shook the stars from his vision and got moving again, but when he had smacked his head on the branch, it had turned him around. He wasn't entirely sure which direction he was now headed.

*Any direction is fine, so long as it's away from Frankie.*

"I can hear you," Frankie shouted, although it was probably a lie. He sounded closer though. "I can smell you."

Smithy dodged under a weeping willow and considered hiding under its dangling branches, but then Frankie shouted again, even closer, and it startled him into a sprint. This time he kept his head low, desperate not to collide with any more low-hanging branches. One more fall and Frankie might find him. He dodged to his right, trying to snake a path away from the demon.

The woods cleared ahead, the space between trees increasing. Frankie's cursing and shouting began to fade. Even the darkness lifted, the moon finally showing itself through the thick canopy. Smithy was home free, about to get back to his life as a lonely, half-starved survivor. He couldn't wait.

A figure stepped out from behind the thick trunk of an ancient oak tree. Smithy managed to put out his hands and stop himself just in time to avoid crashing right into them. Without taking a breath, he squared up to the stranger. He prayed it wasn't Frankie.

It wasn't.

It was a young black man with overgrown hair and fuzzy wisps on his chin. His gaze had a lethal quality to it, like the biggest lion at the zoo.

"S-Shit! You scared the hell out of me, man."

"What you running from, bro? Need help?"

"Yeah! There's a demon on my ass. A demon with some serious mental health problems. Not that I'm stigmatising."

The stranger sighed and shook his head. "The demons were brought here to eradicate you. They almost succeeded."

Smithy frowned. "Yeah, um, look, what's your name, mate, because we really need to get out of here."

"Some people call me Vamps." The stranger offered a hand and Smithy took it, glancing back through the woods to locate Frankie. When he turned back, the stranger was grinning at him. "My true name is Crimolok."

Smithy gasped as the stranger's eyes became inky whirlpools, and jagged fangs erupted from behind his lips. He tried to pull away, but the thing still had his hand. It hissed in his face. "I shall not rest until I extinguish every last one of you insipid creatures."

Smithy could do nothing. He yelled for help where help no longer existed.

"You best leave him alone, blud. His arse belongs to me, yeah?" Unbelievably, Frankie appeared from the trees on Smithy's right and faced the newcomer. He glared and clenched his fists. "Get your own bitch."

Crimolok snarled. "Silence, creature! You address a being equal to God."

"And I'm Frankie fucking Walker."

"Remove yourself, Frankie fucking Walker. I am about to devour this worm."

Frankie didn't back off. In fact, he stepped forward and faced the other demon nose to nose. "But there's no fun in killing him before he's had time to suffer, innit? The real fun don't start till he starts *begging*."

Smithy tried pulling away again, but it was like trying to free his hand from a vice. He couldn't gain a millimetre, despite Crimolok not even paying him any attention. He was staring at Frankie with a curious expression on his cruel face.

Frankie sniffed, a glob of blood disappearing up his nose. "You wanna take a picture, mate?"

Crimolok snorted. "You amuse me, demon. Misery pleases you. It pleases me also."

"Shits 'n giggles, innit?"

Crimolok studied Smithy, boring into him with those jet-black eyes. "You wish to keep this worm alive?"

"Least till we run out of skin to peel off him."

Smithy kicked his legs, but was too weak to fight any more. Crimolok grabbed him by the throat and sneered. "Looks like your eternity of suffering begins here."

Smithy tried to breathe, but his entire throat closed off, his windpipe crushed to breaking point. He saw Frankie out of the corner of his eye, snickering at his torment, and then the darkness of night took over and his misery ended.

## CHAPTER FIVE

AYMUN AWOKE ONCE MORE beneath the trees. David stooped over him and was shaking him gently. "Aymun alive. Good!"

Aymun blinked, his eyes dry and fuzzy. When he pressed with his fingers against his temples, he felt a deep, painful bruise. "Vamps struck me? How long have I been unconscious?"

David frowned.

Aymun tried again. "How long have I been asleep?"

"Short sleep."

"Okay, so Vamps might not have got far." Aymun began to get to his feet.

"Not Vamps. Crimolok. Creator."

Aymun looked at David. "Did you say 'Creator'?"

"Yes, Crimolok made to create. Bad create. Mad create."

Aymun wondered how the demon knew of Crimolok's true purpose. As brother to Lucifer and Michael, his destiny had been to take on God's role as creator, to renew the Earth with life and wonder. The problem was that with creativity came ego, and soon Crimolok viewed himself as God's equal. For his arrogance, he was cast into the darkest pits of Hell for all eternity. Yet somehow he had escaped and taken ownership of Hell's throne, left vacant by Lucifer.

"David, how do you know about Crimolok?"

David tapped his temple with a twisted fingernail. "My lord. In my head."

"In your head? Hold on, David. Has Crimolok been in your head the whole time you've been with us?"

David creased up his face, the bones of his cheeks showing through his translucent skin. He was clearly having to think. "Only while Aymun sleep."

"Crimolok's power is increasing. His influence over demonkind is returning."

David nodded. "I am sorry."

Aymun patted the demon on his back. "Do not be. You have resisted his dark desires before, when he was at his strongest, and you will continue to do so. You are brave, David."

"More people will die. Will not stop."

"Death is a natural part of life. We should not fear it."

David stared at the ground. "Should fear. Hell follow."

"We must find our friend. Vamps needs our help."

David nodded. While he seemed more alert than usual, he also appeared frailer. His skin was taut. His movements were languid.

"David, are you okay?"

"Feel different since gate close. Remember more of David. Things less confusing. And more confusing."

"The gate closing affected you? Why?"

David frowned, trying to find the answer in his rotting, demonic brain. "I think... I think it gate David come through. Gate where David... arrive?"

"That's interesting. Usually when gates close they explode and kill any nearby demons, but when Vamps closed the one here, it was more like he was merely switching it off. If it was the gate through which you came, then its closure may have affected you. Whatever connection you had with it has been broken. Your mind seems less muddled."

"I remember now, name is Davod, not David." The demon frowned. "Prefer David."

"Then David it shall remain." Aymun considered whether David's – or Davod's – ill health had something to do with the gate closing, but decided it might cause the demon alarm and so didn't mention it. "Which way did Crimolok go, David? We have to find him."

"This way. Come."

Aymun chased after the scurrying demon. David was able to dodge through the moonlit forest with ease, but Aymun had to duck and scramble as branches whipped out of the shadows at his face. Fortunately, the trees were thinning out as they neared the edge of the woods.

Aymun was sure he could hear distant shouting.

David slowed and then paused altogether. He tilted his head like a dog.

"What is it, David?"

"Crimolok is close."

"You can sense him?"

"Buzzing in head."

Aymun patted David to get him moving again. The demon took off even faster than before. This time Aymun was sure he would end up knocking himself silly on an overhanging branch, but before that happened, they reached a clearing. They found Crimolok.

The demon was not alone. Another creature stood in the clearing with him, along with a young man who was writhing in pain on the ground. The unidentified demon was kicking and stamping on the young man while cackling with glee. Crimolok – wearing Vamps' face – was watching in amusement.

David ducked behind some bushes, and Aymun moved up beside him, shaking his head in disgust. "They are toying with that poor boy. We must help him."

"How? Two demons, only one of you."

"You are part of this, David. If you want to do good, then you must do it."

David nodded, but he was clearly frightened. "David weak, but David try."

Aymun pulled a long knife from his belt and rushed into the clearing. He couldn't use the weapon on his friend, so instead he confronted the other demon, the one kicking the defenceless young man on the ground. "Leave that boy alone."

The demon looked up in surprise and stopped its assault. His victim was a sorry sight, both eyes swollen, nose gushing with blood. His attacker snarled. "I see the Pakis are still around then? You people are like cockroaches."

"I am Syrian, and you will step away from that young man."

"What if I don't?"

"Then I shall send you back to Hell, fiend."

"The name's Frankie Walker." The demon flashed its fangs then leapt at Aymun, and he sprang aside easily. Frankie swiped the air with bladed fingertips but missed. Aymun sliced the air with his knife and opened a trench in the flesh of the demon's thigh. The skin and muscle tore easily, like wet tissue paper.

Frankie slumped onto one knee and Aymun went to deliver a stab to the neck, but the demon thrust out both arms and struck him in his chest. His sharp fingertips dug into Aymun's flesh and opened bloody divots beneath his shirt. The sudden flash of pain sent him into retreat. David entered the fray, leaping at the larger, taller demon and trying to claw at its eyes. Slithers of skin and globs of congealed blood flew into the air, but Frankie tossed the small demon away from him easily. David fell onto his back, and Frankie lifted a heavy tan boot to stamp on his skull.

Aymun yelled in anguish. "David!"

The beaten young man was still lying on the floor, but he seemed to recover for a moment. He threw out a leg, perhaps instinctively, and tripped Frankie just as he raised his leg to stamp on David.

Frankie swore obscenely and stumbled onto his hands and knees in front of Aymun. Aymun glared at the abominable creature and raised his long knife. "May you find peace elsewhere."

Frankie called out for mercy, but there would be none.

Blood spattered the chilled night air as Aymun stood frozen, his knife still hanging above his head. Slowly, he looked down and saw a blood-soaked fist jutting out of his chest. Elongated fingers twisted and flexed.

And then the fist withdrew.

Aymun wouldn't have believed it if not for the massive circle of blood now staining the centre of his shirt. He tried to turn around, but he could no longer feel any part of his body. He slumped to his knees, desperately trying to breathe but unable to command his lungs. He saw David cowering at the edge of the clearing and, out the corner of his eye, he saw the beaten young man get up and retreat into the woods. He smiled at that. *The boy is saved. Run, and do not look back.*

Vamps' face appeared in front of Aymun, but it was distorted and grim, no longer his friend at all. Crimolok was in full control. Did any part of Vamps still exist?

"You should have fled the moment you faced me in Hell," said Crimolok. "I have no patience for worms who believe themselves to be tigers. Humanity is finished. You have lost."

Aymun laughed, despite his mouth being full of blood. "No. Even in death, we have won. We are the chosen, while you... you are forsaken."

The look of rage that crossed Crimolok's face was satisfying, and Aymun held that image in his mind as he closed his eyes and died.

---

Smithy had no idea what had just happened, but he thanked the stars that the odd stranger had appeared and rescued him. The man had looked and spoken like he'd come right out of the desert, and it seemed he'd had a pet demon. Whoever he'd been, he'd been braver than he was strong, because the dark-skinned demon had shoved an arm right through his chest.

*He died trying to save me.*
*Who was he?*

Smithy still wasn't sure he could get away. He'd taken a beating, and every movement was painful. He couldn't hear the demons following, but there was no way of knowing how close they were. His run had taken him deep into the woods, but he didn't care where he was heading any more so long as he was running.

The woods were pitch-black. The moon only made itself known through the slightest of gaps. Smithy feared he might never make it out of this dark foreboding place, and part of him wanted to give up and cry. He missed his mum. He missed his dad. And he missed his brothers. All dead, ripped apart by demons. This he knew because the first place he'd visited once he'd left his flat above the newsagent was home.

Although it hadn't been home by the time he had got there.

His parents lived in a large house in a small village. A five-bed property set in two acres of lawn beside a church and graveyard. In a zombie apocalypse, it would have been dead central, but this was a different end of the world scenario, and graveyards were no more dangerous than anywhere else. As the house was remote and surrounded by privet hedges and accessible only by a private gated driveway, Smithy held a hope that his parents were okay.

Getting there on foot had been difficult, but he had made the trip in less than a day. Early autumn, and night had arrived around seven o'clock. One hour after that was when he had reached his parent's driveway. The button to open the gate didn't work, and the driveway lights were out, but that was only because the power grid had failed six weeks ago. No reason to think his parents weren't hiding inside the unlit property.

*I know they're in there.*

He hopped the gate and started up the drive, staring up at the bedroom windows. The curtains were drawn over each one.

*Nice thinking, Dad. Keep out of sight.*

The urge to shout out had taken over him, but he knew he'd only got there in one piece by stealth. Being loud and stupid now could attract attention and get him killed. Demons occupied every street in the town, and Smithy had needed to crawl beneath vehicles or jump inside wheelie bins to hide. He'd never known he'd such a talent for sneaking, but he made it four miles across town without a single demon detecting him. Still, he wasn't about to risk his life now by shouting for his parents.

He crept up to the front door and tried the wrought-iron handle. It didn't budge. That was okay, because he knew other ways into the home he had grown up in. He went to the side of the house, where there was a white-painted wooden gate. He tiptoed against it and craned his arm over the top. A moment's fumbling was all it took for him to lift the catch on the other side.

The small courtyard inside was where his mum smoked her cigarettes, and he was relieved to see a large terracotta plant pot full of water and fag butts. Even in the apocalypse, his mum had refused to smoke in the house. His stomach began to flip, though, when he saw his childhood home dark and lifeless. What was making him truly anxious was the fact that, any moment now, he would find out whether his parents were alive or dead.

The back door was unlocked as he assumed it would be. His parents rarely locked it when they were home. It led into a small utility room where an ancient washing machine stood next to a brand-new dryer. The old dryer had packed up several years ago, but the washer was seemingly immortal. The utility room abutted the house's spacious kitchen. The kitchen was where Smithy headed. Inside, he found both of his parents pasted across the tiles, limbs taken off and scattered on the counters. His father's head was sitting on top of the Aga.

Smithy fell sideways against his mum's antique china cabinet and threw up, the entire contents of his stomach spilling on the floor. He heaved until only bile stung his mouth.

His parents... His parents were dead.

*Mum and Dad.*

He couldn't stay in this room, couldn't see them like this. No. Holding his mouth, he staggering around their remains and headed into the dining room, where he promptly threw up. The horror only increased. Both his brothers were dead too. Mike was sprawled against the wall with his dry guts tumbling out. There was a cricket bat in his hand, but the lack of blood on it showed he had never stood a chance. Joey was slumped over the walnut dining table, legs splayed to the point where his pelvis had split apart. A pool of blood had dried beneath him on the dark wood.

What the hell had happened? The demons had clearly attacked, but beyond that Smithy would never know. The only clue was a broken window in the billiards room where the monsters must have got in.

*Got in and killed my family.*

*But I survived. Why?*

Smithy was alive because he hadn't come home. Instead of doing as his brothers had, and making his way back to Mum and Dad, he had cowered in his flat, waiting for the whole thing to blow over. His parents must have died wondering where he was – wondering why only two of their three sons had come home.

*I should have been here. I could have done something.*

But he knew he would only have died with them. Yet that

seemed better than being alive. Now he was alone – utterly and completely. Despite his tiredness, he hadn't been able to bear sleeping in the house, so he had set out into the night and walked until dawn.

Now, months later, he was no longer walking but running. Running through the night on battered legs. But for what? What was the point?

*It's all over. I'm only delaying my death.*

Smithy slowed his run to a jog. Then he didn't even jog. He ambled without caring. Frankie and the other demon might come upon him at any moment, but there was a relief in not fighting any more. Eventually, he stopped altogether. He found a sideways-growing tree and collapsed against its thick, twisting roots. There he waited. If the demons wanted this world, they could have it. All it had to offer was suffering.

An hour passed and his Seiko told him it was past midnight. An apt time to die, and he could sense his fate was due to arrive. Sure enough, a demon approached through the trees.

*A little more pain and then I can rest. Maybe I'll see my parents again. I can tell them I'm sorry.*

The demon crept out of the bushes and stared at Smithy beneath drooping eyelids. It approached cautiously, slinking like a cat. Close enough to pounce, it stopped and stared. "I found you."

"Yes," said Smithy flatly. "Get it over with."

The demon tilted its head and frowned. "We must go. Quickly, we must go. Before bad ones come."

Now it was Smithy who was frowning. "Huh?"

"My friend, Aymun, gave his life to save you. You must live, or he died for nothing. I run when you run. If I stay they would harm me. Hurt David."

Smithy stood from the tree root and glanced around. It felt like a trick, when all he wanted was a straightforward death. Why did they have to toy with him? "What do you want?"

"To help. We must go from here."

"Where? Where is there to go?"

The demon shrugged, a very human gesture. "Somewhere."

"Somewhere? Oh, and here was me thinking you didn't have a plan."

"No plan. Just a name. David. Now come. There are other alive people. Have seen them."

"What? Where?"

"I don't remember, but in time I might. Come, and David will think hard. Try to remember castle in forest with many people."

Smithy couldn't believe it, but for the second time this week, he was about to trust a demon. "Okay, David. I'm Smithy. Let's get the hell out of here."

"David dislike Hell, but yes, let us go."

Man and demon ran deeper into the woods.

---

Night fell and provided an advantage. Mass, Addy, and London were able to sneak right up to the edge of the farm and set themselves up on top of a sloping hill. Addy had pulled the nail out of her face now, but London's hand was in a bad way, shorn almost in two by a chunk of steel. Despite his toughness, the wound clearly tormented him, so much so that he had no hope of holding his shotgun and firing it accurately. Fortunately, Addy and Mass were in full fighting condition.

The farm appeared abandoned, but telltale signs told otherwise. Shadows flittered across the windows, revealing watchful guards, while several firepits told of regular campfires. The biggest reveal, however, was the long white bus parked inside a barn nearby. This was the place. These were the people who had taken Gross and Tusk.

Gemma's people.

But there was no sign of Gross and Tusk. Were they inside the farmhouse? The greystone building rose three storeys high. The kind of place Mass had never stepped foot in before the apocalypse, and far removed from the terraces and tower blocks he was used to. His world had opened up in the last year, all while he had lost everything he knew. It was as though the person he'd been for twenty years was a dream, and this was him finally waking up to reality. Hunting monsters and men through the British countryside.

"What's the plan?" asked London, cradling his hand against his chest. "We have no idea how many there might be. We should come back with more men."

"We don't have any vehicles," Addy snapped. "It would take us the entire night to get back to Portsmouth. Gross might not have that long. And who knows what happened to Tox and the others."

London nodded. He understood the argument. So did Mass. This might be a suicide mission, but they had no choice. The Urban Vampires weren't police officers or soldiers. They were a gang. And any gang worth its salt never backed down from a fight.

"We can't win a firefight," said Mass, "so I'll try to get in and out without being seen. If I can get to Gross and the others without raising the alarm, we can come back and wipe these bastards out. Addy, if they spot me, you know what to do – bring the thunder."

Addy turned and dragged the LMG around to her side. Before leaving, they had gone back to retrieve it from the top of the toilet block. They had about three hundred rounds, which was nothing really, but if Addy made them count, she could give Mass an opening to get the hell out of there. He also intended to put Honeywell's shotgun to good use.

*I can't believe he's gone. He should have fallen in battle, not because of a dirty trick.*

London repositioned himself on his elbow, wincing in pain as he knocked his ruined left hand. "I guess this is it," he said. "It's been an honour that I hope continues beyond tonight."

Mass patted the man on the back. "If we die tonight, it just means we'll be kicking demon arse in Hell tomorrow."

"These aren't demons we're about to face," said Addy. "They're people. I... I haven't had to kill people before. Can't say I like the thought."

"Then I'll do my best not to get caught. I trust you to do whatever you need to do."

Addy gave him a nod.

And then he was gone.

He clambered down the hill towards the farm, the moon at his back helping him stay hidden. The barn was the nearest structure and that was where he headed. If he didn't stay concealed, there was no chance this would work. The bus parked inside the barn was large, more like a luxury coach than anything municipal. Large black lettering marked the side: **HUMANISTIC RELIEF FOUNDATION.** Had it belonged to some kind of charity? Stolen? Or were these people charity workers gone bad? He doubted it.

What was the point of all this? What did Gemma and her group want? The woman had murdered half a dozen people who had only been trying to help.

Mass tried the coach's door but found it locked. He'd thought maybe he could find some intel on board, but he was undeterred by the setback. He crept out of the barn and moved towards the main farmhouse. If Gross and the others were being held on the upper floor, it would be difficult to get to them without being seen. No turning back though. He would kill a hundred people if he had to. That was the worth of an Urban Vampire.

Mass crept around to the back of the house, searching for a way in. Eventually he found a back door with a tiny windowpane that allowed him to see inside. Although dark, it appeared deserted and the door was unlocked. He began to fear that the place might be abandoned.

*No, there were people in the windows. I know what I saw.*

Speaking of the windows, they had been boarded up from the inside with only slight gaps at the top remaining. *Somebody had made this place secure.* Furthermore, the kitchen itself was well-stocked with supplies. Tin cans, pasta, and various other non-perishables were piled up on the counters. People lived here.

Mass kept low as he moved through the kitchen, holding his shotgun at the ready. He knew if he fired it then the jig was up, so the goal was to remain undetected. Two men occupied the adjacent room, sat around a dining table playing cards by candlelight. One was chubby and white while the other was tall, lean, and Asian, with a long black beard. Neither saw Mass as he crept into the corner of the room. The problem was how to creep past them into the house's front reception. The darkness would help, and the candles might make the two men blind to what lay beyond the circle of light they cast. All the same, Mass needed to stay absolutely silent in an unlit, unfamiliar room.

Carefully, he tucked the shotgun under his arm and got down on his knees. Holding his breath, he began to crawl. The floor was tiled, which made the journey hard on the knees. It also made his boots a danger as his toecaps struck the tiles softly with every movement. Mass paused. His heart was beating rapidly, not because he two men in the room frightened him, but because he knew Gross, Tox, Tusk and the others were relying on him getting through the house unseen.

The reception beyond the dining room was lit by more candles, which meant he would be visible once he passed into it. If the men happened to look his way... He watched them playing cards, waiting for the right moment. The white man had just lost a hand, sliding over a bundle of notes with a disgruntled moan. "I thought it was illegal for Muslims to gamble," he said, "so how come you're the best poker player I know?"

The darker-skinned man chuckled. "This isn't gambling. Money has no worth any more. It's just paper."

"So it would be illegal for you to bet with anything of value?"

"Not illegal, just frowned upon. For me, wiping the floor with you is enough of a thrill."

"You're a cocky prick, Imran, you know that?"

"It's not cockiness if you win. Okay, shuffle."

Mass saw the two men divide the cards and begin shuffling them. It meant their eyes were fixed downwards, focused on what they were doing. Mass slipped into the next room and held his breath.

The hall was empty, but voices came from what Mass assumed was a lounge. Benign chit-chat. It seemed unlikely Gross would be inside.

*He must be upstairs. Damn it. If I get seen, escaping will be impossible. What choice do I have?*

Mass located the staircase and crept upwards. The old panels creaked, and after each step he paused, waiting to see if he'd been discovered. Eventually, he found himself on the upstairs landing, still undetected. Stealth wasn't his forte, but he was pulling it off so far.

*Maybe this can actually work.*

Now fully ensconced in enemy territory, Mass raised Honeywell's shotgun. He still hoped not to fire it, but he was more than ready. More voices floated out onto the landing, but not ones as laid-back as downstairs. The tone of this conversation was adversarial – an interrogation. Mass moved up beside a door and listened.

"How many soldiers in Portsmouth? Where are you finding new supplies?"

"Piss off. There's enough people in Portsmouth to wipe you idiots off the map. By the time we're—"

It had been Gross talking, but a meaty slap interrupted his words. These people were interrogating him, but why? What did they want? If it was intel on Portsmouth, they were biting off more than they could chew. Even if the farmhouse was chock-a-block with people, there couldn't be more than twenty or thirty. Thirty against the thousands at Portsmouth.

"Just answer my questions. I promise you, my mission is more important than yours. I serve a higher purpose."

"You're a dead man. I ain't telling you jack shit."

"So be it. You're not here to answers questions. Tomorrow, you shall discover your own worth. Until then, you should learn to watch your mouth."

A moment of silence was broken intermittently by the scuffling of footsteps on floorboards. Gross began to swear. Then he began to scream.

They were torturing him.

Mass flinched, which caused him to bash his shotgun's barrel against the door. He froze, hands trembling, but no one inside the room seemed to hear over Gross's screaming.

Then Mass heard something to his left. Someone stared at him from down the hall.

Gemma.

The woman's eyes went wide with shock, but she recovered enough to shout out a warning. Absurdly, Mass put a finger against his lips, urging her to keep quiet, but of course she had no interest in obeying his commands. She was the enemy.

"Luan, Michael! There's someone in the house."

Mass hissed with frustration. He was fucked. The only thing he could do now was go down fighting. He raised his shotgun at

Gemma and pulled the trigger. She leapt out of the way just as a chunk of wall exploded. He'd missed.

*Shit on it!*

A door opened further along the hallway and an Asian man rushed out with a handgun. Mass pulled the second trigger on his shotgun and put a hole in the man's torso. Then the door right beside Mass opened, and he had to leap out of the way as someone came at him with a bloodstained knife. The blade sliced at Mass's neck, but he ducked and struck his attacker's knee with the butt of his shotgun. The man hit the ground, howling. Then Mass hurried backwards, desperately trying to load another pair of cartridges into his shotgun. Usually, he would have a line of Urban Vampires covering him while he reloaded, but now, alone in the enemy's house, the low-capacity shotgun was a liability.

He fumbled the second shell and cursed, his hands trembling. No time to retrieve the ammo, so he made use of the single cartridge he had inserted successfully and lifted the shotgun to find another target. Another Asian man, more demonic than human, came raging down the hallway. He had a milky left eye and an ugly hate-filled face. Mass aimed for that wicked face but didn't have time to pull the trigger. The milky-eyed man batted the shotgun aside and threw Mass against the wall. He raised an arm that ended in a nasty steel hook, and with a snarl he demanded, "Who are you, trespasser?"

"You have my friends. I came to get them."

That milky eye bore into Mass as a smile crept across his face. "Your friends are not leaving here, but you are free to join them in the morning."

Mass screamed as the man slashed at his throat with his hook. Blood cascaded over his shoulder as he found himself tumbling backwards into a nearby room. He collapsed against the worn carpet, right at Gross's feet. Gross stared at him miserably, his face a twisted clown's mug. His mouth had been sliced open at the corners and his eyes were wide and full of terror. He was clearly shocked to see Mass, but he could do nothing to help because he was tied to a chair.

The hook-handed man entered the room. "There are bandages

over there," he said. "If you're still alive in the morning, you and your friends shall get to see the sun."

Mass clutched his bleeding throat and stared in disbelief. The door closed and a bolt sounded. He was trapped inside. And he was dying.

# CHAPTER SIX

MADDY WAS DRUNK, which was a beautiful feeling. If the end of the world wasn't a good time to get pissed, there would never be one. Wickstaff and Thomas looked a little the worse for wear, but Thomas clearly had the larger constitution of the three of them. Had he possessed a personal supply of booze these last eight months? It wouldn't be a surprise.

"I have to admit, Amanda," said Thomas, now on a first-name basis, "you have survived against impossible odds here. The things you've described... You're a formidable woman."

Wickstaff raised her glass in salute. "Thank you, Henry. It's been one long trial, I won't lie, and it's good to have someone else to lend a hand."

Thomas sipped his brandy and appeared thoughtful for a moment, then he looked at Maddy. "What did you do before all this? You already told me you weren't in the military."

"I was a paramedic."

"A noble vocation. I can see why Amanda thinks so highly of you. It's not everybody who could stand up to a general like you did me."

"I had a leader to bring out the best in me." She smiled at Wickstaff, who seemed abashed by the compliment.

General Thomas sniffed. "Yes, I'm quite aware of the hero

worship that goes on here in Portsmouth. I hope, in time, I can inspire such confidence in you too."

Maddy hadn't meant the comment to be a petty jab, so she tried to backtrack. "I suppose we've survived so much here that it feels impossible for anyone else to understand. I forget things are the same everywhere."

Thomas nodded slowly, seriously. "There's nary a corner of the Earth not soaked in blood. The things soldiers used to fear were random IEDs and snipers in the hills. Now those things are positively humane compared to our new threat. When we first started fighting back, regaining the territory we had lost, I led a mission to liberate an oil field and refinery in Iran. It was vital to our supply lines as our tanks were starting to splutter. The problem was, a gate had appeared there and brought a massive enemy presence along with it. We couldn't go in all guns blazing because we would risk igniting the oil and razing the place to ashes."

Wickstaff sipped her brandy and cleared her throat. "So what did you do?"

"I sent in a thousand men with nothing but rifles. I knew the demons would overrun many of them, but the oil was too important. Without our tanks, our planes... We would have been sitting ducks out there in the desert."

Maddy leant forward and put her elbows on her knees. "How many men did you lose?"

"Eight hundred and twelve."

Maddy gasped.

Thomas went on, a far-off look in his eye. "I remember walking the battlefield afterwards; it was like stepping on a carpet of flesh. The sand was red and clumped with gore. Lumps of flesh and skin were scattered all over. The demons had bitten and torn men apart like meatballs and spaghetti. The few hundred who survived were broken – wounded either psychically or mentally. One of them was so shell-shocked he wandered into the gate and closed it. And that was the end of it. The mission was a success."

Maddy shook her head. "A success?"

Thomas nodded. His eyes seemed to look right through her into the past. "We counted almost two thousand demons amongst the dead. The biggest kill ratio we'd ever seen until that point –

over two to one. It gave the remaining forces hope by showing that the monsters were less than us."

"But was it worth it?" asked Maddy. "All those soldiers..."

"The next day," said Thomas. "We refuelled our armour and pushed towards Tehran. We reduced the city to rubble. We closed several gates and killed one of the fallen. That time, we lost three hundred men. The demons lost three thousand. Without the oil, we never would have been able to take Tehran. The demons had too much cover without our tanks and missiles. Within two months, we had secured seventy per cent of Iraq while the German Confederation and other allies did their part in Syria, Turkey, Iraq, Israel, western Afghanistan. The fight is still ongoing, but we're winning. So, I'll leave you to decide whether the sacrifices were worth it."

"They were," said Wickstaff, surprising Maddy with the speed of her answer. The former general gave a shrug of apology. "Humanity needs to survive. We have to do whatever's necessary. It's the tough decisions that keep me awake at night, but it's the tough decisions that will get us through this."

Thomas nodded. "I came home because mainland Europe is going to become a consolidated superpower in the years ahead – so will the United States, Russia, and China. This war with the demons has led to the biggest land grab in history, and eventually mankind will be resurgent. Then there'll be no place left for small independent nations like ours – unless we are prepared to defend ourselves. When that time comes, Great Britain will need to stand as it always has, an unyielding bastion of freedom and compassion. We need to restore our country to the place where all are welcome, where all are protected. If we don't reclaim our lands quickly, however, there won't be enough time to gather strength. Deterrence is what will keep us safe. Great Britain must become more trouble than it's worth."

"We have a nuclear sub," said Maddy.

Thomas eyeballed her. "Really? I thought we lost both of them."

Wickstaff chuckled. "No, it's not a British vessel. It's a German sub with a German crew. They defected to us."

"You're joking? Chancellor Capri never mentioned it in his cross-command meetings."

"I'm sure he didn't. He's been rather insistent about getting it back."

"He mustn't have it!" Thomas almost shouted it. "It might be the only thing that keeps the wolves from the door. The German Confederation won't risk trying to absorb us if we can fire a nuke straight at Berlin. Amanda, you are a gem of the highest order."

She laughed. "I have my moments."

"I shall meet with this German Commander in the morning," said Thomas. "Position him in the most strategic way possible."

Wickstaff cleared her throat and stared into her glass. "That might be difficult. Commander Klein considers his submarine somewhat of a sovereign nation and has made it very clear that he will not utilise his missiles under anyone's judgement but his own. Meet him, by all means, but he won't take orders."

"And you've allowed this insubordination?"

"What do you want me to do? He's here voluntarily."

"He's enjoying our protection. I assume he comes on land and enjoys our facilities, consumes our supplies?"

Wickstaff nodded, but she seemed unashamed by the admission. "I decided a nuclear submarine with a full crew was worth feeding. Feel free to send them on their way."

"I shall do no such thing. What I will do is clarify that he is either in or out. He wants to be a sovereign nation, he can produce his own food for his own people."

Maddy noticed they were nearly at the end of the second bottle of brandy. They'd been swigging it neat for several hours now. A third bottle might kill them. The conversation might too. "Perhaps we should call it a night," she suggested. "It's early morning and we're going to feel like shit as it is."

Wickstaff and Thomas glared at one another. Were they merely drunk, or were they enemies pretending to be friends?

"Perhaps you are right," said Thomas. "We shouldn't be talking shop. Tonight was about getting to know one another, and I feel I know enough."

Wickstaff bristled. "What does that mean?"

Thomas waved her off. "I didn't mean anything by it. I only

meant I see what an accomplished leader you are, and that people are right to respect you. Don't doubt that I respect you too, Amanda. You are as strong-minded as any man I ever served with."

Maddy rolled her eyes. "Just don't expect too much from her when she's on her period."

Wickstaff grimaced, then exploded with laughter. Thomas looked unsettled for a moment, then he started cackling too. "I'll take that as my cue to leave, ladies. Oh, hang on, this is my office, isn't it?"

Wickstaff chuckled. "It is."

"Okay, well, bugger off then, the two of you. And leave the other bottle of brandy, Maddy. We never even opened it. I feel positively ashamed."

Wickstaff stood. She wobbled for a moment, then was straight and steady. She pulled Maddy up by her arm and dragged her out of the office. Maddy's head was spinning like a hula hoop. "There's a good chance I might puke," she said.

Wickstaff rubbed her back. "Have a good lie-in and you'll be right as rain."

"You don't mind if I sleep in?"

"Of course not. I shall be."

They exited the port authority building into the salty night air. Thomas's guards watched from various perches, but all was quiet. You could hear the sound of the waves. It must have been three in the morning.

"W-What do you think of Thomas?" asked Maddy in a drunken whisper. "I can't make up my mind."

Wickstaff sighed. "He's a good man, but whether he's good for Portsmouth is another question entirely. We are not a professional army surrounded by desert; we are a ragtag group of survivors fighting for tomorrow. I fear some won't take to Thomas's rigid command style. That's not his fault, it's just who he is, but that's the problem with assuming command rather than rising to it. One can never guarantee a good fit. Anyway, it's time for bed, Maddy. Let's save tomorrow's headaches for tomorrow, shall we? Whatever happens, Portsmouth isn't in any imminent danger.

"So, you're telling me the main villain, the monster behind all of this, is trapped inside your friend who's a vampire? And you're a demon who was originally a young boy from thousands of years ago?"

The demon – apparently named David – had a strange way of speaking. Sometimes he hissed for no reason. He seemed adamant about what he was saying though. "Crimolok is one of God's three eldest sons. Very bad. Stuck inside Vamps."

Smithy nodded. There was no point doubting the demon after all that had happened. Anything was clearly possible. In fact, it was a kind of comforting that all this hell might be for a reason, if only because of the ego of some demigod named Crimolok. Better than billions dying for nothing at all.

Smithy and the diminutive demon had fled through the woods until they'd made it out into some fields. There was no way of knowing where Frankie and the other demon were, but Smithy finally started to feel a little safer. For months he had coped with the apocalypse better than he would ever have thought, but now he felt as vulnerable as he had in those early days. The horror never stayed static. It evolved. The early frenetic assault had given way to a systematic extermination followed by a lull. Perhaps that lull was ending, because he'd been attacked by two demons in a single day. A third scampered along beside him.

"I need to sleep," said Smithy. His Seiko told him it was three in the morning.

"I sleep too."

"I thought demons didn't have to sleep."

"Don't have to. Want to. When sleep, David dream. Dream of before."

"When you were alive?"

David nodded.

"We should try to find some shelter. It's not safe to be out in the open like this. It'll be light soon and we don't want to be exposed."

David peered up at him quizzically. "That demon wanted to kill you?"

Smithy shrugged. "That's what demons do, right? Frankie

seemed okay at first, a bit like you – confused but friendly. Then he turned."

David scratched at his arm, and a chunk of flesh sloughed away. The wound released a smell, but the demon didn't seem to notice. "Crimolok control Hell, but when become trapped inside friend, Vamps, he lose connection. Now, David think he only influence demons close. Only demons that accept him. Other demons confused and... afraid."

Smithy raised an eyebrow and tried to consider things from a different point of view. "It must be pretty shit being a demon. Were you in Hell?"

David lowered his head towards the silvery, moonlit grass. "Yes."

Smithy sensed he was asking painful questions, but how often did you get to question someone who actually knew about life after death? "Do you... do you remember any of it?"

"Flashes. Waves. Memories. Empty place. Forever place. There is pain too, but emptiness is what makes lose self. Forever of nothing."

Smithy shivered. "Is there a Heaven too?"

David shrugged. "You ask about place never been. Wish to been."

"I'm sorry. I shouldn't pry. I appreciate you and your friend saving me. You're obviously a good demon, David."

"My friend's name was Aymun. Brave warrior. I miss already."

"I've lost people too. The worst part about it is— Hey, wait! Tell me I'm not imagining things."

David squinted. His eyes glinted bright white like a wolf's. "Buildings?"

Smithy could only make out shapes, but the moon was full, and it cast enough light to show a familiar outline. "I think it's a farm. I can see barns and a house."

"We sleep inside house tonight. Would be nice, yes?"

"Houses usually have bodies, and I'm too tired to be dealing with that right now. Maybe we can break into one of the barns and sleep there. We can find somewhere better tomorrow night when we head north to find this group of survivors you mentioned.

Shouldn't be hard to find a castle in the forest, right? Not like there're hundreds of the things lying around."

"Okay," said David. "We sleep in barn. Walk tomorrow."

Smithy considered the time and corrected the demon. "I think you mean later today. Although, after all I've been through, I might sleep a full twenty-four hours."

They started down a sloping field towards the distant farm. Smithy wondered, for a moment, whether anyone was there. He'd scavenged a dozen farmhouses during the last few months, and he always held a hope of finding a family alive and living off the land. All he ever found though was bodies. Farming families had been determined to live and die on their land, no matter the cost.

Once they were halfway down the slope, it became clear they were indeed approaching a farm. They even passed an old tractor abandoned in the field. Weeds grew around it in place of whatever crops had originally been planted. Startled movement inside suggested rats, or something bigger.

A pair of barns rose ahead, and Smithy visited the nearest. The sally port was open, and a mountain of rotting hay lay inside. Fortunately, there was also a rack of body warmers meant for horses, which Smithy decided to use as a sheet and mattress. They were musty, but there were worse stenches to endure nowadays. He and David climbed the hay mountain and made beds towards the back beneath the sloping rafters. No one would see them from below. They were hidden. Safe.

Smithy rolled himself up in the body warmers and felt his eyelids clamping shut immediately. "Hey, Dave," he muttered, "I know you're a good demon, but don't eat me or anything while I'm asleep, okay?"

David gasped. "I would never."

"I'm kidding. See you when I wake up, okay?"

"Sleep good, Smithy. I sleep too. Then we walk."

Smithy tried to nod but his head was too heavy. *Yes*, he thought, *tomorrow we walk, searching for a castle in the forest with an army of survivors. What a lovely dream to have.*

Mass awoke on the floor. He opened his eyes and his vision spun. His stomach turned over and over. He heard a voice – "Y-You're alive?" – and glanced up to see Gross staring at him. He was still tied to a chair and blood stained his naked chest and most of the floor. Mass didn't know where it had all come from.

Then he remembered being cut. His throat bleeding.

He looked around and saw piles of bandages. He raised a hand to his throat and felt a clump of bandages there too. Somehow he had stopped himself from bleeding to death.

"I thought for sure you'd bled out," said Gross. His words were a quiet mutter as his mouth had been sliced wide open. He had to be careful to only part his lips a tiny amount with each word. "You stemmed most of it, but I still didn't have much hope. You've been out a few hours. Where are the rest of the guys?"

Mass didn't know if he could speak, so it was a surprise when he managed it more or less normally. "They... They're dead. There was an injured man with a bomb strapped to his waist. A trap."

"Fuck!" Gross groaned as his mouth parted slightly. More quietly, he swore again. "Fuck it! Addy!"

"No, not Addy. Addy's alive. London too. They're outside, set up on a hill. Tox and a couple of guys came here separately before the bomb went off. They could still be alive too."

Gross sighed. "We're still in the game."

"Barely. We've lost half-a-dozen of our guys. And Honeywell."

"We lost Tusk too. He tried to make a run for it when they marched us off the coach. His body is probably still out there somewhere." Gross gritted his teeth and looked away, fighting tears.

Mass sat up. When the hook-handed bastard had cut him, he must have missed the jugular – or the artery or whatever – and just given him a nasty gash in the meat of his neck. He'd evidently lost a lot of blood, but he wasn't dying. In fact, other than feeling woozy, he didn't feel that bad. It was time to get the fuck out of there. "We need to search for Tox and the others. That bitch Gemma probably led them into an ambush." He shook his head in anger. "She's gonna pay for this."

Gross tugged at the ropes around his arms. "Why are they doing this, man? What are they trying to achieve?

"I heard them asking you about Portsmouth. Seems like they want to attack us or something."

"They'd have to be crazy. There can't be more than twenty guys here. The guy with the hook is leader. He kept going on about finishing what Allah had started."

"Bloody Allah. Will we ever be free of fucking religion?"

Gross rolled his eyes. "I suppose demons arriving from Hell kind of reinforces the whole Heaven and Earth thing. Mass, can you get me out of this goddamn chair, man?"

"Let me try." He stood and went behind the chair. For a moment, his vision blurred, but he managed to focus on the knot. It was well tied, but fortunately his captors weren't the cautious type and hadn't checked him for weapons. He could still feel the penknife he kept in the thigh pocket of his baggy jeans. It wasn't a weapon he could defend himself with, but it would be just fine for cutting through ropes. "Hold still, mate."

As soon as the ropes gave, Gross pulled his arms forward and moaned in pain. Mass had to hiss at him to be quiet. "Give me a break," he said. "My arms have been wrapped around this goddamn chair for hours."

Mass got to work on the ropes around Gross's legs. "If they hear us, you'll have to fight them with your legs tied together, so bite your lip."

"Not funny, man."

Mass looked up at Gross's ruined mouth and grimaced. "Sorry, man."

"Ladies like scars, huh?"

"I'm sure Addy will love it."

The comment caught Gross by surprise and his eyes went wide. "What, why would you say—"

"Easy, man. We can discuss you and Addy later. Let's focus on our actual problems right now. There, you're free. Now we have to escape with only a penknife between us."

Gross rubbed his ankles and groaned again. "You know kung fu, right?"

"Kung fu's for show-offs. Krav Maga is what the professionals use."

"Great, so you know Krav Maga?"

"I think you just have to elbow people a lot. Come on, we can do this."

Mass tried the door. It was locked. He swore under his breath, but he wasn't beaten yet. It was just a normal interior handle with a keyhole, not the latest in apocalyptic security. He took his penknife and started unscrewing one of the screws holding the handle against the frame. It was a fiddly task and took a minute, but then he moved onto the others. Eventually, he removed the handle from the door.

"Great," said Gross. "What do we do now?"

Mass wasn't sure, but he could see the mechanism of the door now, and he reached his thick fingers inside and started twisting at the various bits of metal. It didn't take much pressure for him to feel something *click*.

"You got it," said Gross. "Nice one."

Mass tried pulling on the door, and it slipped the catch and began to open. They were out.

But not yet free.

Mass crouched and moved into the hallway. He whispered for Gross to follow, and together the two of them crept across the landing. It was quiet – no chatting voices or the heavy breathing of sleepy guards. They had been left unattended. "Don't these people have any concern about us escaping?" said Mass. "There's not a single guard."

"Maybe they assumed you'd die – and *I* was tied to a chair."

"Still, it ain't clever, and it don't feel right."

Gross paused at the stairwell's bannister and looked at Mass. "You're right. Even more reason to hurry up and get out."

They started down the creaky wooden staircase but, despite the noise, no one came. Even when they reached the downstairs reception, the house remained empty.

"I don't like this," said Mass. "Where are all the guys from last night?"

Gross fingered the bloody cuts on his face. "Gone, I hope. That hook-handed bastard is a nutcase."

"We're all nutcases now. It's the only way to survive."

They passed into the dining room and Mass noted the pack of cards stacked neatly on the table. Half-melted candles took up several surfaces, and candles were not something you abandoned. They were too useful. Like the rest of the house, the kitchen was deserted too. Mass made straight for the drawer beside the sink and searched for the biggest knife he could find. He handed Gross a steak knife and took a slightly longer paring knife for himself. They were more than capable of killing someone with the blades, but it wasn't ideal. Where were the guns they'd been carrying? Honeywell's shotgun?

Gross raised an eyebrow. "Maybe they went to the shops."

Mass moved towards the back door and tried to peer out, but the windows were boarded up. "Did you hear any LMG fire last night? I didn't hear Addy engage, but I was unconscious. Did you hear any gunfire?"

"I heard nothing after they caught you."

"Then Addy could still be out on the hill, or heading back to get help."

"Or they caught her," said Gross angrily, which caused his slashed mouth to spread. He fingered his wounds and winced. "If they hurt her…"

Mass grabbed his friend by the back of the head and looked at him. "She's fine, Gross. I know it. If they had come for her, she would have fired that LMG. She would have… Hey, why didn't you get a shot off back at the car park? You only sent up a flair."

"Because I was an idiot. I heard a woman screaming for help so I jumped down from the roof and headed to the road. Tusk tried to stop me but ended up chasing after me. We found a blonde woman lying at the side of the road, clutching her ankle. I thought she'd fallen, but as soon as I made it over there to help, a bunch of guys exploded out of the hedges with shotguns and pistols. I had no choice but to drop my weapon. Tusk couldn't do anything or they would have gunned him down too. Next thing we know, they're bundling us onto a coach. I managed to pop a flare, but they beat Tusk half to death for it so I behaved from then on. Wish I hadn't sent up that flare. If you guys hadn't come they wouldn't have ambushed everyone. I think it was only our supplies they were interested in, but they know how to handle themselves."

Mass nodded. "They got it all. Fuck knows how many people

they've robbed in the past, how many survivors they've killed. We found a bunch of people in the fields, burned alive."

"We need to stop these fuckers. We can't be killing ourselves any more. We're barely hanging on as it is."

"Come on, let's go."

They headed to the back door, and it opened easily. Mass almost felt like he was being allowed to escape. It was possible his captors assumed he was dead, as it was still a surprise to him that he wasn't. If he'd been a cat, he would have used up several lives not bleeding to death. As he yanked on the door handle and stepped outside, he wondered if he had enough lives to get him out of this.

The weather lately had been mild, but this morning was chilly. The day was young, and a gloomy grey clung to the rolling fields surrounding the farm. A dozen people knelt on blankets in the gravelly courtyard, but they didn't notice Mass and Gross exiting. Only one man faced them, and he grinned a brown-toothed smile. "Ah, you have joined us for morning prayer," he said. "Your piety is to be commended."

The kneeling men looked back and then jumped to their feet. Several pulled handguns from the folds of their clothing while others only scowled. None of them spoke, yet all acted in unison. A well-trained group of survivors.

The hook-handed man stepped forward, showing no fear of their knives. He studied the bandages around Mass's throat and appeared impressed. "You survived your wounds. Allah wishes you to live."

"Fuck Allah."

"Yeah," said Gross, "and your mother."

"Words are not weapons," said the hook-handed man. "You waste breath assuming they have power. Actions are what define a man."

"Then I'll fuck your mother personally," said Gross.

"We're leaving," said Mass, "and unless you want trouble from Portsmouth, you'll let us go about our business."

"Your Babylon is no threat. The things I fear are beyond your comprehension, so cease your posturing. If you attempt violence, you shall be shot. If you attempt to flee, you shall be shot. You are my prisoners, but I do not need bars to hold you."

Mass frowned. "What, so we're like minimum security inmates? You'll give us the run of the garden so long as we eat our meals and go to bed on time. Why? Why bother capturing us?"

"Because you are warriors, and warriors deserve to choose their fates."

"Sorted then. We choose to leave."

The hook-handed man smirked. His odour was foul, even from three feet away. "Yes, you have that option, but as I said, if you flee you shall be shot. Nonetheless, the choice is yours."

"So what then?" Gross demanded. Fresh blood trickled from his cut cheeks. "What the fuck do you people want?"

The hook-handed man turned, so he was addressing his people as he talked. "To reclaim the Earth. To start again. To finish what the demons started. Allah's second great flood. The flood of flesh and blood."

His people cheered and prayed. A lot of noise.

"The Reclamation," said Mass. "That's what you people call yourselves, isn't it?"

The hook-handed man turned back to face Mass fully. "No, the Reclamation is the name of our mission. Allow me to demonstrate our glorious purpose to you first hand. Come."

Mass and Gross looked at one another. They didn't move.

The hook-handed man sighed. "Come with me or die here. Once again, your choice."

A staccato of clicks as weapons cocked. Mass studied the crowd briefly and saw the two men who had been playing poker. No women were present, and only a third of the men were white. Had they been praying to Mecca? Did they still believe in that rubbish? God – or Allah – wasn't listening; didn't they get it?

Mass gave Gross a nudge, and the two of them followed the hook-handed man, who led them around the side of the building and into a paddock beyond. Instead of horses, the small fenced-off paddock was filled with graves. A fresh one had been dug. A blanket-covered body lay next to it.

"The man you killed last night," the hook-handed man explained. "He shall receive his reward in the next life, as will all those who dedicate themselves to the mission."

Mass still didn't get it. "The mission to do what? Side with the demons?"

"The demons are not our allies. They are a mere device. A punishment upon the wicked delivered *by* the wicked. Our mission is simply to prevent interference in Allah's will."

"Interference? People trying not to die is an offence to you? You're an idiot."

The man sneered, flashing his crumbling brown teeth. "If the last year has shown us anything, it is that we are all idiots. We know nothing but our own sin and have been sentenced for it. Only a few will receive the duty of living on and reforming the Holy Kingdom. That is why—"

Mass cut the guy off with a yawn. He then shook his head like he was fighting to stay awake. "I know you said words don't have power, mate, but yours are putting me to sleep. You're just another religious nut – full of the same old shit. Power is the only thing you're interested in, and you want people to follow you so you don't have to admit what a worthless bag of shit you are." Despite the hook-handed man's assertion that insults couldn't harm him, Mass detected a hint of irritation on his face. His rheumy left eye twitched. Mass smirked and kept on. "I can smell your ego from here, mate. It's as big as your cock is small."

The hook-handed man breathed out and forced a smile to his face. "Soon we shall see what you are made of. Let us pray it is more than hollow words."

Gross elbowed Mass and whispered, "You're going to get us killed."

"We're dead, anyway. Might as well have a little fun."

Gross sighed.

They headed through the paddock and into a hedge-lined field. Another half-dozen strangers milled about, but Gemma was the only woman. She held a deadly 12-gauge that must have once been military issue. When she saw Mass and Gross arrive, she waved a hand smugly as if they were old friends.

A trio of steel shipping containers took up most of the small field and had been converted into living space. Sad-looking women sat inside on plastic chairs or on the floor, performing various tasks like sewing or cleaning. Many of them sported bruised cheeks and arms. Mass's biceps tensed and his fists clenched by themselves. Gemma and the men outside the containers had weapons – obviously there to guard the women. If he tried anything, they would shoot him, but it still took everything not to grab the hook-handed bastard by the throat.

Gross exchanged a look with Mass suggesting he was as sickened as he was. The sight of the beaten women made Mass think about Addy. There was no evidence she'd been captured, but where was she?

*Are you out there, Addy? If you are, I hope you have a plan.*

Cows, pigs, donkeys, and sheep nosed at the grass in the adjoining fields, but the thing that captured Mass's attention next was a line of three people kneeling by the nearby fences. Bags covered their heads, and a massive hole had been dug out in front of them the size of a small swimming pool. A single guard stood behind them with a ball-peen hammer.

Gemma came to greet the hook-handed man. "*As-salāmu 'alaykum.*"

The hook-handed man nodded. "*Wa 'alaykumu s-salām.* You deserve a rest after last night's struggles, Gemma. Your passion encourages us all."

"I serve the Reclamation with my every breath."

"Are the offerings ready?"

"Yes, they are ready to be reclaimed."

"Excellent."

Mass eyeballed Gemma and considered the ways he could kill her before catching a bullet. Shoving his paring knife into her eye was the leading option. It was absurd that they had allowed him to keep his weapon, and he had even forgotten he was holding it. Should he go down fighting? Yes. Every time, yes. The question was when to *start* fighting.

The three men kneeling on the other side of the hole had their hoods removed. As Mass had feared, it was Tox and the two men who had gone with him to follow Gemma yesterday. With their eyes cast downwards, they began to moan.

Mass stepped forward to see what was inside the pit, and was shocked by what he saw. It was filled with demons. The kind that resembled twisted chimpanzees. The deadliest of all the infernal creatures on Earth.

"Let my people go," Mass demanded.

"I found them unconscious in this very field," said the hook-handed man, pointing to the demons. "It was at that moment I understood what Allah demanded of me. These beasts were sent to me by him, for I was to become a shepherd. Mankind has grown beyond its limits and must be pared back, but in our arrogance we resisted the cull. People fought back, refused to give up. The demons were sent as a cleansing tide, but mankind found hiding spots among the rock pools. The demons alone were not enough to complete Allah's task. They needed assistance."

Mass sneered. "You're off your head, mate. Why are these idiots even following you? Zippy and Bungle speak more sense than you."

"They follow me because they have faith. Faith that we are destined to rebuild Allah's kingdom, A righteous place full of beauty and devotion. I was the first to go into this pit after the demons woke up." He lifted his hook and loosened the straps holding it in place, revealing an unsightly stump. The flesh was puckered and badly knitted, but the wound patterns resembled bite marks. "I left a hand in this pit, but I gained a most holy mission. I am to test the sinners and lead the righteous."

"You're testing people by throwing them in a pit full of monsters," said Mass, staring down at the writhing mass of pale, pock-marked flesh. "Very fucking holy. It's murder, and you'll pay for it. You can have faith in that."

The hook-handed man stepped closer, looking Mass right in the eye. He was close enough now to stab, but Mass couldn't summon his arm to do the deed. He wasn't done listening. "People thought God was kind and forgiving, but that only proves their arrogance. God is the most almighty of beings and we are mere ants beneath His feet. Allow me to demonstrate."

Sensing the talking was over, Mass reached for the hook-handed man and decided now was the time to stab him in the face.

Gemma fired her shotgun.

Gross crumpled to the grass.

Mass stopped reaching out and gawped at the bloody hole in Gross's chest. "You fuckers! You fucking monsters! I'll kill y—"

The hook-handed man swiped his hook through the air and struck Mass in the temple with the blunt side. He fell to the ground beside Gross, his vision exploding with stars.

The hook-handed man walked away, barking orders. "Throw them in."

## CHAPTER SEVEN

Smithy knew it was early, which was why he tried hard to go back to sleep. Dawn had just arrived, which meant he had got two or three hours sleep max. After last night's ordeal, he needed more than that. Try as he might, though, he couldn't nod off. The birds were in full chorus and he could even hear the mooing of cows. Most annoyingly, the little demon next to him snored like a motherfucker.

"Hey, Dave! Wake up."

David opened his eyes immediately. Impressive, considering how deeply he'd been sleeping. "He is near."

"What?"

The demon hopped up into a crouch. "Crimolok is near. Buzzing in head, sending war cry to kill."

Smithy rubbed the fuzziness from his eyes. "That don't sound good. If you can hear him, other demons can too, right?"

David nodded. His demonic eyes were somehow sad and vulnerable – a pit bull with the heart of a poodle. "Must go. Quickly."

"All right, Dave, I hear you. Is there time to check the farm for food? Do we have that long?"

David squinted as if accessing the inside of his own brain. "Small time."

"We best hurry then. Nothing like a cold morning on two

hours' sleep to make an empty stomach feel worse." Smithy kicked the musty horse blankets away and shuffled on his butt along the hay. The rotting fodder turned to mush between his fingers, but he managed to descend without sinking or breaking his wrists. David, light as a feather, scampered down with ease, although Smithy noticed the demon had left an ear behind in the hay. It fell off as though it'd been attached with putty. Knowing little about demonic health-matters, Smithy left the grisly fact unmentioned.

The door to the barn was ajar, allowing in a slice of daylight that illuminated a thin wedge on the concrete floor. When a shadow moved across the gap, Smithy froze, but he failed to stop himself from swearing. "Shit!"

The shadow outside paused, blotting out the wedge of light on the ground. David crouched, not readying to attack but cowering. Smithy realised he was cowering too. After last night, he had nothing left in the tank. If Frankie and Crimolok found him, then so be it.

The barn door flew open and two strangers rushed inside pointing shotguns. Smithy wheeled backwards, hands out in front of his face. "Don't shoot! Jesus, I think I pissed myself."

One of the strangers, a female, snarled at him. "Say your prayers, because I am most definitely going to fucking shoot you."

"What? Why?"

"Because *your* people have taken *my* people hostage. Because that bitch Gemma killed my friends. And because I think I'm getting my fucking period."

Smithy stared into the shotgun's angry mouth, waiting for it to roar fire and death, but it didn't. Perhaps there was still time to beg for his life. "I-I have no idea what you're talking about, I swear."

"This not right," said David. "We do not know you peoples."

The woman glanced at David and her mouth fell open. The man standing beside her gasped. He held his shotgun awkwardly as if he only had one functioning hand. As he stared at David, it looked like he might pull the trigger. "That's one of them," he muttered. "A demon."

"Demon, yes," said David. "Please, not hold against. Am friendly. Smithy sleep with me all night. He is good."

Smithy winced. "Choose better words, man."

The women thrust the shotgun at Smithy as though it was a pitchfork. "What the hell is this?" she snapped. "Some kind of interspecies relationship?"

"Demon and human same species," said David. "Just... different."

Smithy sighed. He put a hand out to David and realised he was about to vouch for a demon. "He's friendly. He was with some other guy last night when I was being attacked by demons. They saved me."

The man's eyes narrowed and he looked around the barn. "Where is this other guy?"

"Crimolok kill friend Aymun," said David. "Was brave warrior."

The woman flinched. "Did you... did you say *Aymun?*"

"Yes. Aymun and Vamps. We travel many months. Family."

The two strangers looked at each other. Then the woman turned her gaze back to David. Smithy tried to figure out what was happening, but he only grew more confused.

"Vamps?" said the woman. "Black guy? Gold fangs?"

"Yes! Shiny teeth!"

"And you definitely said *Aymun?* Araby-looking guy who speaks like he knows the answer to every question before you've even asked it?"

David wrinkled his stumpy nose at Smithy and grunted. "I do not know this word, *Araby*."

"That's because it's not a word."

David turned back to the woman and shrugged. "Aymun was a... *Syrian.*"

The woman lowered her shotgun and shook her head as if she couldn't believe it. "I was at Portsmouth with Vamps. I fought alongside him. After I survived the battle, I joined a unit named in his honour."

Smithy was astonished. "Wait? Are you telling me you and David mix in the same social circles? Shit, you might have been Facebook friends in another life."

The woman resumed her interest in Smithy. "Vamps and Aymun went into a Hell gate with a team. Their mission was to take the fight to the enemy. Soon after they left, the demons started to change. They stopped fighting."

David had been crouched this whole time, but he now stood taller. "Crimolok prisoner inside Vamps."

The woman was gobsmacked. "Wait? What? We didn't even know if Vamps was still alive, but you're saying he returned from Hell and took Crimolok prisoner at the same time?"

David nodded. "Yes, left Hell. Came back."

"I didn't know them," said Smithy, feeling rather left out of the conversation. "They sound swell."

The woman narrowed her eyes and lifted her shotgun, but not all the way. "Then who the hell are you? What are you doing here?"

"Dave and I crept into this barn last night to sleep. We thought the farm was deserted."

"It's not. There's a group of people living here and they're bad news. 'Burning innocent people alive' kind of bad. They have my friends – my boyfriend."

Smithy put his hands up. "I swear, me and Dave have nothing to do with it. It was the middle of the night. I was tired. We just crept in here and crashed."

"Smithy sleep with me all night," said David.

Smithy winced again. "Seriously, will you stop saying it like that?"

David frowned. "It is truth."

"Yeah, but still…"

The man with the shotgun nodded towards the door. "You should get out of here. The people who live here took our friends outside with hoods over their heads. We've been waiting for a good chance to strike, but it looks like it's now or never. Leave, or you might get hurt."

Smithy considered making a run for it, but it felt like another death sentence. He couldn't survive out on the road much longer. He'd already beaten the odds. "Wait! Is it… is it safe where you people come from? You mentioned Portsmouth, right? I heard about there. There are still soldiers fighting?"

The man nodded. "We're all soldiers at Portsmouth. All ten thousand of us."

"T-Ten thousand? I didn't even know there were that many people still alive on the planet."

"A lot, yes," said David. "Only a hundred at Kielder Forest."

The woman stared at David, apparently now used to conversing with a demon. "What are you talking about?"

"A castle. Forest north. Many miles north. I remember all now. They fight demons. They close gate. Strong, but need help. Aymun and Vamps head to Portsmouth to tell about castle in forest. They —" David suddenly coughed and blood dribbled down his chin. "Am sorry."

"Are you okay?" Smithy asked.

David nodded, but he suddenly seemed smaller. He half turned away and wiped at his mouth.

"We're still in this fight," said Smithy, feeling a massive relief to learn that he wasn't alone in a world full of monsters and bark-chewing strangers. "Your friend Vamps is with another demon called Frankie. They're after me. Please, take me back to Portsmouth with you."

The woman shrugged. "Okay, sure. Everyone is welcome at Portsmouth, but there's one rule."

"What's that?"

The man beside her pulled a knife from her belt and shoved it at Smithy, handle first. "Everybody fights."

---

Mass crawled to the edge of the pit and tried to reach his men – but they were too far down. The demons didn't swarm like they would've several months ago, but they could still kill if given the chance. Even now, they glared at the men in the pit with hungry interest.

Tox was on his feet, swinging his fists at whatever came close. One of the other men was injured, having fallen badly on one shoulder, and he lay in the mud while Tox fought to protect him.

Mass could do nothing up top, so he did the only thing he could think of – he threw himself forward into the pit. He landed hard on his side and lost his breath.

"What the hell are you doing?" said Tox, dragging Mass to his feet. "We're going to die down here."

"No, we ain't." Mass was still groggy from the whack to his skull, but he put his brute force behind a punch that collided with a nearby demon and sent it cartwheeling backwards. Mass could fight, but he was too weak to kill. The paring knife he had taken from the kitchen was now lying somewhere in the grass up top.

The demons formed a huddle at the other end of the pit. They eyeballed their prey but didn't attack. Not yet. They were working up to it.

Tox moved everyone to the back of the pit. The demons, although wary, moved with them, their contorted faces and sinewy limbs even more nightmarish while covered in mud and the dried blood of previous victims.

Mass clenched his fists. "We fight until we're dead."

Tox took a deep breath and nodded.

The demons approached, salivating as they drew nearer. Too many of them for four guys to fight. Vamps had sacrificed himself to strike a blow at the enemy, but Mass was going to die in a muddy hole in the ground.

*I'm sorry, man. I let you the fuck down.*

The edges of the pit were eight feet high, at least. No way to climb out. If they tried, the demons would attack as soon as they turned their backs.

"Shoulder to shoulder, lads," said Mass. "Don't let anyone get dragged down."

The demons finally launched their attack. Mass watched as two of his men died in seconds, their throats slashed open by deadly claws. That left Mass and Tox standing alone, throwing punches while dodging deadly swipes from demon claws. Mass headbutted a demon in the face and sent it back, but as soon as it stumbled, another monster took its place. He could already feel himself growing tired. The bloody bandages around his throat had come away. His exposed wound seemed to arouse the demons.

"Let us the fuck out of here!" Mass shouted up at the edge of the hole, hoping someone with an ounce of sanity would put a stop to this madness. "We're human beings!"

No one answered – but then a sharp snap of lightning sounded. Voices erupted and angry gunfire rattled.

"There's a fight going on up there," said Tox, dodging backwards to keep from being sliced open. He was right. A fight had broken out. Someone was shooting.

"Help!" Mass shouted. "Help us!"

More gunfire. More shouting. Fortunately, the demons were equally confused by whatever was occurring up top and they paused their attack. But the gunfire grew distant, the fight moving away. Mass despaired. Whoever was shooting wasn't there to pull them out of the pit. Did they even know Mass and Tox were down there?

A demon leapt to attack, but Mass smashed it in the face with a hard right hand. With the other demons distracted by the gunfight, he tried climbing the muddy sides of the pit. It was useless, but it was all he could think to do. Digging in with his fingers, he hooked onto some buried roots and pulled himself up more than expected. Suddenly, his body rushed with adrenaline as he contemplated getting out of there. Then he looked down and realised he would be abandoning Tox. His man – and friend – was now battling with two demons. He'd already been sliced open by one.

Mass could get out of there if he just focused on making it up those last few feet. Freedom was in reach. He could do it. Except he couldn't.

"Goddamn it!" He leapt off the wall and landed on top of one of the two demons attacking Tox. He kicked it hard enough to launch it right into the other, and both monsters hit the mud wall.

Tox grabbed Mass's belt and hauled him to his feet. "You should've gone, man."

"Don't want to live that way." He put his fists up. "I would rather die *this* way."

The demons regrouped and approached again. The more the fight went on, the more they seemed to wake up and rediscover their vicious instincts. Meanwhile, Mass and Tox were only getting weaker.

Tox pressed up against Mass, shoulder to shoulder. "Urban Vampires for life, mate."

Mass nodded. "Urban Vampires for life."

The demons snarled, reared back, and pounced.

A shotgun blast filled the pit. Light and noise echoed off the mud walls and caused Mass and Tox to close their eyes and cover their ears. It was like standing inside a broom cupboard with a lit firework.

"Come on!" someone shouted.

Mass looked up, expecting to see a familiar face – Addy or London – but it wasn't either of them. A stranger. The young lad had a shotgun set on the ground beside him and was dangling a horse's bridle over the edge of the pit. "Come on, before they all come back!"

Mass wanted to know who was rescuing him but decided to leave the questions until he was safely out of the hole. He shoved Tox against the wall, then used his muscles to shove the man upwards. Tox grabbed the bridle, and the stranger grabbed his shirt, pulling him to safety. Immediately, Tox grabbed the shotgun and fired it into the hole, taking out a demon right as it was about to pounce on Mass.

Disorientated from the noise, Mass took a wobbly run-up and hopped off the mud wall, giving himself a three-foot boost. He grabbed a hold of the bridle and heaved. The stranger grabbed a hold of his arm and yanked. A demon grabbed hold of his ankle and tugged. For a moment, he feared he would fall back into the pit, but he threw out a kick and freed himself. He rose quickly out of the hole and was back on solid ground.

*Thank fuck!*

The people who lived at the farm had scattered, firing at a distant target on the hill. From the sound of the rapid return-fire, it could only have been Addy or London with the LMG. A dead man lay bullet-ridden in the grass nearby, but everyone else had moved into the adjacent fields.

The stranger helped Mass get moving. "Your people drew them all away," he said, "so I could sneak up and get you out of this hole."

"Who are you?"

"Smithy. You're Mass, right? Addy said to look for a big muscly guy. Thought you'd be bigger, to be honest."

Mass shook the lad's hand more vigorously than he had ever shaken any hand. "You just made yourself a new best friend."

"We need to go," said Tox, checking the shotgun for ammo. "Addy and London won't be able to hold out for long. Eventually, that LMG will run out of teeth."

Despite the gunfight taking place elsewhere, there were other people still in the paddock. Mass went over to the anxious women in the containers and told them to get out of there. "Quickly, before those bastards come back."

The women stared at him as if they didn't even understand what he was saying, more like startled rabbits than people.

"I don't get it," said Tox. "Why aren't they moving?"

Mass felt sick to his stomach. "Because they're terrified. They'd rather live in a harem than be alone."

"We need to get them to Portsmouth," said Tox.

"First things first. Smithy, what did Addy ask you to do once you'd rescued us?"

"She said to meet back at the gravel car park. Said you'd know where that was."

A good plan, thought Mass. It was the only place nearby that all of them knew. The place where all this had started. "Okay, let's move."

"Not so fast!" Gemma appeared from amongst the women in the container. She brandished a shotgun and a pissed-off snarl. "You killed two of my friends last night. You think you're going to get away scot-free? Naseem might want to test you, but I just want you dead."

"You started this fight," said Mass, "but I promise we'll be the ones to end it."

Tox levelled his shotgun. "Too right."

Gemma pointed her shotgun at Mass. "You shoot, I shoot. Want to play?"

Mass rolled his eyes. "Pull the fucking trigger, Tox."

Gemma shook her head and sneered. "Idiots. You think I'm joking? I fire this thing and it will take the three of you out. Give yourselves up and I might—"

Gemma's eyes went wide and she dropped like a sack of potatoes. A woman appeared behind her, clutching a large tin of chopped *tomatoes* in her trembling hand. Mass wasted no time and grabbed Gemma's shotgun. The 12-gauge was heavy, but it had five spare shells racked along the top of the barrel and three more in the chamber. Apocalyptic fried gold. "Now we're talking."

The woman with the chopped tomatoes was panicked as she spoke, but her words were defiant. "That bitch helped trick every woman here. She and Naseem deserve to burn in Hell."

Mass reached out a hand cautiously. "You'll be safe with us. We'll get you out of here."

"The other women won't come," she said flatly. "They're too afraid. Some of them prefer it here to what they went through before."

Mass looked over at the containers and watched the women retreat back inside. The sight of Gemma unconscious seemed to frighten them, as if they feared repercussions. "We'll come back for them, but first we have to make it out of here alive. My people are meeting us back at a nearby car park."

The woman's eyes widened. "Do you have a lorry parked there?"

Mass nodded. "Yeah, we do. Although it isn't going anywhere without four new tyres."

"You need to avoid it! I heard Naseem order some men to go back and siphon whatever petrol is left in the tank. They took guns."

Tox swore. "If Addy and London make it back before us, they'll be ambushed."

"We have no choice then," said Mass. "We dig in here and fight. If Addy sees us staying put, she'll come back to provide cover. She won't retreat without us."

The woman began to shake her head. "There's too many of them. There're twenty men staying here."

"But you said four have left to go steal our petrol. Those plus the two I killed last night leaves fourteen. Fourteen piece-of-shit scumbags versus four Urban Vampires – and my friend Smithy here. I like those odds."

"And Dave," said Smithy.

Mass frowned. "Who's Dave?"

Smithy shook his head. "Never mind. Now ain't the time."

"You people are crazy," said the woman. "We need to get out of here before they come back and kill us. They've turned this place into a death trap. The farmhouse's basement is stacked with enough weaponry to blow up the moon."

Hearing that caused a grin to spread across Mass's face. Tox was smiling too. Mass turned to the woman in all seriousness. "What's your name, love?"

"Harriet."

# RESURGENCE

"Okay, Harriet. I need you to show me that basement."

---

Seeing Gross take a shotgun blast to the chest had been too much. Addy should've acted sooner. Now, the most important person in her world was dead. If only she hadn't delayed, waiting for the right moment.

She set up the LMG on the hill and prepared to start taking lives. Human lives. Her moral reservations faded. This entire operation had been a fuck show. After months of fighting demons and taking zero losses, they had lost most of their unit in a day. All she wanted now was to make these people pay. Her first shot from the LMG went wild, but it helped her find her aim. The next barrage took out two bewildered gunmen standing in the fields. Then she took out a third standing by the containers in the paddock.

The people at the farm scrambled in a dozen directions. London and the demon, David, were with her, but neither had weapons. London had given his shotgun to Smithy in case he had needed firepower during his mission to rescue Mass and the others from the pit. They both began spotting targets for her, helping her suppress anyone trying to climb the hill.

But she was already running out of ammo.

The LMG could spit seven-hundred rounds per minute, but it wasn't accurate, and all the bodies buzzing around below made it difficult to see if Smithy had got Mass and the others out of the hole. The last thing she needed was to shoot them accidentally. "I don't see them, London. Did they get away?"

London came back up the hill. He'd descended as much as he safely could. "They ran into some trouble, but they got away. Tox, Mass, Smithy, and some woman who helped them escape."

"A woman?"

London shrugged. "Looks like they found support on the ground."

"Then Smithy will have told Mass about the rendezvous. We need to fall back and make it to that car park. We can't win here."

London agreed. "Let's make tracks. Hey, where's that demon got to?"

"I am here," said David, appearing from further down the hill.

"We're leaving," said Addy. "Are you coming with us, David?"

"No, must aid Smithy."

London raised an eyebrow. "He has all the help he's going to get. The plan is for us all to meet back at the car park. You'll be safer with us."

The demon was conflicted. It glanced down the hill to where men were now cautiously advancing. "Something feels wrong."

"No shit," said Addy. "That's why we're retreating."

Gunshots cracked below, but not aimed at the hill. It seemed to come from the farmhouse. Addy dropped back down and got on the LMG, squinting to find a target. She fired off a barrage, almost emptying the weapon, but bought herself enough time to make out what was happening below. "They're not leaving. They're heading for the farmhouse."

London crouched to keep his cover on the hill. "What? Why?"

Addy scanned the farm. A dozen men dove into cover, not knowing whether to continue attacking the hill or to head towards the farmhouse. "I don't know what's happening, but if they're in trouble, we can't leave."

"Something isn't right," said David, but he went ignored. Addy didn't have time for the demon and his nonsense. She needed to cover her squad mates.

Mass was cutting between the barns and heading for the farmhouse. He must have thought it was the best place to find cover, but once he entered there would be no getting out again. The enemy would surround the house.

Addy did the only thing she could – she tried to even the odds. She aimed the LMG at the largest group of enemies she could spot, which was four men taking cover behind an old tractor. She fired off a spread and cut down two men before the others could duck into cover.

The LMG grunted, finally out of breath. She wouldn't be laying down any more covering fire, but at least she had made her final shots count.

"We need to go," said David. "We need to go. We need to go."

Addy hissed at London. "Shut him up, will you?"

"How?"

"I don't know, but if we don't think of something, Mass and Tox are screwed. They can't fight off all of those men with a pair of shotguns."

"He's coming," said David, clutching his head and dancing. "He's coming. He's coming. Ahhhh... He's here."

Addy turned away from the empty LMG and glared at the irritating demon. It was only its ties to Aymun and Vamps that had kept her from putting it down like a rabid dog. The demon was an enemy. And right now it was losing its shit.

Addy checked no one was climbing the hill, then leapt up and marched over to the demon, intending to strike it until it shut up. Before she got there, she paused. Something was coming up the other side of the hill, a rapidly moving mass approaching their rear. She gasped. "Oh no!"

They'd been flanked.

Any second now, they would be riddled with bullets. Mass and the others too.

Game over.

London noticed the advancing army as well, but he noticed something she hadn't. "Demons," he said in disbelief. "Those are fucking demons. I haven't seen so many in months."

Addy's stomach hit the floor. The two dozen bodies advancing up the hill weren't human. They were demons. A wiry, young black man led the pack, roaring like a hellish beast. When she realised it was Vamps, she might have fainted with relief, but it wasn't really him. It was whatever the tiny demon had spoken about. The wicked creature imprisoned inside Vamps' body.

David, breaking out of his stupor, grabbed Addy's arm and pulled her. He glared with his soulless black eyes. "We must run!"

And so they did. Right down the hill towards their other enemy. They weren't getting out of this alive.

## CHAPTER EIGHT

MASS and the others were intercepted mere metres from the farmhouse's front door and forced to take cover behind an old brick outhouse. Four men unloaded on them from behind a tractor.

Mass had his 12-gauge and Tox had reloaded his shotgun with spare cartridges. They were low on ammo, but Addy needed to hear that they were dug in. She had to hear them shooting. If she did, she would head back for the farmhouse instead of the car park.

Mass fired a shot around the corner of the brick building. Harriet and Smithy crouched behind him.

"If we don't move from here," said Tox, firing a shot of his own, "we'll end up surrounded. Everyone's coming back down the hill. The distraction Addy brought us is about to expire."

I know," said Mass, flinching as a gunshot obliterated the brickwork right next to his face. "We need to take out those bastards behind the tractor."

"We're going to die," said Harriet. "We should just make a run for it."

Mass rolled his eyes at her. "Thanks for the positivity, sweetheart."

Smithy ducked and fired a shotgun he'd found on a man Addy had killed. His shot struck the tractor's rear window and shattered it, causing glass to rain on the men hiding behind the massive tyres.

"Ooh, I nearly got the sods, did you see? Not bad for my first shoot-out."

Tox raised an eyebrow in surprise. "You've never used a shotgun before?"

"Nah, but you just point and shoot, right? Piece of piss. Oh, and I totally agree with Harriet, by the way. We're absolutely going to die."

"Probably," said Mass, "but anyone still alive nowadays is on borrowed time, anyway."

"Good point."

Tox hissed as more brickwork exploded and spat debris into his face. He rubbed his eyes, frantic for a second, but relaxed when he realised his vision was okay. "We're pinned down. What the hell do we do?"

One of them had to break cover to try to get an angle on the men behind the tractor. The problem was that whoever volunteered would probably get shot. That was why it had to be Mass. "Get ready to break for the farmhouse," he said. "Okay, on three. One... two... three!" Mass lunged from behind the brick wall and levelled his shotgun towards the tractor. He pulled the trigger and sent a blast into the giant tyre. The men behind it ducked, but were right back up again, knowing they had a chance to shoot at him in the open. He fired again, his last cartridge before he needed to reload. Behind him, the others made a break for it. If he ducked back into cover too soon, it would leave them exposed. That couldn't happen, so he knelt and pulled a pair of cartridges from the holder on top of the shotgun. He started loading them as quickly as he could, hoping to get off another shot before the enemy broke cover and shot first, but it was an unfamiliar weapon and his hands were shaking. As soon as he fumbled the first cartridge, he knew he wouldn't make it in time.

One of the men behind the tractor stepped out into the open and raised a stubby shotgun at Mass. If they missed, he would have time to finish reloading. If they didn't...

Thunder boomed and the man pointing a shotgun at Mass did a dance. Then one of the other men behind the tractor flopped forward onto the gravelly courtyard as the thunder continued.

Addy was firing from up on the hill. She'd heard the fighting and returned.

*Right on time, sister.*

Mass got the time he needed to run after the others, hopping a low stone wall outside the farmhouse and making it up to the front door. It was locked.

"Damn it," said Tox, battering a fist against the wood. "This thing's as thick as a mattress and hard as a rock."

Mass kicked the ancient oak door and knew it wouldn't budge – not without some impressive persuasion. "Stand back."

Everyone moved away from the door and Mass pumped several cartridges into his shotgun and fired a shot at the door. The wood splintered around the lock but was unaffected otherwise. The wrought-iron handle bent slightly.

Tox tried the door again. "It still won't budge! Shoot the lock again."

"Okay, stand back."

Mass levelled the shotgun a second time but was distracted by movement to his left. One of the two remaining men behind the tractor had moved out of cover and was approaching the small stone wall surrounding the house. Mass twisted his hips and adjusted his aim, pulling the trigger and placing a hole in the sneaking man's shoulder. The other man leapt back behind the tractor's tyre.

Most of the enemy were nearing the bottom of the hill now, breaking cover and moving back towards the farmhouse. Addy and London were legging it down the hill, too, with what looked like a small demon.

"What the hell are they doing?" Mass shook his head. It made no sense.

But then he saw what they were running from.

"No way."

A stream of demons crested the hill and released a bone-chilling screech. A platoon of the damned.

Addy and London were only halfway down the hill. The creatures bellowed and hissed after them like blood-crazed monsters. Animal noises came from the paddock, too, and when Mass looked around, he saw demons from the pit leaping out and attacking the nearby livestock. The sound of terrified cows was hellish.

Smithy took cover behind the brick wall. "Where the fuck did those demons on the hill come from?"

Tox looked sick. "They're going to get Addy and London."

Mass didn't disagree. No way were Addy and London going to make it. The demons rolling down the hill behind them were like a crashing wave, gathering speed every second. By now, the men who lived at the farm had stopped fighting altogether and were running for dear life. Mass spotted the hook-handed man amongst them, dashing inside one of the barns and taking cover behind the white coach that had taken Gross yesterday. Mass considered rushing over and snapping the bastard's neck. If he did that, though, the demons would get him.

The last surviving man behind the tractor had wandered out of cover and was staring at the approaching horde as if he couldn't believe his eyes. Mass lifted his shotgun and was about to fire but changed his mind. He couldn't shoot a man in the back. Instead, he shouted, "Hey! We need to get inside the house. Anyone who stays out here is dead meat."

The man turned slowly. Dark-skinned and white-eyed, he didn't lift his shotgun to shoot at Mass. Instead, after a moment's thought, he hurried over to join them at the farmhouse door.

"Tell me you have a key to this place," said Tox.

"No," said the man in a mild African accent, "but we can go around back."

Mass nodded, knowing it was the right course of action. They needed to hurry, but he couldn't pull his eyes away from the hill. He couldn't pull his eyes away from Addy and London running for their lives or the weird little creature running alongside them. Of the three of them, only the demon seemed quick enough to have any chance of getting away. He grabbed Tox by the arm. "Get to the kitchen around back. Then get whatever weapons are inside that basement and put them to good use."

"I'm on it!" Tox got everyone moving while Mass raced away from the house, yelling at the top of his lungs. Addy set eyes on him and ran full tilt towards him. All the armed men of the farm had taken cover, and some now fired shots at the demons on the hill. One man, though, was aiming not at the demons but at Addy.

*You son-of-a-bitch.*

Mass rushed forward and shot at the man. At that range, he missed, but the explosion of dirt near the would-be assassin's feet was enough to send the man scrambling for cover.

Addy and London finally made it onto flat ground. They wheeled towards Mass as he continued to yell to them. The small demon with them seemed disorientated, and it scurried out of view behind the barns. The demons on the hill began to spread out like a concertina fan, seeking human targets. Men began to scream. The battle had begun.

Addy and London weren't going to make it. They had too much ground to cover. Mass hurried to reach them, wishing there was some way he could save them from being slaughtered. All the armed men began to flee – all except one. The hook-handed bastard exited the barn with a hunting rifle tucked against his shoulder, not yet retreating. Did he hope to take out the demons single-handedly? Why wasn't he running with everyone else?

Then it became clear. Mass watched in horror as the man balanced his rifle against his hook and fired off a shot.

London cried out in pain and dropped to the floor, grabbing his thigh with both hands.

The hook-handed bastard lowered his rifle with a smirk, then departed, disappearing back into the barn.

London dragged himself along the ground, hands covered with blood. Addy turned back to help him, but the demons were already on him, biting into him and tearing at his body with their claws. His screams echoed through the fields. Mass lifted his shotgun and fired at a primate about to tackle Addy. Then he took a second shot and struck a burnt man. There was no time to reload, so he yelled at Addy to get the hell out of there before it was too late.

Addy pumped her arms and legs, cheeks puffing out like giant raspberries. Most of the demons had found other targets, or were occupied by London's screaming death throes, which meant she now had a slim chance. She could make it. Then another primate appeared, right at her back. She didn't even know it was there. She didn't know she was a dead woman. Mass fumbled with his shotgun, trying to reload, but he knew it was too late. He needed to turn and run – to save himself – but he just… couldn't.

Addy was only a dozen steps away, but the demon would be on her in six. It leapt into the air, rising over her with outstretched talons.

*Boom!*

Someone shot the primate clean out of the air. It landed in the grass, rattling and choking. Mass turned and saw Smithy standing behind him, a smoking shotgun in his hands. He gave Mass a silent nod and ran back towards the farmhouse.

Mass finally gathered Addy into his arms and dragged her towards safety. "Come on," he said. "We need to get inside that house or we're screwed."

Addy was panting and moaning. "We're screwed no matter what. Vamps is here."

Mass had no idea what that meant, but he decided to ask questions later.

---

Maddy was sharing a bowl of baked beans with Diane in the dining room. It'd been a long, arduous day and General Thomas had run everyone ragged implementing his changes in Portsmouth. It was now six o'clock, and she was done for the day. Wickstaff had told Maddy to take a couple of days to herself while she and General Thomas learned to work together. Fine by Maddy.

Diane was off the clock too. As Wickstaff's head of security, she could never truly take an evening off, but now that there were so many more armed men on base, it was as good a time as ever to take a break. It felt strange, sitting together just to chat. Almost normal.

"So, you hooked up with anyone on base yet?" asked Diane. The girl had once been a shy mouse, but months of survival had hardened her. She was now one of the scariest people on base – all smiles until she had to pull her gun and shoot something in the face. Diane never hesitated. That was why she was still alive despite her previously meek nature. The apocalypse had unlocked the deeper parts of her soul.

Maddy had changed too. This time last year, she'd been a married paramedic thinking about having kids. She'd never found out what had happened to her husband, but she had resigned herself to the fact he was almost certainly dead. For the most part, she never thought about him any more. She never said his name or pictured his face. He was from a different time – a different time when monsters didn't exist. She couldn't encumber herself with thoughts of what was lost. Not just *her* husband, but the millions of husbands all over the world. Billions of people torn to pieces with their lives unfulfilled, their goodbyes unsaid.

Maddy turned her mind back to the question Diane had asked her. "Have I hooked up with anyone? Erm, no, I haven't. How do you even find time to think about that stuff?"

Diane smirked. "Are you kidding me? I barely think of anything else. I swear, if I don't find a man soon, I might dry up down there."

"Jesus, Diane."

"Hey, we might die tomorrow."

Maddy looked over at a table crowded with naval officers at the rear of the dining room. The newcomers were friendly enough, but mostly aloof and unwilling to make small talk. That might change after a little time for them to settle in, but for now it created an awkward atmosphere. "I feel as far away from dying as I have in a long time," she admitted. "Wickstaff was right; we're better off with Thomas and his people, even if it puts our noses out of joint."

Diane shrugged. "More the merrier, I suppose. More men, for one thing. Time to start living our lives again."

Maddy rolled her eyes. "You think this will ever truly be over? Something sent the demons into hiding, but they're still out there. I can never shift this feeling that they'll just reappear in force one day and wipe us all out. There are still so many gates open."

Diane reached over and took Maddy's hand. "Hey, we're alive. We survived the end of the world. All that's left is a new beginning. Perhaps things won't ever get back to normal during our lifetimes, but I'm proud to be part of the reason that future generations might one day get to live happy, normal lives. Maybe even better lives than the ones we had before. Maybe once the demons are gone, mankind will finally live in peace."

Maddy huffed. "We'll always find a reason to fight. As long as one man can have something another man doesn't, there'll be war. It's who we are."

Diane shook her head. "It's who we *were*."

A high-pitched whine filled the dining room, followed by a crackle and a hiss. Mass looked over at the naval officers and saw that one of them was receiving a call from a shoulder-mounted walkie-talkie. He was sitting too far away for her to hear his conversation, but she saw his eyes widen. After a few seconds, he got up from the table and hurried out of the room, taking his colleagues with him.

"Something's going on," said Diane, her smile replaced with a thin-lipped grimace.

Maddy stood. "I need to get back to the office. You coming?"

"Nothing gets to happen around here without me knowing about it. Yes, I'm coming."

The two women exited the dining room and followed the naval officers outside. Portsmouth was a ruin, which had ironically made it easier to fortify. The concrete and wood from destroyed buildings had been used to erect barricades and watchtowers in numerous places. The roads were blocked by cars and lorries, and a two-mile palisade had been erected north of the docks. If Portsmouth fell, people could fall back to the waterfront. If the waterfront fell, people could fall back to the ships. Wickstaff had drilled them all relentlessly about staying alive no matter the cost.

The naval officers were hurrying. Maddy spotted other personnel gathering ahead. Clearly, a call had gone out. Most of those present were Thomas's men, but she was relieved to see at least some of Portsmouth's militia making their way to the gathering too. Then she spotted Wickstaff and was even more relieved.

The brigadier stood beside Commander Tosco. Maddy hurried to join them. "Ma'am, what's going on?"

Wickstaff nodded to both Maddy and Diane, then explained. "There are demons at the north-west edge of the city. A lot, by all accounts."

"Define a lot," said Diane.

"Sixty or seventy. Nothing to wet our knickers about, but it's been a while since we saw a group this large."

"Months," added Tosco, his hands on his hips and foot tapping. He seemed nervous.

Maddy glanced around at the gathered personnel and estimated there being two hundred men and women, nearly all armed. "Why are Thomas's officers gathering like this?"

Wickstaff rolled her eyes. "Because this is a chance to flex his muscles. He wants to send a team out to deal with the threat."

"And I agree, it's a good idea," said Tosco, stating his words defiantly. "General Thomas should solidify his authority as soon as possible. Last thing we need is a weak leader."

"I take no issue with a bit of posturing," said Wickstaff, "but I see no reason to risk men outside our defences. Fifty demons are not a threat so long as we hold our position behind the barricades, but Thomas fears they might multiply."

"And might they?" asked Maddy.

"Yes," said Tosco. "The longer we leave this group, the bigger it could grow."

Wickstaff shrugged. "Perhaps. We should tread cautiously though and not send men out without getting all the facts first."

"What facts?" asked Tosco. "We've killed enough demons by now to know what we're doing."

"But the demons have changed," said Maddy. "Who knows how they'll behave if we attack them?"

"Exactly," said Wickstaff. "I'm about to tell General Thomas the very same thing. We should wait this out and try to gather a bit of information on how best to proceed. No one is in imminent danger. There's no need to be hasty."

Speaking of the devil, General Thomas appeared from amongst a group of officers and approached Wickstaff. "Brigadier, we shall conduct a full sweep of the city at twenty-one hundred hours. I want every last enemy dispatched in a five-mile radius."

"That's unnecessary," said Wickstaff. "I know it might seem counterproductive to leave enemies within our borders, but they're not a threat unless they gather in greater numbers. They could be stragglers, but we have no way of knowing until we learn more. Sending men out in darkness is a bad idea. It would be better to at least delay until morning."

Thomas looked at Wickstaff as if she were a waitress who had brought him cabbage when he'd ordered steak. "I have been wiping out these beasts for nigh on a year, Brigadier, while you've been idling behind your walls. Perhaps it's been too long since you had to get your hands dirty, but I assure you these smalls groups can grow like a fungus. Better to mow the lawn while the grass is low than wait for it to tower over us."

Wickstaff stood for a moment like a malfunctioning robot. Then she blinked. "General Thomas, we do not have the benefit of open desert or aerial drones here. Send men out into the ruins in the dark and they could be walking into anything. Demons haven't gathered in Portsmouth like this since the Great Battle. I fear they are here for a reason. Who sighted them anyway?"

"One of my scout teams. They went a mile past the barricades to verify the integrity of our perimeter. They reported several dozen demons congregating on the outskirts of the city, spilling out of some parkland. Hundreds more may be on the way."

"Which is why we should stay behind our defences. That's what they're for."

"Defences are for hiding. Those days are gone."

Wickstaff pressed the bridge of her nose as if she were getting a migraine. "You're risking people's lives for no gain. I respectfully disagree with your intentions."

Thomas turned away. "That is your right, Brigadier, and as general, I have the right to do as I please."

Wickstaff stepped after the man, not allowing him to turn his back. "Not with my people you don't!"

General Thomas growled. "They are *not* your people any more."

Wickstaff closed her eyes and took a breath. It looked like she was meditating, but then she exploded into action. "Commander Tosco, call the unit leaders. None of my men are to leave the barricades. We have an hour of daylight left and I want them all on guard duty by the time night falls. Also, call the boats and have them light up the ruins with their spotlights."

Tosco took a half-step to leave, but then paused. His eyes darted between Wickstaff and Thomas. "I-I'm afraid I can't do that, ma'am. You handed operational command to General Thomas. I can't contravene his orders."

General Thomas gave a smug grin, but Wickstaff didn't relent.

"Well, Commander Tosco, I am taking back control of my people. You can serve who you damn well please, but I refuse to send men and women into unnecessary danger."

"You have no right!" Thomas roared right in her face, but Wickstaff didn't even blink. "We had an agreement, woman! You answer to me."

"We *agreed*, General Thomas, that you would take things steadily and not charge in like a bull with the clap. As far as I'm concerned, you have not kept your word, which frees me from obligation."

"You'll catch a bullet for this. This is mutiny."

"No," said Wickstaff. "This is survival, which means doing everything you can to keep people alive." She turned to Maddy. "Tell our people they report to me and *only* me."

Maddy grinned. "Gladly, ma'am."

"You will not give that order, girl!"

Thomas pointed a bony finger right in Maddy's face, but it only infuriated her. She stuck her middle finger up at the old fart and kept her focus on Wickstaff. "Anything else I can do for you, *General* Wickstaff?"

"Yes, would you kindly move General Thomas's things out of my office, please?"

Thomas went bright red, a stark contrast to his grey, colourless hair. "I am not leaving Portsmouth, you fool. I'll have you, and anyone who joins you, locked up or shot."

Wickstaff faced the man, and it was then Maddy realised the woman was an inch taller. "General Thomas, you may command your men in whatever way you wish, and you're welcome here at Portsmouth, but if you fight me, you'll regret it. I'll wipe the floor with you."

Wickstaff nodded. "And by the end, you'll be left with half your army and none of mine. Good luck liberating the United Kingdom then. I'm sure Commander Klein will take his nuclear submarine elsewhere too. That would make the German Confederation far more of a threat."

"Don't you dare blackmail me, woman!"

"I just did, and you can suck my dick if you don't like it." Wickstaff turned on her heel and marched away. Maddy couldn't help but smile as she looked back and saw Thomas trembling in abject fury.

*Your move, asshole.*

---

Smithy was waiting at the back door, ready to close it at the first sign of anything unfriendly. He didn't know what had made him go back to help Mass, but he couldn't forget that a stranger had saved his life last night — a stranger who had apparently once been a friend of these people. Aymun, they had called him. He could still remember the sight of the man being impaled through the chest.

Once Mass and Addy were inside the kitchen, Smithy slammed the door. A heavy china cabinet stood beside it, so he put his shoulder behind it and heaved until it was blocking the door. He immediately felt safer, but then a pang of worry struck him. "H-Hey, where's Dave?"

Addy looked him in the eye for a moment then glanced away. "I don't think he made it. I probably wouldn't have either if he hadn't started freaking out."

"What d'you mean?"

"He was clutching his head like he had bugs inside his brain or something."

Smithy nodded. "He can feel when Crimolok is near. It's like demon-sense or something."

Mass was rooting around the drawers for knives, but he looked up now. "Crim-a-who?"

Tox entered the kitchen from the other side. "We don't have time to chat. We need to get this place squared away."

Smithy looked back at the china cabinet, wondering if it would hold. Then he hurried to catch the others as they exited the kitchen. They all gathered in a large reception hall at the front of the house. It was dimly lit, but Harriet was busily lighting candles.

"Where's the basement?" asked Mass.

"Over there." Tox pointed to a door beneath the stairs. "Cam is gathering weapons right now."

Mass frowned. "Cam?"

"The dude who was trying to kill us. He said his name is Cam. We should watch him."

"Too right," said Smithy. "I'll go give him a hand." He rushed to the door Tox had pointed to, and when he opened it, light splashed up a short, wooden staircase. At the bottom, he found a survivalist's wet dream. The damp-stone room was crammed with supplies. Crates of bottled water and tinned food took up the entirety of one wall while a stockpile of assorted weaponry filled the two far corners. Smithy hadn't eaten in days, so he threw etiquette aside and grabbed some kind of protein bar from a box and bit into it. It was the best shit he'd tasted in months.

*At least if I die tonight, I'll die happy.*

"Some of the weapons have no ammo," said Cam, "and some are untested. We take whatever we find, but this is not a gun-wielding country – part of the reason I come here from Nigeria. Now, I wish I were back home."

Smithy huffed. "Don't we all? What stuff here do you know has ammunition?"

Cam looked around, moving stocks and barrels aside as he searched the stash. "This hunting rifle." He handed Smithy a long, lightweight weapon that could have been an air rifle for all he knew. "It fires the bullets in that red box."

Smithy picked up the ammo box and was pleased by its weight. "Anything else?"

Cam picked up a few handguns and put them in a duffle bag alongside a plastic tub box full of loose rounds. Then he grabbed a pair of shotguns. "These are old, but they should do."

"Let's get it upstairs where it can do some good."

Smithy turned his back and carried the tub of ammo upstairs. Cam followed with the duffle bag. It was strange, but he didn't sense any threat from the man despite them having been shooting at each other only ten minutes ago.

Everyone grabbed a weapon and positioned themselves at the hallway windows. Smithy hadn't noticed earlier, but the they were boarded up with only a few inches clear at the top. Wooden boxes had been placed on the ground so people could step up and aim their guns over the top of the boards. Despite the age of the house, the windows were double-glazed with opening panels at the top. They made perfect parapets.

"What's happening out there?" asked Smithy. "It's starting to get dark."

"Chaos," was Mass's reply, as the big man peered through the gap at the top of one of the windows. "The demons are everywhere. Can't you hear the screams?"

Of course he could hear the screams.

"What about the women?" Harriet moved with a candle into the centre of the room. "They're out there by themselves."

Mass flinched. "Shit! I forgot about them."

"They'll be sitting ducks out there," said Smithy. He hopped up on one of the boxes and peeked through the window gap. The writhing mass of demons and the static, bloody corpses turned his stomach, but he blanked them out and searched for the paddock and those shipping containers. There had been two dozen women out near the pit.

When he spotted the containers, he assumed the worst because he didn't see a single woman, not one screaming for their life or trying to get away. All he saw was two unmoving containers. But then he realised something. "The containers are closed! I think... I think they locked themselves in."

Harriet sighed. "Thank God. We need to rescue them."

"Let's rescue ourselves first," said Mass. He cocked his shotgun, still standing on one of the boxes. "Everyone ready to kill some demons?"

Tox stepped up to the last of the three windows. "I should have already died twice today. Let's see how long I can keep this going."

Mass turned to the others, those not at windows – Harriet, Cam, and Addy. "Make yourselves useful wherever you can. They won't all come at us through the front door."

"The house is boarded up well," said Cam, "but we will not be safe forever. How many fiends do you believe are out there, my friend?"

Mass sneered. "I'm not your friend. You were trying to kill me."

"And *you* were trying to kill *me*. Now you are the enemy of my enemy."

"Which makes us friends for now," said Smithy. "Let's keep

things civil and see who's alive at the end. Cam, to answer your question, there are a shit tonne of fiends out there, so get to a window and start shooting."

Cam lifted a pair of handguns and nodded, then he, Addy, and Harriet disappeared into the house.

Smithy looked to his right, to where Mass was standing. "You've survived worse odds than this before, right?"

"Sure, once. Except that time I had a buddy with a flaming sword and an ageing pop star with angel powers."

"Oh," said Smithy. "Well, I have chewing gum, if that helps?"

"You're shitting me? Of course it helps. Hand it over, man."

"Heads up!" Smithy tossed the squashed green packet from his jeans pocket and Mass caught it.

Mass popped the gum into his mouth and nodded his thanks. "Have to admit, for a bunch of murdering wankers, the people here knew how to plan ahead. If we can keep these barricades in place, we might have a chance."

"What went down here?" Smithy looked out at the demons. They were almost done with their victims. Soon they would turn their focus on the farmhouse. "The people here, they – what? – kidnapped you?"

Mass grunted. "To be more accurate, they stole from me, lured me into a trap that killed most of my men, and then slit my throat."

"I was going to ask you about that," said Tox in a low and miserable voice as he peered through the third window. "Looks like it was a bit of a bleeder."

Smithy looked at the blood-soaked bandages around Mass's throat and imagined how it must have felt. "Yeah, I reckon that's going to leave a scar. I hear apple cider vinegar helps."

Mass smirked. "It's just a paper cut. We get out of this and—"

The attack started. Their conversation ended at once.

Finished with everyone out in the open, the demons now rushed at the house. They threw themselves at the boarded-up windows and the thick front door, and for a second, the sheer force of the assault made it seem certain the barricades would splinter like wet matchsticks. Miraculously, they held.

Smithy angled his shotgun at a demon right beneath his

window and fired. The top of its head exploded, which made him even more glad of the boards because they shielded him from the spatter. Mass and Tox fired their weapons too. Elsewhere in the house, Addy and the others joined the fight. The world became a disorientating barrage of ear-battering noise – animalistic screeches and relentless gunfire. Smithy had never been in a fight like this, and it made him realise how detached he'd been from the end of the world. There were still people in the world fighting to stay alive. He had never been alone.

Mass was firing the hunting rifle Cam had brought from the basement. It was single-action, so he had to reload it after every shot. It meant the demons were piling up at his window. When he went to shove the barrel back out through the gap for another shot, it was yanked from his hands. "Damn it!"

Smithy watched the demons toss the rifle into the yard. He managed to shoot the bastard that had yanked it away, but the others hooted and yelped with glee. For a moment, they reminded Smithy of the monkeys at the zoo – mischievous scamps – but then one leapt up and tried to claw his face through the gap in the window. He reminded himself how wicked they were.

"This is like how they used to be," said Tox between shotgun blasts. "They're relentless and blood-crazed."

"Looks like they're done taking it easy," said Smithy, groaning. He never could have survived on the road if the demons had remained in berserker mode. All of a sudden, things seemed hopeless again.

"I need to get the 12-gauge," said Mass. "Can you two hold on without me?"

"What choice do we have?" said Tox. "Try to keep hold of your weapon this time."

Smithy pulled his trigger and obliterated a primate trying to barge open the front door. He stopped to reload and was about to tell Mass to go, but the big guy had already headed into the kitchen where he must have left his shotgun. From the rear of the house, Cam and the others continued firing. Demons surrounded the house.

"Hey, Smithy! You in there, bitch?"

Smithy recognised the voice, and it sent chills down his spine like an icy tongue. He stared out the window and saw Frankie standing beside the tractor, kicking at one of the dead men lying there. His face was contorted, flesh dripping away like hot candle wax. "Smithy, I know you're in there, blud. I can smell you."

Tox glanced aside to Smithy. "You two know each other?"

"Yeah, we met recently. It didn't go well."

"Enough said. I'll leave him for you to kill."

"No, feel free to take a shot. I'm not fussy."

Other demons surrounded Frankie, and he stood far enough away that Smithy would never hit him with a shotgun. Was that why he was keeping his distance? In fact, all the demons had stopped assaulting the house and were now standing back. It was as if they had been ordered to pull back.

Frankie called out again. "Hey, Smithy, I'll make you a deal, yeah? Come out and let me bugger you against this big old tractor tyre and I'll let your friends live. Go on, take one for the team."

Tox looked at Smithy in a way he didn't care for. What must the guy be thinking? Frankie was one unhinged piece of shit – even for a demon.

"Sounds like a good deal to me," said Mass, coming back into the hall with his heavy shotgun. "Get out there and drop your kecks, boy."

Smithy swallowed. "He-He'll kill me. Frankie is a complete psych—"

Mass shook his head and smirked. "Chill out, I'm just pissing around. We don't negotiate with demons. He wants you, he can come get you."

Smithy nodded. "Thanks."

"You're one of us." Mass filled his pockets with shotgun shells from the tub and got back to his window.

"They've fallen back," said Tox. "Maybe they've decided it's not worth it."

Mass squinted. "No, they're going to drag this out. We're in for a long night."

"And I don't have any more gum," said Smithy. "Anyone fancy running to the shops?"

"Maybe later," said Mass, and then fired a shot out into the growing darkness.

# CHAPTER NINE

A CHEER SOUNDED from all corners once word got around that General Wickstaff was in charge again. Maddy didn't hear an objection from a single man or woman, and none seemed worried by General Thomas. Portsmouth had faced worse monsters.

General Thomas, unwilling to take the insult lying down, had ordered his men to secure Portsmouth immediately. The armoury, the port authority building, and most of the guard towers were now controlled by him. But Wickstaff's loyalists were unconcerned. They gathered on the docks, fully armed and full-spirited. Maddy wondered how long it would be until things came to blows.

It was fantastic that Wickstaff had stood up to General Thomas, but Maddy was smart enough to know things wouldn't end there. Civil war was inevitable, and neither side would back down. Everyone would fight each other while far greater threats went ignored. Surely only disaster lay ahead?

For tonight, however, Maddy allowed herself to feel good. Good about the woman she had vowed to serve. Wickstaff valued every life under her command, and there was comfort in that fact, while General Thomas cared only about his own agenda. His plan to send men outside Portsmouth's barricades was still in full swing despite the strong objections.

What Maddy estimated to be a hundred armed men now congregated in the main road leading away from the waterfront. It would take them all the way to the barricade near Portsmouth's Spinnaker Tower. There, they could climb ladders up and over a massive supermarket lorry blocking entry into the docks. Then they would be alone in the dark ruins of a corpse-littered city. Maddy shuddered at the thought and felt an ominous weight attach itself to the air as she watched them head off. Unlike Portsmouth's militia, Thomas's soldiers were professional and silent, using hand signals and whispering into radios. Whether or not they were scared was a secret only they knew, but Maddy was afraid *for* them.

As much as she didn't want the men here, she hoped to see them return.

With a yawn, she decided to head to her room for sleep, but then realised it was inside the port authority building. Would she be allowed to get inside her own quarters? Or would Thomas's soldiers prevent her access? She supposed she'd find out.

On her way back across the docks, she spotted Commander Tosco – *that dickhead* – and made a beeline for the man. He spotted her coming and stood to attention. "Maddy," he purred. "What can I do for you?"

"Absolutely nothing, you spineless shit. How could you betray Wickstaff like that?"

"What are you talking about?"

"You chose General Thomas over her."

Tosco sighed and let his shoulders slump. "I obeyed the chain of the command. Just like I have always done. Just like I pledged to do when I joined the service."

"Bullshit! The chain of command doesn't mean anything any more."

"It does to me and it should to you. If people pick and choose who they follow, it'll lead to factions and infighting. That should be obvious from what's happening now. Wickstaff went back on her word and now we're split in half – enemies within and enemies without."

Maddy's fists clenched. "General Thomas went back on his word first! How can you serve him after all we've been through? We're family at Portsmouth."

"My family is most likely all dead," he said flatly, "but I have others to consider. Over a thousand people are under my command. I can't get them involved in a pissing contest. I owe it to Guy to keep them all safe." He shook his head and looked away. "To keep Alice safe."

Maddy hadn't seen Guy's daughter for a while, and she suddenly felt ashamed of it. The young girl had lost everyone. "How is Alice doing?"

"She's tough – really tough – but I worry that any more bloodshed will make her *too* tough. I was really hoping General Thomas's arrival might have bought us some breathing room, an opportunity to focus on things besides merely surviving. It seems it's only made things worse."

"Of course it's made things worse. He had no right to come here and take command." Maddy looked around the docks, at the scattered chairs and tables, at a child's football lying near a makeshift goal. They had made this place a home. "He had no right."

"He had every right," said Tosco. He seemed angry for a moment, but then his gaze softened. "Look, Maddy, I have the utmost respect for General Wickstaff, and I would die fighting for her – for *everyone* here. It's not a question of loyalty. It's a question of what I believe in and what you believe in. We don't have to fall out over it."

Maddy smirked, and it clearly confused Tosco, because he asked her what the joke was. She told him. "You said *General* Wickstaff. Maybe you'll come around. Until then, I still think you're a dickhead."

Tosco huffed and then rolled his eyes. With his slightly overgrown dark hair, he reminded her of Tom Cruise. It led her to wonder whether the actor was still alive. Would there ever be actors again?

He cleared his throat and looked at her. "Whatever happens going forward, I am dedicated to protecting what we have built here. I won't do anything I believe would cause more harm than good. You should know that by now, Maddy."

Maddy sighed and suddenly she didn't hate the guy any more. While Tosco was known for being arrogant, he had done as much as anyone had over these last few months to keep Portsmouth safe.

"I do know that, Tosco. You're a good guy deep down. Hey, it's late, and I'm not sure I have anywhere to sleep, so do you fancy going to get a cup of—"

"Maddy!" Colonel Cross came marching across the dock. At first he seemed confrontational, but once he neared her, he smiled warmly. "I was hoping to run into you," he said. "When the top brass bicker, it's the likes of you and me that have to keep things from getting out of hand. We should talk."

Tosco gave a slight bow to the colonel and then bid Maddy goodnight. "I'll catch up with you tomorrow," he said.

Maddy gave a short wave. "Yeah, erm, I'll see you around, Tosco. Good night."

"Sorry," said Cross. "Was I interrupting something?"

"No, just an argument. What can I do for you, Colonel? I don't really want to get caught fraternising with the enemy."

"The enemy? You offend me! As far as I'm concerned, we're still all friends here."

"And what about Thomas? Does he think that?"

Cross folded his arms and leant in towards her. "Thomas is a stuffy old Etonian who thinks he was born and bred to lead lesser men. Anyone lower than a major might as well be a gnat on his nut sack."

Maddy was taken aback. "I... wasn't expecting that. You don't like Thomas?"

Cross shrugged as if what he had said shouldn't be so surprising. "I spent my entire career disliking men like Thomas, but they're a necessary evil, unfortunately. Leave too much room up top and everyone will want to call the shots. Like it or not, people respect those who respect themselves, and Thomas is a legitimate commander."

Maddy groaned. "You sound like Tosco."

"The handsome young American you were just talking to?"

"I can get his number for you if you'd like?"

Cross broke out in smiles. "That won't be necessary. I could use a coffee though. It's going to be a long night."

Maddy had been about to ask Tosco to join her for a coffee, but she supposed Cross would have to do for company. It was late, and she was tired, but she wouldn't sleep. "Well, your people are probably in charge of our supplies by now, but I might be able to hook us up somewhere on neutral ground."

"You're a woman with means. I like that."

She wasn't sure she could get her hands on coffee, but she took Cross to a place that Thomas and his people wouldn't have yet discovered. A secret place.

Commander Klein came ashore twice per week, and whenever he did, he played poker. For weeks now, he and a small group of eager gamblers had been meeting inside a train carriage parked at the far side of the docks. It had once been destined for service on the country's railways but had never made it that far. Its many windows were still covered in protective foam, which made it completely private inside.

"What is this?" Cross asked as she took him inside the open engineer's cabin at the front of the carriage.

"Portsmouth's best-kept secret."

From the driver's compartment, she squeezed through a slim metal door and entered the carriage's interior. Commander Klein looked back at her without concern, even though the other dozen men inside all flinched.

"Madeline, how *wunderbar* to see you. Shall I deal you in?"

"After last time? No thanks, I'd rather keep the shirt on my back."

Klein frowned. He was the quintessential German, tall with floppy blonde hair, but despite his gruff accent he was constantly smiling. "You English have such strange expressions, *ja*? Who is your friend? A colonel, it *vud* seem?"

Cross took a step forward into the aisle. He saluted Klein, but it made the German grimace. "Colonel Cross. Pleasure to meet you, Commander Klein."

"We are all equal at ze poker table, Colonel. You may call me Hans."

"All right then, you can call me Tony."

"Tony, *ja*. A good name. Do you play, Tony?"

There were several bench set-ups in the carriage, but Klein's table was full, so Cross remained standing. "I've been known to play a few hands, but what I really came for was coffee and a chat with Maddy."

"You come inside my train, you play." Klein waved a hand and the men in his booth moved to other seats. "Sit, both of you. We shall play, chit-chat, and drink coffee, *ja?*"

Maddy put a hand on Cross's back and eased him into the booth. "Take a load off. You could be dead tomorrow."

Cross gave her a look that suggested she shouldn't tempt fate, but he did as she asked and sat opposite Klein. Maddy slid in next to him. Their thighs pressed together, and it made her realise how chilly she was.

Klein started dealing cards, smiling as he did so. Someone brought over two steaming mugs of coffee and a tumbler full of vodka for Klein. Cross palmed the hot coffee and sipped at it. "Christ, that's good. We ran out of the stuff early on in the Middle East."

"I hear they call it East Germany nowadays," said Klein with a playful smirk.

Cross rolled his eyes. "That's what your lads call it, yeah, but Chancellor Capri didn't liberate the place all by himself."

Klein started the game, pushing in a stack of chips. "Capri always was an ambitious man. I knew him when he was Federal Minister of Defence, but it was obvious he would climb higher. I doubt he will rest until he's conquered ze entire world. Perhaps that is a good thing considering our current enemy. He is as relentless as the demons."

Cross picked up his cards and examined them. "Maybe. Or perhaps he's no better than all the other tyrants who use a crisis to give themselves power. What's the point of surviving this nightmare if it leads to more of the same?"

Maddy sipped her coffee and placed it on the table. "Because the alternative is the extinction of the human race. We can't fix everything right now, but by surviving we at least give future generations a chance to do better."

Klein lifted his vodka in salute. "*Vell* said, Madeline. A wounded dog smells better than a dead dog, *ja*."

Cross chuckled. "Looks like you Germans have some strange expressions of your own."

"A few, *ja*. So, Tony, tell me about your superior, General Thomas. Is he a good man?"

"He makes it hard for people to see, but, yeah, he's a good man. A good leader."

"You like him?"

"No."

"*Vy* not?"

"For the same reason I don't like Chancellor Capri. He's a tyrant. He does whatever he thinks is for the greater good, but the thing about the greater good is that it shits all over the small good affecting normal people's lives. Sacrificing a hundred men to kill a thousand demons might seem worth the loss, but not if you ask those hundred men. Thomas has sent thousands of brave soldiers to their death for the greater good. Now that we have the upper hand, it's time to focus on the little people and the smaller goods."

Klein placed his cards face down on the table and leant back in the bench. "Tony, we are all equal in this train, yes, but it is alarming to hear you talk so disrespectfully about your commanding officer. What if I were to tell him your *vords*?"

Cross huffed. "I've heard a lot about the German submarine commander who refuses to pay fealty to anyone but himself. I'm thinking that if I can speak freely to anyone, it's you."

Klein grinned. "But what about ze other men here?"

Cross glanced at the other men in the train carriage. They were a chilled-out, laid-back bunch, but they were clearly listening to the conversation. "I imagine only a certain type of person gets invited to play poker on this train. Those with big mouths probably don't make the guest list."

Klein swigged his vodka as if it were beer. "I like you, Tony. We are both men in authority who hate authority, and nature loves a contradiction. Here's to a future without leaders."

Tony lifted his coffee in salute.

Maddy realised something, sitting here with these two headstrong, moralistic men. They could be allies, senior officers with common interests. "Wickstaff should be in charge of Portsmouth," she blurted out. "She doesn't like authority either. The reason she took charge is that there was no one else, not because she wanted to. When Thomas arrived, she stepped down rather than see people hurt. Now she's stepped back up for the same reason."

"Thomas won't take it lying down," said Cross. "I'm sorry,

Maddy, I like Wickstaff a lot already, but she's going to come off badly. Thomas will have her shot once the dust settles."

"He does that and half of Portsmouth will rebel."

Cross looked at her and raised his patchy eyebrows. "Greater good, remember? Thomas will consider it acceptable losses."

"I have an understanding with General Wickstaff," said Klein. "I doubt I would extend it to this new man, Thomas."

"Thomas doesn't reach understandings," said Cross, running a hand over his shaved and scarred head. "You're either with him or against him."

"Then I am, unfortunately, against him."

Maddy nodded. "So am I."

"I'm a colonel under his command," said Cross. "I know we're talking freely here, but there's still a line."

"No," said Maddy. "The lines have been blurry for a while now. In fact, I think they've been rubbed out. There can only be one leader in Portsmouth. We're all going to have to pick a side."

Cross sipped his coffee then placed it down carefully. He rose slowly and studied Maddy and Klein. "I understand where this conversation is going, and it ends with us all lined up against a wall. Trust me, it's better to let the top brass sort it out amongst themselves. I might be a colonel, but that's only because all the qualified people went and died. I'm nothing more than a sergeant at heart, and this conversation is a little above my station. Look, Maddy, General Thomas is a bastard, I agree, but he's no idiot. If Wickstaff is serious about opposing him, a lot of people will die. Best thing anyone can do is convince her to step down. Even that might not be good enough after what she did tonight."

"Thomas is sending people into danger, Tony. Wickstaff is trying to keep them alive."

"Well, she's going to achieve the exact opposite. Talk to her, Maddy, before the skid marks won't wash out."

Maddy glanced at Commander Klein, and she was crestfallen when she saw him shrug noncommittally. "Talk at the poker table cannot be taken too seriously, Madeline," he said. "I believe Wickstaff would be safer stepping down, but I wish her the very best whatever happens, *ja*? If it makes you feel better, she is my pick to win. God help anyone who crosses zat warrior of a woman."

Tony raised an eyebrow at that, but Maddy got up and shoved past him before he could say anything. She left the carriage in disgust. It was irrational, but she was just so... *overwhelmed*. For months, she had fought alongside Wickstaff and the people of Portsmouth.

*Then some dinosaur arrives and threatens everything.*
*Screw you, Thomas.*

Cross caught up with her on the docks, despite her attempts to hurry away. It was late now, and the moon was a rare gem sparkling overhead. It made her want to cry even more, so she turned towards the sea and stared at the silvery glint of the waves to disguise her expression. Her attempt to ignore Cross failed. He put a hand on her back and made her shudder. "Don't think what you're thinking, love, okay?"

"And what am I thinking?"

"That you would die for Wickstaff. Kill for her."

It was true she would like to march up to Thomas and shoot the old bastard in the face, but she wouldn't seriously do it. She didn't have it in her. No way.

*Although there are a lot of things I never used to have in me. Truthfully, I don't know what I'm capable of any more.*

"I just wish you people hadn't come here," she said. "We were fine before."

Cross removed his hand from her back and sighed. He stood beside her and looked out at the sea. "But for how long? I'm well aware of what people did to survive here, but you're undermanned and undergunned. It really is a good thing Thomas came here. You just need to stop resisting."

"Because resistance is futile, huh?"

"No, because resistance is never as good as cooperation. I understand you don't like Thomas, and I admit he's not my cup of tea either, but he *is* here to help. He wants to put a stop to the demons and make the world safe again. I wouldn't serve him if I didn't believe that."

"No matter the cost, huh?"

He shrugged. "Perhaps that's the difference with men like him. Perhaps seeing the big picture is what makes someone suited to lead." He rubbed his brow and chuckled. "Christ, I only wanted a coffee and a chance to get to know you, Maddy. I didn't realise it would be the start of an insurrection."

Maddy turned to him. "Why do you want to get to know me?"

"Are you kidding? Most of the women I served with in the desert have more scars than me."

"I wear my scars on the inside."

"I sense that, but there's still light in your eyes. Somehow your heart is still beating inside your chest."

"Isn't yours?"

"Barely. I've seen so much fighting and death this last year I can barely feel anything besides fear."

Maddy frowned. His face looked like cloth-covered oak. "You don't look afraid to me."

"That's the thing about fear, love. Endure enough of it and it gets under your skin and forms callouses. I used to fear getting shot or being taken prisoner by the Taliban. Then I feared the demons – feared them more than anything else. Now, it's something else that keeps me from sleeping at night."

"What's that?"

Cross let the air out of his lungs and stared out at the ominous, unmoving shapes of the massive ships and tankers. "What if we win, Maddy? What if we beat the demons and have to go back to being human again? I'm not sure I remember how."

Maddy saw the fear he was referring to, and for half a second this battle-hardened warrior was a frightened five-year-old boy. Instinctively, she reached out and took his hand. "Then I guess, if that time comes, we'll have to help each other."

Cross looked at her for a long moment. His lips parted as if he wanted to say something else.

But distant gunfire spoke first.

---

Mass took a breather by sitting on the stairs. He quickly realised that if he hadn't sat down voluntarily, he would've collapsed. Blood from his throat covered every inch of him, and while most of it was from the initial wound, it had bled steadily over the last several hours. His hands trembled and his stomach sloshed uneasily.

"I can help you with that," said Cam. He was holding a bottle of water and a small plastic box. The water he handed to Mass, then he opened the box. Inside were some cotton reels and a needle. "It needs disinfecting and sewing up. It is very bad wound."

"Thank your mate with the hook for me."

Cam sighed. "Naseem used to be a good man. It pains me to have seen him fall to such ruthlessness."

Mass had accepted that Cam was inside the house with them, but he didn't consider him a trustworthy ally. Harriet had admitted she knew little about him, but she did state he had never taken liberties with the women in the containers – one of only a few who hadn't. That counted for something, Mass supposed. It was enough to give the guy a chance at least.

"Who is Naseem?" asked Mass. "What's his deal?"

Cam took a packet of alcohol wipes from his pocket and tore them open with his teeth. "May I clean your wound?"

Mass nodded and prepared for the pain to begin. He'd never been good with needles. The TB jab at school had given him nightmares for months.

While he worked, Cam answered the question. "Naseem was a Muslim youth worker and I met him when he came to Nigeria. He helped the children in my village and it inspired me. The stories he told, of the lives we could lead if we threw aside fear and despair, were mesmerising. He taught us we did not have to accept poverty or oppression, and that our lives could be tools to build a better world. I, and a few others in my village, came to the UK to help spread the message of Islam. We petitioned the rich to help the poor."

Mass rolled his eyes. "You and me wouldn't have got on, mate. I won't even tell you about the time a Jehovah's Witness knocked on my mate Ravy's door. You ever seen a man covered in baked beans? Anyway, I'm not a big fan of religion."

Cam merely shrugged. "My intentions were good. I wanted to live a life Allah would deem worthy, to help others find a better path. Now, I'm unsure if Allah is real. Perhaps all that exists beyond this life is monsters."

"The only monsters we need to worry about are the ones outside this house. One of those monsters out there might be an old friend of mine, Vamps. He was the bravest guy I knew – my best friend – and he went to Hell to fight the enemy on their own turf. It was all for nothing, though, because here we are, still fighting for our shitty little lives."

"It is our nature. The ant avoids the spider. All things wish to live. Even those fiends outside." Cam finished cleaning the wound and threaded the needle. "This will hurt."

Mass huffed. "Everything hurts. I still don't understand why your man did this to me."

"Naseem has his reasons, but I long ago stopped understanding them. When the demons first attacked, Naseem had a pair of sons. One died early. The other was shot by a police officer who wanted our bus. It was packed with supplies. Naseem's surviving son had been filling it with petrol when the police officer appeared and ordered him to hand over the keys. He refused, so the police officer shot him in the face."

"But he didn't take the bus though," said Mass. "I saw it parked in the barn."

"Yes, he did take it, but Naseem got it back. He tracked the police officer for three weeks, avoiding demons at every turn. There were only six of us back then, but we followed Naseem because we didn't know what else to do. We also grieved for his son who had bravely refused to give up our supplies. Eventually, Naseem found the police officer hiding at this farmhouse. We expected Naseem to kill the man, but he did not. Instead, he burned the man's hands and feet to a crisp before chaining him up in the barn. A week later, he burned the man's eyes. One more week and he placed a tyre around the man and set fire to him. His suffering lasted three whole weeks."

"I found a group of bodies burned in tyres near here. Why did Naseem kill them? Why did he torture them?"

"In Nigeria, Naseem saw the villagers execute a rapist in this way. The people you found burnt in the field were a group who tried to leave us. Naseem believes only a chosen few are supposed to survive this apocalypse, and that he has been chosen to lead them. Everyone else must die. Allah sent the demons here to wipe out the unrighteous, but after their failure, Naseem reclaimed their mission in the name of the righteous."

Mass rolled his eyes. "He thinks he's Noah."

Cam shook his head sadly. "No, he does not. He thinks he is Christ. A saviour meant to rescue us from ourselves."

"And you all follow him!"

"You saw what happened to those who did not. I no longer believe in Naseem, but the people here are still my friends. I could not abandon them." His gaze lowered. "Now they are dead anyway."

Mass almost said sorry for the man's loss, but stopped himself. "What about that bitch, Gemma? What's her deal?"

"She was a police officer."

Mass frowned. "Like the man who shot Naseem's son?"

"Yes, that was Gemma's husband. When Naseem began torturing the man who shot his son, Gemma begged for mercy. She promised to do whatever Naseem asked – and she has done so ever since. Naseem's most devout follower."

"This place is a cult. You see that, right?"

Cam nodded. "I fear it is so, yes. I am sorry you found your way here. Naseem took your man when he stole your supplies because he wanted to know more about Portsmouth. He sees it as the new Sodom. They survive in defiance of Allah's will."

Mass sighed. "Okay, enough. It's all bullshit. It was bullshit before the end of the world and it's bullshit now. Just get me patched up so I can fight."

Cam held up the needle. It glinted in the light of the candles Harriet had set up. Mass took a long swig of water and nodded. "Do it quick."

The pain was immense: a precise, white-hot agony, a thousand tiny bee stings one after another. But it was still just pain. He was more than used to it. Once Cam was done, he stood up with clicking knees that betrayed his age. "Keep the wound clean. If you live."

"Yeah, *if* I live. Thanks."

"You are most welcome. I am sorry I tried to kill you."

Mass tested his legs and held onto the bannister as he stood. "You want to make it up to me, kill as many demons as you can."

"I will do so."

Mass patted Cam on the back and took a walk. The demons

hadn't attacked in over an hour, which had left everyone standing around anxiously, peering out windows and checking doors. He found Addy in the lounge, lining up shotgun shells on an oak coffee table. It was almost ritualistic how she straightened and positioned each one. "You okay, Ad?"

"Right as rain." She positioned another shell.

Mass didn't sit down on the sofa because he wasn't sure he would get back up again. He'd never felt so weak, not since he'd been a sickly little kid with asthma trying not to get his ass beaten in Brixton. "I'm sorry about Gross," he said. "Once we make it back to Portsmouth, we'll have a drink in his name."

"I'm not going back to Portsmouth." She kept her eyes on the shotgun shells. "I'm going to kill those animals outside and then I'm going to find that hook-handed bastard's corpse and piss on it."

"Then what?"

"Then nothing. I do that and I'm done."

Mass sighed. He went to the room's large boarded-up window and peered through the gap at the top. The demons were still out there – he could see their shadows dancing back and forth. Now and then the moon would strike a pair of eyes and light them up. Several demons fell in the battle earlier that night, but Mass suspected another dozen, at least, surrounded the house. It might not sound a lot, but in the darkness of night, and with everyone in the house growing weary, it was a demoralising threat. Not to mention that Vamps might be out there somewhere.

*What the hell happened to you, mate?*

Addy was certain it had been Vamps she'd seen, although apparently it hadn't been him any more. Vamps was a demon now – possibly a demon more terrible than any other. Mass needed to see it with his own eyes though. He couldn't give up on his friend until he knew there was no hope. "Addy, we will kill every last demon out there, I promise, but you need to promise me you won't stop after that. There are more demons than this, and we all made a promise to each other that we would fight until the death to keep them at bay. Gross might be dead, but thousands of people at Portsmouth are still counting on us. *I* need you with me, Addy."

Addy didn't answer. She kept on counting shells.

Mass left the room to check on everyone else. Tox was in the kitchen, making a sheath out of a tea towel. He'd found a large chef's knife and wanted to fix it to his belt. Mass chit-chatted for a minute then left him be. "Let me know when the killing starts back up," was the last thing Tox muttered as Mass left.

Harriet was bringing more ammunition and guns up from the basement. That left Smithy, who he'd seen go upstairs earlier. He had wanted to see what was happening outside from a higher viewpoint. Mass took a candle and went looking for him. He liked the lad. They were about the same age, yet Smithy had retained a sense of humour that Mass had completely lost. Perhaps it was because Smithy had survived on his own. He hadn't lost as many people as Mass. They had both survived but in different ways. Mass liked knowing people could still be different. Not everyone was the same shattered soul. Two vases never broke the same.

No sign of Smithy on the landing, so Mass checked the room where he'd had his throat slit. His blood still stained the carpet, but it was dry now – more black than red. The metallic scent of it coated the air. Other than the chair Gross had been tied to, the room was empty.

A thud from further down the hall alerted him, and he ducked down, candle in one hand, shotgun in the other. "Smithy?" he whispered. "That you?"

No answer other than a series of light thuds.

"Shitting hell, here we go!" Mass crept down the hallway towards the noise. It hadn't ceased, and he could still hear awkward fumbling – like someone trying to climb in through a window.

*Damn it.*

Mass had expected the demons to sneak in, eventually. He raced down the corridor and shouldered open the door at the end. Inside, he found a cramped bathroom. A small demon hung from a narrow rectangular window. It had made it through the opening but had somehow got its leg twisted between the frame and the window. It was flapping around like a wounded crow, grabbing at the sides of the bathtub and trying to right itself.

Mass smirked and placed his finger against the trigger. "Nice try, dickhead."

"Me David!"

Something struck Mass in the side just as he pulled the trigger.

It sent his aim wide by a thumbnail, but it was enough to make him miss. The bullet buried itself in the tiles above the bath taps.

"What the hell?" Mass spun around and pointed his shotgun at his attacker's chest. It was Smithy. The lad was a heartbeat away from taking a hole through the lungs.

"Don't shoot."

"It's a demon."

"No! I mean, yes, but don't shoot, okay? He's... he's..."

Mass shook his head in utter confusion. "He's what?"

Smithy went and helped the little demon get free from the window. "He's my mate."

"Me David," said the demon. "Please, may come in? Yes to enter?"

Mass lowered his shotgun. "Start explaining."

---

Nine months. For nine months, Smithy had survived against impossible odds, but right here, in this bathroom, he had been sure Mass would shoot him dead. Somehow the big lad had managed not to pull the trigger – not even when Smithy had helped David out of the window and into the bathtub. What must it have looked like?

"Start explaining," said Mass, standing there with his thick forearms crossed and his shotgun thankfully propped against the door.

Smithy moved in front of David, whether to protect him or hide him, he didn't know. "He's a good demon. He doesn't kill humans. He can think for himself – on some occasions more than others, admittedly, but he's not like the others."

David peered out from behind him and waved. "Hello, friend."

Mass waved back. "Um, hello."

Smithy got straight to what was important. "I think he used to run with some mates of yours. Aymun and Vamps?"

Mass frowned. His gaze went between David and Smithy several times before he spoke. "This demon knew Aymun and Vamps? How? What happened to them after they went to Hell?"

David crept out from behind Smithy. Smithy had an urge to keep the demon behind him, but Mass made no move for his shotgun. "Vamps and Aymun leave Hell. Crimolok go with. Is inside Vamps."

"Who in the blue hell is Crimolok?"

"Red Lord. Not blue."

Smithy saw a minute shudder run through Mass's shoulders. While the name Crimolok clearly meant nothing to the guy, mention of the Red Lord stirred something. "The Red Lord is the thing inside Vamps? The monster behind this entire shit show is inside my friend? The exterminator of mankind?"

David nodded and grinned oddly. Smithy understood it was because he had been understood, not because he was glad of the situation. "Yes! Crimolok, God's son. Brother of Lucifer and Michael. He is outside."

Mass raised both eyebrows. "For real?"

"Yeah," said Smithy. "Bit of a head fuck, right? Not every day you get to meet the destroyer of worlds."

"This is our chance," said Mass, suddenly growing excited. "We kill him and this will all be over."

David eeked, then stared down at the grimy tiles with a shudder. "Vamps weak. Soon body give out and Crimolok free. Vamps close gate. Red Lord wake up."

Mass frowned and looked at Smithy. Smithy shrugged. "This is all stuff from before I met Dave. I don't really understand what he's talking about. I get that it's bad though."

Mass grabbed his shotgun. "Real bad. Come on, let's get back downstairs. I need to put this Crimolok down."

"No," said David. "Kill Vamps. Crimolok go Hell. Take control of demons again. No kill."

"You mean that killing him will free him? If that's the case," said Mass, "then why doesn't he just top himself?"

"Sin."

"What?"

David gave a lopsided shrug. "Kill self go Hell. Yes?"

Smithy was struggling to understand. It looked like Mass was too. "But you just said that Crimolok *wants* to get back to Hell."

"Yes, but all kill selves belong Devil. Devil judge. Own soul."

Smithy spoke again, trying to keep up. "But the Devil's a bad guy, right? Wouldn't he just release Crimolok?"

Mass smirked and then chuckled. "Nah, he wouldn't. I met the Devil once – he's a good bloke."

Smithy realised he had clearly missed a lot surviving on his own. Why was it that everyone else seemed to talk about Hell and the Devil and other powerful creatures like it was all completely normal? Then he looked down at the little demon he had just called his 'mate' and realised that the definition of the word had changed.

Suddenly there was noise downstairs, and it made them realise they were standing around chatting when they were still in a huge amount of danger. "Let's discuss this over tea and crumpets later," said Smithy.

Mass nodded. "Where's your weapon?"

"Shit, I left it in the other room while I was looking out the windows. I'll go get it."

"Do it fast," said David, clutching his head. "He is coming."

Mass looked at Smithy for an explanation. Smithy sighed. "Yeah, he does that sometimes. It's never good. I'll meet you downstairs, mate."

Mass nodded and rushed off, leaving Smithy with David. He grabbed the demon and pulled him closer. "Come on, Dave."

David loped after him, in obvious pain as he clutched his head. It seemed like the closer Crimolok got, the harder it was for the little demon to think. He wondered if there was any chance of him turning violent if that influence grew too strong. It was a struggle to imagine the small creature being much of a threat, but he was still a demon.

Smithy grabbed his shotgun from where he'd left it standing against a bedside cabinet in one of the bedrooms. Just as he got a hold on it, the sound of gunfire rang out below. "Showti—"

David barrelled into Smithy and knocked him forward. Smithy fought to keep his balance but realised he had just narrowly avoided being decapitated by the swiping claw of a demon. The hunched monster clattered into David and threw him against the wall. Before it had a chance to tear into the smaller demon, Smithy aimed his shotgun and pulled the trigger. The blast pasted the demon's skull on the wall. Its lifeless body slumped on the bed in the centre of the room.

Smithy went to David, who was cowering on the ground. "You okay, buddy?"

David nodded, but his eyes were rolling all over the place. There was a divot in his naked chest where he'd been clawed. It didn't bleed. "Yes, am okay."

"Good. Stay down." Smithy ran to the window that was now hanging open. Its rotting boards were lying on the threadbare carpet. The demons had found a weak point and sent in an assassin. But this couldn't be the only one.

It had started to rain, which caused a slinking shadow on the sloped roof above the kitchen to glisten in the moonlight. While it was too dark to aim, Smithy fired a blast in the shadow's general vicinity. The pained screech that followed was enough to let him know he'd hit his target.

There were more creatures' shadows along the roof, all making their way for the open window. Smithy shoved in another pair of shells and fired them at once. He couldn't tell if he had hit his targets because his temples were thudding in panic. There was no way he could fight off all these demons alone. It was too dark, and reloading took too long. "Shit! Dave, get up. Get out of this room."

David shuffled out into the hallway and Smithy leapt out after him, dragging the door closed. Desperately, he searched for a lock on the door, or something he could throw across the entrance, but the hallway was bare. So he did the only thing he could think to do. He placed his shotgun against the wall and grabbed the door's brass handle, waiting for the room beyond to flood with demons. The door opened inwards, which meant he couldn't help the situation by placing his weight against the wood. The only thing he could do was try to keep the handle up.

He heard demons flood in through the open window, hissing and chattering like rabid monkeys. Did they know he was standing right outside the room?

A thud struck the door and made him yelp.

*Looks like they know.*

His yelp gave his presence away, causing the thuds to multiply. The wood cracked. The hinges rattled. There was no pressure on the door handle yet, which meant he wasn't dead yet as none of the demons had thought to try to open the door in the traditional way.

They would get through eventually, but at least he had some time. "Help! Someone! The demons are getting in up here. I need help."

The gunfire downstairs was deafening. Smithy lacked hope anyone would hear him. Then Cam appeared at the top of the stairs. He wasn't holding a candle, which caused him to glance around the shadowy corridor for a moment, but once he saw Smithy backed up against the door, he came rushing over.

"The room is filling up with demons," Smithy explained. "They got in through a window."

Cam nodded to David, slumped on the ground nearby. "There is one here."

"No, leave him. He's... not a threat."

The door thudded constantly, the wooden frame beginning to rock back and forth as the nails loosened. From the force of the blows, Smithy decided there was either a giant demon in the bedroom, or half a dozen of the normal-sized ones with a hell of a hard-on for eating him. Downstairs sounded no better.

"What's happening with the others, Cam?"

"It is bad. The demons are attacking on all sides."

Smithy flinched as the door tilted at the top. It would come away from the frame at any moment. Smithy reached out with one hand and grabbed his shotgun. "David, get downstairs. Tell them what's happening."

David dragged himself to his feet and got. If not for the fact the demon started down the stairs, Smithy would have thought he hadn't heard.

Another blow shifted the door out further. The thick wood clonked against the side of Smithy's head. His hand slipped from the handle and he raised his shotgun, firing off a blast into the widening gap between frame and door. Cam poked his shotgun into the gap on the other side and fired. Then both of them grabbed the door and shoved it back into place, trying to push it back into the frame. The pair of shotgun blasts had bought them a little breathing room, but the onslaught resumed almost immediately. The door was now completely unattached by the hinges, held in place only by their heaving shoulders.

But the weight was too much.

"We cannot hold this for long," said Cam.

"No shit. I'm sorry I called you up here."

"It is okay, but it is time for you to leave now, friend. Go warn the others. Fall back wherever you can."

Smithy studied the man who was only one level above being a stranger and wondered if he'd heard correctly. "If I step away from this door, the demons will flood out and kill you."

"I understand this. I will hold them off as long as I can."

Smithy winced as the wood clonked against his head again. He heaved the door back into the frame, losing his breath as he used up the last of his strength. "Y-You'll die."

"Yes. Now go."

"Why?"

Cam smiled, but it was full of sadness. "Because I followed a man once who taught me that Allah respects sacrifice above all else. That man lost his way, but I shall not. Go, my friend, and live."

The door thudded against Smithy's head again and this time dislodged him from the door. The gap between the frame widened. Smithy hurried to get his shoulder back up against the door, but Cam moved in his way and blocked him. "Go! Now!"

Smithy clutched his shotgun and backed away. "Shit. Thank you. Thank you, mate."

The door flew open and Cam leapt back.

Smithy turned and ran for the stairs, listening to the sound of gunfire behind him and praying it would last forever. Once it stopped, it meant Cam was dead.

It stopped by the time he was halfway down the stairs.

The demons were inside the house.

## CHAPTER TEN

Mass rushed into the kitchen as soon as Tox called for help. Shadows moved past the windows. The demons were launching their attack.

"Shit's about to go down," said Tox, checking his shotgun like a surgeon checking his scalpel.

The back door was blocked by the cabinet Smithy had pushed into place, but the kitchen had more windows than the other rooms, and while they were all boarded up, it could be the weak point in their defences.

"Addy has the front," said Mass. "I'm with you, mate. Ready?"

Tox cocked his shotgun. "Urban Vampires for life."

Mass nodded. "For life."

The first attack came – a thud at one of the windows that shook the wooden board nailed in place. A small cloud of brick dust erupted from the wall. Mass ran and hopped up on the worktop, his weakness taking a break as adrenaline flooded his system. If this was supposed to be his death, he intended to send it packing. As with all the other windows, there was a gap at the top to shoot or stab through. Mass fired his shotgun into the shadow-filled night.

The other window boards shook as the demons attacked several places at once. Tox got to work firing out of the two windows near to him, rushing back and forth. Pictures and utensils rattled on the walls. Candles flickered. Rain began to beat at the roof tiles. Demonic howls surrounded the house.

Addy started shouting from the lounge. Gunfire exploded upstairs. There was no way to be everywhere at once, so Mass would just have to hope the others could handle their own personal battles.

One of the windows burst open, its wooden board detaching from the crumbling brickwork and clattering into the kitchen's large metal sink. The glass panes shattered, and a demon was suddenly inside.

Mass was still standing on the worktop, and he leapt off to get a better angle on the monster. It glared at him in the flickering candlelight and let loose a roar. Mass replied with a roar of his own and the shotgun blast tore clean through its leg, sending it tumbling to the tiles. He finished the demon off with a vicious stamp to its misshapen skull.

Another window burst open, letting in the rain, the howling winds, and the demons.

Tox leapt down from the worktop too. "We need to get out of this bloody kitchen. We can't hold it."

Mass nodded. "We need to find somewhere we can dig in and keep from being surrounded."

The two of them moved back towards the door, letting off shots as demons flooded the kitchen. Candles flickered in the flurry of activity, elongating the ghastly shadows and sending them up the walls.

In the dining room, Mass slammed the old wooden door shut and shoved a chair beneath the handle. He had no idea if the trick worked, but it was the only thing he had time to do. The demons were already banging against the wood by the time he and Tox made it into the front hallway. Addy and Harriet were there, trying to hold a board in place over a window. No sign of Cam or Smithy. Mass suddenly realised how massively outnumbered they were.

*We're not getting out of this alive.*

"We're totally screwed!" Harriet sobbed, echoing the thoughts inside his head. "There're too many."

Footsteps sounded on the staircase. Mass turned to see the demon, David, hurtling down the steps. There was blood leaking from its one eye and its movements were jerky. "Inside upstairs," it yelled shrilly. "Inside upstairs. Smithy need help."

Mass stood at the bottom of the stairs and aimed up towards the landing. He could hear the commotion, the sound of demons inside the house. He could hear Smithy shouting for help. There was no time to do anything. Tox tried to help Addy and Harriet keep the window board in place, but another window was also under attack, its board loosening with every blow. The sound of splintering wood came from the dining room too.

"We need to get the hell out of here!" said Tox. "We've lost."

"Where the fuck is there to go?" Addy shouted, grunting as the board shifted out of her grasp. Her hand was bleeding.

"We're screwed," said Harriet, holding a shotgun but doing nothing with it.

Mass searched around, not knowing where an attack would come from next. His eyes spotted something that should have been obvious – the basement door. "Get downstairs," he yelled. "Get into the basement."

Tox turned from the window with a frown, but then the frown shifted into a look of shocked relief. "Damn it, yes! Come on. Move it."

Harriet moved first, sprinting for safety. Addy and Tox leapt back from the window and let the board fall away to reveal a dozen demonic eyes glaring in at them from the rain-streaked darkness outside. They raced to the basement door and clattered down the wooden steps. Mass went to join them, but David grabbed his leg. The demon slumped like it could barely hold itself up, but its eyes were clear and lucid. "Smithy!"

Mass looked up the stairs. Smithy was no longer calling out for help. "I'm sorry, mate, but he's a goner. We need to get inside the basement."

"He is alive. I go." The weak little demon began to slither up the stairs on its hands and knees. Suicide. There was no way to help Smithy. The demons were invading the house.

"For Christ's sake." Mass started up the stairs. He owed Smithy. The lad had got him out of that pit and helped save Addy. "Smithy! You alive?"

To Mass's relief, Smithy appeared at the top of the stairs and began legging it downwards. "They're coming," he screamed. "Shit, they're coming."

On the upstairs landing, demons raced towards the stairs. Mass leapt back down into the hallway and aimed his shotgun, but before he pulled the trigger, he sensed a more imminent threat to his right. He turned and let off a shot at a demon racing at him from the dining room. "We have to move!"

Smithy's face was an oil painting of terror. "Where?"

"The basement. Move!"

Mass took another shot and hit a primate leaping down the stairs. Its body tumbled like a boulder and almost took out Smithy, who made it into the hallway just in time. Like a parent, he grabbed David and pulled him close. "Come on, little buddy, you're with us."

Mass knew he was out of ammo, so he turned the heavy 12-gauge sideways and used it as a club. He swung for a demon climbing in through the window and dented its skull. Smithy emptied his last shell into a demon in the dining room and then did the same, swinging his long-barrelled shotgun like a baseball bat. The two men moved towards the basement door, unable to turn their backs and run.

Demons came from everywhere, spilling into the hallway from every window. A burnt man leapt off the stairs and collided with Smithy, grabbing him by the arm and tearing his flesh with its bony claws. Taken by surprise, Smithy dropped his shotgun and yelled. Mass skipped across the tiles and swung his shotgun at the burnt man, knocking its head clean off. It was as if its flesh was made of slow-cooked pork.

Smithy was bleeding, but he was able to continue towards the basement door. Mass put a hand on his back and pushed him faster. Then they were at the top of the stairs, inches from safety.

Smithy started downward, David right behind him. Mass turned and grabbed the door handle and saw a dozen demons rushing towards him. He slammed the door closed and the demons struck the other side, rattling the door in its frame. The wood was thick, the handle made of heavy iron.

A demon screeched in pain.

*Then another one.*

*The thudding against the door stopped. Mass frowned.*
*The iron!*

Iron was some kind of kryptonite to demons. They couldn't touch the door handle. Their only option would be to smash in the thick wood panels. Mass joined the others in the basement. "We have a little time. Enough to try to think our way out of this."

"There's a hatch," said Harriet. "Whenever Naseem and the others brought back supplies, they would head in and out through a hatch at the back of the house."

"It's over here," said Addy, pointing up at a trapdoor overhead. There was a stubby wooden ladder attached via hooks.

"We have a way out," said Mass, breathing a sigh of relief between heaving gasps for air. "We're not done yet."

Smithy started rooting around, moving aside boxes and examining various antique firearms. "We need to rearm. I doubt we'll get an easy— Yah! Jesus!"

As Smithy had shoved aside a stack of food crates, he uncovered someone hiding. Gemma cowered, holding up a shaking hand in defence. "P-Please!"

Addy's face turned to stone. She threw down her shotgun and pulled out the knife she always carried. "This bitch is mine."

Gemma moved behind Smithy as if he would protect her. Of course, he wasn't about to do that, and instead he shoved her into the centre of the room. "Don't know you, sweetheart."

"Sorry, love," said Mass, "but I think Addy's earned a little payback. Don't worry, I won't let her get too carried away."

Addy stalked towards the woman with her knife. "Gross was worth ten of you," she snarled. "I'm going to make this hurt."

Gemma shook her head, looking for help but finding none. "No," she begged. "No, please. I... I can get us out of here. There's a way!"

"We already know about the hatch."

"I don't just mean out of this basement. I mean I can get us off this farm. I can get us out of here in one piece."

Mass moved to Addy and placed a hand on her arm. "One sec, Addy. We're going to hear what this bitch has to say."

Maddy was dead on her feet. Time was an imprecise thing nowadays, but her body told her it was closer to dawn than dusk. The fact she was fully armed and about to travel beyond the barricades for the first time in months was surreal. That she was doing so to help rescue a bunch of soldiers who had arrived, uninvited, only yesterday was even more bizarre.

The gunfire in the city had continued for about ten minutes before the first maydays started coming through the radios. The calls were unfiltered and went to both Thomas's and Wickstaff's men, which meant everyone knew what was happening. The soldiers outside the barricades were being slaughtered, surrounded by the enemy on all sides. They needed rescuing. Thomas's face had turned pale at the news, but Wickstaff went to work with grim determination. "I still think you should stay behind and man the fort," she told Maddy. "There are more than enough of us heading out on this fool's errand."

"No way," said Maddy. She was a survivor but not necessarily a fighter, yet she couldn't sit this one out. It felt like vindication. The men and women of Portsmouth were banding together to save Thomas's men because that was what they did. They rescued people. She couldn't sit by while others risked their lives. "I'm going, ma'am, unless you object."

Wickstaff cocked the lever on her SA80. "I would never tell a woman not to fight. Having you next to me will be a comfort. It's been a while since I was in the field. You promise to tell me if my pants are showing?"

"Why are you going out with us at all?" Maddy asked, ignoring the attempt at humour. "You're our leader."

"Exactly. Let everyone see I'm willing to get my hands dirty, hierarchy be damned. We all need to fight together when the time comes. Now, let's get on with this grim task, shall we? The sound of screaming is not something I enjoy."

Maddy agreed. The constant screams and shouts coming from the ruins were disturbing, and the only positive was that it meant men were still alive out there.

Wickstaff moved to the front of her cohort, a hundred men and women of varying ages, creeds, and colours. "Okay, you lot. We all know what we have to do. There are a bunch of idiots out there who need our help. They might be brave, professional men, but when the shit hits the fan, it's always us who has to clean up the mess. We've been cleaning up other people's mess for the best part of a year, and while the rest of the country went and died, we held out. We faced the monsters and told them to get back under our beds, to go back to hiding inside our closets, to banish themselves only to our nightmares. We refused to accept their new reality. We refused to be afraid. Tonight we will remind them of that."

The cohort cheered. They were about to face monsters in the night, but every face was determined. Every weapon was loaded. Portsmouth did not cower.

Wickstaff raised her assault rifle to show she was ready. "You people of Portsmouth make me proud to be human. Now, let's go send some demons back to Hell."

Another cheer, but as it died down, a shouting voice took over. "Stop this at once." General Thomas marched through the crowd, a group of uniformed soldiers trailing behind him as well as Colonel Cross. "Brigadier Wickstaff, you are under arrest for insubordination and incitement of mutiny. You are to stand down immediately."

Wickstaff chuckled. "And I say, *fuck you*, General."

Thomas's men raised their weapons, but they were met with the cacophonous clicking of a hundred weapons being cocked and primed. Wickstaff's army aimed at Thomas and his men.

In the white glow of the spotlights, Thomas looked like an enraged phantom. "This is treason! I am in charge of what is left of this ruin of a country and I will restore it. If you oppose me, you will be shot." He lifted a pistol and pointed it right at Wickstaff.

Wickstaff opened up her body, presenting a larger target. "So shoot me, General. If you think that's the right call, do it!"

Thomas's hand shook as though he would actually do it. Maddy went to step in front of Wickstaff, but the woman shook her head and shooed her away. "I don't need a bodyguard, Maddy. Not inside my own city."

Thomas's moustache flickered in anger. "Colonel Cross, you are to relieve Brigadier Wickstaff from her duties and lead these men out yourself. We are wasting time, and our men need rescuing."

Colonel Cross was clearly not happy with the unfolding events, but he obeyed the command, although he left his rifle hanging from his neck strap and approached Wickstaff with his palms out. He was forced to stop when a guardsman stood in his way. It was Tom, the guardsman. He didn't aim his rifle but held it firmly across his chest. Then another three men stepped up beside him, forming a wall. Cross didn't know what to do. He still kept his hands off his weapon.

"This is mutiny," Thomas screeched. "You will all be shot."

Tom smiled. "I was a painter and decorator when the world ended. I never made an oath to serve anybody. I serve General Wickstaff because I *choose* to, not because I *have* to. No matter what happens, I won't serve an asshole like you."

Thomas pointed his pistol at Tom, but Tom didn't flinch.

Cross turned to his superior. "Sir, I advise caution."

"You do not caution me, Colonel. You were nothing but a grunt when you staggered out of the desert. Don't you see what's happening here?"

"Yes, sir, I do, and if you pull the trigger on any of these people, I fear things will continue to happen. Let's just focus on the priority right now. We need to pull our guys out of the fire."

Thomas bristled. His grey-white moustache twitched. Meanwhile, more men stood beside Tom, obscuring Wickstaff with a bigger and bigger wall. Maddy could no longer even see the woman, but she hoped she was smiling. She hoped that General Wickstaff appreciated what was happening here. Portsmouth was voting. And the result was a landslide.

Thomas lowered his pistol with a growl. "This isn't over. There shall be a reckoning."

Wickstaff parted the men in front of her so that she could face Thomas. "That, you can guarantee, General. Now, get your men out of my way. We have a mess to clean up."

Wickstaff turned and climbed one of the ladders leading up onto the top of the parked lorry and that prompted everyone to get going. There were four ladders in total, with the same amount leading down over the other side. Many of the barricades were dependent upon parked vehicles and ladders like this.

Maddy made it over and joined the assembly on the other side. Despite their eagerness, everyone fell to silence and caution. They spread out in a line and began to stalk the main road. The screaming was less than a mile away. The gunshots sounded close. So did the monsters.

Maddy heard hurrying footsteps behind her and turned to see Colonel Cross beside her. "What the hell are you doing?"

"What's it look like? I'm going to rescue my men."

"Does Thomas know?"

"It was his idea. Wants me to keep an eye on Wickstaff. Probably hoping I'll put a bullet in her back."

Maddy glared at him. "I'd put one in you first."

"Relax. There's only one reason I'm here, and that's because a bunch of my men need help. I wasn't always an officer. I served with those soldiers. Maybe if I'd gone out with them in the first place..."

Maddy saw the torment and knew it was real. Cross had a face that seemed incapable of fallacy. "We'll get them out of there," she said. "Don't worry."

"Looks like Wickstaff was right about everything. We went rushing out for a fight without knowing a damned thing."

"The demons have changed back to what they were," said Maddy. "I think we've been sensing it in the wind for a while here, but you and Thomas had no way of knowing. It should've been a routine search and destroy. Maybe it's no one's fault."

Cross grunted and then nodded. "You have a nice way of looking at things. I hope we can keep this from turning bad."

"I think we're beyond that, Colonel."

"Yeah, I know. Sorry. Maybe if we're lucky we'll die out here tonight."

She looked at him. He wasn't apologising for anything he'd done, he was apologising for the man he served. He was a similar man to Tosco. Both men had their beliefs and stayed true to them for better or worse.

Wickstaff gave a hand signal to *halt*. Everyone took a knee and raised their weapons. Then Wickstaff gave another signal to *advance*. The line moved forward, weapons pointing towards shop windows and alleyways. Whatever had befallen Thomas's men, it had happened nearby. The screams were dying out and the gunfire had reduced to a trickle, but it was close. Another block or two.

The Spinnaker Tower jutted out of the ruins less than a mile away and they were nearing the city's pleasure pier. Its tall Ferris wheel was undamaged, and Wickstaff often spoke about her desire to reclaim the area for morale.

A man ran out into the road, a soldier dressed in fatigues. He didn't see the advancing army as he was utterly terrified and focused only on running. A moment later, a primate leapt out from a doorway and pinned the man down, tearing into his back with ferocious claws. Wickstaff raised her rifle and emptied four rounds into the demon, enough to see it dead.

Then the battle began.

At the sound of new gunfire, demons spilled out from the roads ahead, the usual variety of primates, burnt men, and zombies. One zombie was articulate enough to shout out in garbled tones, "Tear their throats!"

Wickstaff fired again, which prompted her army to do the same. Before long, the streets were lit up with gunfire and spotlights from the boats. The demons came in droves, leaping from roofs and emerging from alcoves. In the harsh light, their skin seemed translucent and serpentine.

Maddy hadn't fired a weapon in some time, and her hands were shaking as she aimed her MP5 and pulled the trigger. Her very first shot hit a burnt man in the chest. After that, her confidence quickly grew. She knelt and started picking her shots while Cross did the same beside her. "There's more than I expected," he said as he pumped round after round through his rifle. "There's fifty at least, if this is any indication."

Maddy knew he was right. In this one street alone, Maddy estimated a few dozen demons, and there must have been more that had attacked Thomas's men. It was the biggest enemy congregation in Portsmouth since the Great Battle. The smell of rancid flesh filled the air as yet another wave of them rounded the corner.

"Hold fast," shouted Wickstaff. "Stay together."

The gunfire increased, demons dancing and jittering in the street as they were ripped apart, but as was always the threat, they kept on coming. Their advantage had always been in numbers and lack of fear.

The first soldier went down, torn apart by a sprinting zombie.

Thankfully, his screams were drowned out by the gunfire. More men fell. The sight of so much blood took Maddy back to the battle against Lord Amon. There had seemed no hope back then, but somehow they had survived, even if the cost had been significant. It'd been the last time she'd seen her friend, Rick. She wondered if he was still alive somewhere, still fighting. Or did he have the peace of death?

A man to Maddy's left hit the ground as a primate leapt on top of him. Immediately, she aimed and fired, killing the demon with her first shot to its skull. The man beneath was already dead though, his throat torn open.

"Heads up!" Cross shouted.

Maddy glanced up to see another demon coming from the direction of the first, slinking out from behind a parked minibus. She raised her rifle to fire, but an ear-piercing blast stunned her into inaction. Cross pulled her back behind him. His aim had been deadly, and the approaching demon now lay dead with a smoking bullet hole between its eyes.

"Thanks!"

"Don't mention it, but you owe me a pint."

"I owe you a bottle."

"Advance," yelled Wickstaff, signalling by throwing an arm forward. The crowd of demons was thinning. Thomas's men were still alive and shouting for help. The line moved at a quick march, popping off shots left, right, and centre. Demons came from everywhere, but the balance had shifted and they could no longer swarm in sufficient numbers to overwhelm. Every time one appeared, they put it down with a deadly barrage of gunfire.

They found Thomas's men at the next intersection, holed up inside a corpse-littered petrol station. They were trying to maintain cover inside a small supermarket at the back of the forecourt. Its glass panes were thick and reinforced, but the sliding entry door was lying shattered on the ground. A stream of demons had already fought their way inside and were now stalking the remaining men around the aisles.

Wickstaff sent everyone forward, and men and women rushed inside the building and shot up the demons from behind. The breathing room allowed Thomas's remaining men to recover and fire from the front. Eventually, between them, they mopped up every demon and then the two groups met in the middle of the aisles, jubilant and grateful. Earlier that night, they had been untrusting strangers. Now they were battle-forged allies. Maddy still didn't know what would happen later, but she knew that, if anything, tensions would at least be eased by this rescue mission.

Cross came up behind Maddy and placed a hand on her back. She was full of adrenaline, so the sudden contact made her flinch. "Sorry," he said. "I didn't mean to startle you."

"It's okay. I'm glad most of us are still alive."

"Your people are warriors. I'm not surprised, but it's still impressive to see. They put their necks out for a bunch of men who tried to look down on them."

Maddy studied the scene inside the petrol station, saw Wickstaff's men and Thomas's men exchanging handshakes and pats on the back, and suddenly felt a pang of hope. She felt what Diane had spoken of: that she was a part of making sure there would be a tomorrow. There was more to do though – much more. She turned to Cross, all seriousness. "I'm going to kill General Thomas."

---

Smithy sat on a crate eating stale biscuits while the others talked. The door at the top of the stairs was holding up well, and every now and then a demon would screech as it accidentally made contact with the iron handle. They still wouldn't have long, which was why he had thrown down his empty shotgun in exchange for a handgun he'd found in a carry case with twenty-four short round bullets. Until tonight he had never fired a shotgun or a handgun. It was surprisingly easy once you got used to the pure, explosive force of pulling a trigger.

Gemma was still pleading her case, going over her plan for the third time. "I have keys to the coach," she said. "We make it to the barn and drive the fuck out of here. Nas and I reinforced the coach inside and we have an iron chain wrapped around the front bumper. We'll mow down any demons stupid enough to get in our way."

"Why don't we just kill you and take the keys?" asked Addy

quite reasonably. She hadn't taken her eyes off the woman once in the last five minutes – barely even blinked.

Gemma swallowed. "You could kill me, but you people are better than that, right? You can take me back to Portsmouth and lock me up. That's what the good guys do, isn't it?"

Mass smirked. "We ain't the good guys, love. Sorry."

"Wait," said Smithy. "If the plan is to escape this basement, all guns blazing, then it would be better to have another pair of hands. We can't afford to be killing our potential allies."

"Oh," said Addy, "so we're going to arm her now as well?"

"We need her," said Harriet. She too was glaring at Gemma. "Some of the girls in the containers are chained up. The ones who misbehaved, or the newer girls who haven't been beaten into submission yet. There's no key on their chains, just a padlock. A padlock only she and Naseem know the combination to."

Addy took one step forward and slapped Gemma in the face. "Spit it out, bitch. What number did you use to chain up a bunch of women like animals?"

Gemma held her face in shock, but then a smile crept across her face. "You want the number, you'll have to take me with you."

Mass folded his arms and grunted. "You really want to play this game?"

"What other choice do I have?"

Addy punched Gemma to the ground. Then she booted the woman in the ribs. The air escaped Gemma in one long, pained groan. Smithy winced. He'd never liked violence, especially when it was one-sided, but there was nothing he could do about this. Gemma had harmed these people, and it was their choice how they responded. While they might not be the 'good guys', they were certainly better than the people who had lived at this farm.

Mass pulled Addy back to keep her from killing the woman. "Smithy is right," he said. "We need every body available. It'll be a nightmare as soon as we open that hatch. I would rather she gets torn apart by a demon while we make a run for it."

Addy growled, her eyes seeming like they might summon lasers and fry Gemma to a crisp. "Once we get those girls on board that bus, she and I have unfinished business."

Gemma spat blood and nodded. "Looking forward to it."

David piped up from the corner. He'd shaken off some of his daze but still seemed weak and sickly. Smithy felt sorry at the state of him. "We need to go soon. Crimolok is... he is still outside... outside front of house. I don't think he knows we plan to escape from back of house."

Mass was grasping his ribs and wheezing a little, but he nodded enthusiastically at this. "Then maybe we have a shot at this. Everyone arm up and take a breath. We're moving in five minutes, and then— Hey!" He stooped down and pulled an old, battered shotgun from one of the lower shelves.

"What is it?" Smithy asked him.

Mass looked at the old shotgun in his hands and smiled. "This belonged to a friend. Two minutes everyone. Be ready."

Smithy shivered, realising he might die in the next few moments. It wasn't the first time he'd felt that, but this time it felt... *undeniable. Mass looked like he might drop dead even before they left the basement. Dried blood caked his neck, and his face was the colour of bacon fat.*

"You're hurt," said Harriet, standing in front of Smithy and nodding at his arm. The gash left by the demon that had grabbed him was bleeding steadily. His wrist was slick and wet with his own blood.

"Just a deep, agonising wound. I'm not dead though."

Harriet rummaged through a couple of boxes. Eventually she pulled out a yellow scarf. "I was hoping for bandages, but this will have to do. It's too ugly to wear anyway."

"Oh, you don't have to—"

"Please, let me. Every time the demons come, I fall to pieces, so right now, while I'm not a screaming mess, please just let me be useful."

Smithy smiled and let a little chuckle sound between them. Harriet was a good-looking young woman, but there were tiny cuts and larger bruises all over her. Her wrists were almost purple. "You've been through a lot," he said.

She didn't look him in the eye as she shrugged. "We all have."

"Yeah, but there are different kinds of Hell. Some worse than others. Whatever happens, this place is behind you now. It's over."

She stepped back from him for a moment, almost like she was

afraid, but then she started wrapping his arm gently with the scarf. "I don't think this world has anything left but horror. You don't need to try to create a fantasy for me."

"I'm not! These guys are from Portsmouth, a real-life city with people and walls. There's still hope for us – for everyone."

"Just have to make it through the *Night of the Living Dead* first, right?"

"That was zombies, not demons, but close enough. After all the shit we've been through, getting out of here should be a cakewalk."

Harriet laughed. It was genuine, and obviously unexpected, because she covered her mouth and blushed. "I don't remember the last time I laughed."

"It's nice. I hope to see you do it more often."

"There! You're all wrapped up. Want me to kiss it better?"

Harriet was chuckling at her own joke, but Smithy one-upped her by holding up his bandaged arm. "It would be the most action I've had in nearly a year."

She smirked and shook her head. "You'll have to work harder than that."

As she walked away, Smithy felt butterflies in his stomach. Had he just engaged in a bit of good old flirting?

*Shit, that felt good.*

The brief moment of humanity reminded him of the stakes he was playing for. As long as there were still people alive, he had to keep fighting.

The door at the top of the stairs rattled as demons thudded against it. A sharp *crack sounded* as part of the frame gave way.

"Okay," said Mass. "Looks like our time just ran out. Once the hatch is open, we need to get out as quickly as we can. Stick together, head for the barn, don't die. Ready?"

The butterflies in Smithy's tummy turned bad, and the stale biscuits he'd just eaten threatened to revisit him. Tox must have seen his apprehension because he came over. "You know how to work that?"

Smithy lifted the pistol in his hand and looked at it. "I'm not sure, to be honest. The clip was loaded, and I just jammed it in.

"It's a semi-auto. It'll keep firing until it's empty. This is the safety. It's on."

Smithy saw a small lever and pushed it with his thumb. "Now I can kill things, right?"

Tox grinned. "Right. It's been good meeting you, Smithy. Let's have a beer back in Portsmouth."

"A beer? God, yes."

"Let's go!" Mass threw open the hatch and scrambled up the ladder. Then he was gone, swallowed by the night. Addy went after him, and, of all people, Gemma went next. Tox told Smithy good luck and then disappeared. David scrambled out next, and that just left Harriet – but she wasn't moving. She stood there, trembling, with a shotgun cradled awkwardly in her arms.

"You need to move," Smithy told her over the din of the door rapidly cracking at the top of the stairs. "It'll be okay. I'll be right behind you."

Harriet nodded at him, but she still didn't move. There was nothing he could do, except…

"Sorry about this!" Smithy slapped her cheek hard and then shoved her towards the ladder. To keep her moving, he yelled at her nonstop, using her timidity as a harness and his unkind voice as a whip. It worked, and Harriet scurried through the hatch. Smithy kept his word and stayed right with her, putting a hand against her back as they left the basement and started across the field. The darkness was disorientating, and it was difficult to know which way to go. The others were ahead, but they were almost invisible. Only the sound of their hurried panting allowed him to keep up.

The demons could have been anywhere, hiding behind every shadowy shape. Not being able to see them was even more terrifying than them coming right at you.

"I can't see anything," said Harriet. Her wide eyes shone.

"Just keep moving. We're fine."

Harriet grabbed hold of him and stared into his eyes. "Promise me I'm not going to die."

It was absurd to ask such a thing. Death waited around every corner and most of the world had already succumbed. He couldn't promise her she wouldn't die tonight. "You're going to be fine," he said. "I won't let anything happen to you. Just… just keep moving. Look, over there. I can see the others."

Smithy pointed his handgun forward with one hand while

shoving Harriet with the other. While he couldn't promise to keep her alive, he could promise not to let her go.

One of the others was just ahead, their silhouette taking shape in the dark. Smithy wanted to call out, but he knew his voice would be too loud – too anxious. If the demons were still gathered at the front of the house, then there was a chance they didn't even know they were making a break for it. He might make it to the bus in one piece.

The figure ahead was standing still, as if they were waiting for Smithy to catch up. He was grateful because he didn't know where the hell he was heading in the dark. With the moon gone from the sky, there was no sign of the barn.

"Tox? Mass? Is that you? Addy?"

"Nah, blud, it's me, innit?" A demon stepped out of the darkness. "And this time, you ain't running nowhere."

## CHAPTER ELEVEN

THERE WERE STILL DEMONS in the streets of Portsmouth as they made their way back, but they were backing off now, retreating into alleyways and shopfronts. They'd lost the fight but had managed to tear apart two dozen of Thomas's best men. Another dozen were injured. Spotlights cast from nearby boats lit up their misery and made their many cuts glisten.

Cross grabbed her arm as she tried to hurry ahead, a little harshly for her liking. "Tell me you were messing around," he snapped at her. "You were just telling a bad joke, right?"

Maddy shrugged free of his grasp. "Take a look around, Tony. Your men are carrying the bloody remains of their friends. No one needed to die tonight. If killing Thomas and his ego prevents more deaths, then so be it. I'm sorry but I wasn't joking at all."

"D'you realise what you're saying? You're threatening to murder a ranking general in what is basically a martial state. I can't just pretend you didn't say it."

Maddy kicked a flattened pop can into the gutter and glared at Cross. "Who's asking you to?"

"Why did you even tell me? I'm the man's second in command."

"I told you because I thought you were a good man who would be as pissed off about men dying as I am."

"I *am* pissed off, but that doesn't mean I'm about to kill this country's highest-ranking officer. We're at war; people die."

"You think I don't know that? Tony, I've watched people die in front of me by the thousands, crushed and mangled beyond recognition. I've lost friends, family, and people I respect, but until tonight I hadn't seen a single person die simply because someone ordered them to. We fight at Portsmouth because we're family, not because Wickstaff tells us to. Your people don't belong here so long as Thomas is in charge. Either he goes or you all go."

Cross stopped her by grabbing her arm again, but this time he was gentler. He looked around, making sure no one was listening. Everyone was so weary and glad to be alive that they kept on marching towards safety with no regard for each other. "Okay, Maddy, let's say I agree with what you're saying. It doesn't mean you can just kill Thomas. He has a personal guard. You'd be shot before you even pulled the trigger. Even if you got him alone, you'd catch a bullet as soon as they discover the deed."

"I don't care. Every day people around me die trying to make the world a better place. Maybe this is my turn."

Tony leaned in closer, his breath hitting her lips and making them tingle. "Maddy, don't do anything stupid, okay? At least sleep on it for a night. We've been in battle and your blood is up. Things might look different tomorrow."

Maddy sighed. The decency in his eyes was too much to bear after the madness of the last hour. His gaze made her feel safe, like a silly girl with silly fears. To look at, Tony was a hardened, rough-edged warrior, but his eyes gave away his kindness. "Fine. I promise I'll think about it before I do anything, but I won't let Thomas throw away any more lives."

Tony put a hand on her shoulder and gave it a tiny squeeze. The warmth of his hand made her shudder. He said nothing else to her, just turned towards the docks and resumed marching with the other men. Maddy had no choice but to do the same. While she did so, she stared across the ruins at the shattered remnants of the Spinnaker Tower. Its remaining panes and steelwork glinted with silvery light as dawn approached. That the monument was still standing, even though battered and burned, gave her hope.

*Beaten but still standing tall.*

The returning army neared the barricaded lorry that blocked access into the docks. Everyone breathed a sigh of relief.

But the relief didn't last long.

A trio of men stood on the roof of the lorry with rifles, and they began to wave at the sight of everyone making it back home. Two of them were from Portsmouth, but one of them was a soldier from Thomas's contingent. The men were working together.

Then they were dying together.

A group of primates appeared from nowhere and leapt up onto the lorry in a single, collective leap. In their recent fugue state, the demons had been incapable of such feats, but it seemed they had now broken free of their daze and were once again out for blood. Unstoppable killing machines.

The three men on the lorry were blindsided, torn down before they could even acknowledge their attackers. More demons spilled into the streets from multiple directions. Maddy started shooting, launching into action even before Tony did. A second later, every man and woman was firing in a dozen directions. The demons were everywhere.

"It's a sodding ambush." Tony raised his rifle. "I think they meant to set us up this whole time."

"Everyone, close in," Wickstaff bellowed from the front. "Keep a tight formation and let the bastards have it."

Blood and gunfire filled the air, getting in Maddy's nostrils. She didn't know if the blood stench was demon or human, but it made her sick. And angry. She levelled a primate with her MP5, putting four rounds right in its skull. Then three more took its place. Men began to fall again. Portsmouth men. People Maddy knew. More anger rose in her guts and turned her vision red as she pumped round after round into the demon forces.

Tony shouted at her. "Maddy, get back. You're too far out."

Maddy knew she'd moved away from the group, leaving herself vulnerable, but she didn't care. She just wanted to kill. She imagined every demon she shot was Thomas and slammed in her next clip like a lifelong-trained soldier.

"Maddy, damn it! Get back!"

Maddy was out at sea, space all around her that demons could exploit. Her survival instincts finally snapped back into place and she began moving backwards as she pulled the trigger, moving back towards the safety of the group. But it was too late. She was cut off.

A burnt man reached out for the back of her neck and another burnt man lunged at her from the left. She swung her MP5 and fired into their chests. A primate appeared and slashed at her face. She leapt back but caught the bladed talon across her collarbone. She bit down on the pain and lifted her MP5, emptying it into the primate and tearing it to shreds.

She was out of ammo.

The problem with weapons like the MP5 was that if you fired them out of desperation or panic, they were liable to run dry on you in a matter of seconds. Hers had done just that. Now she was defenceless. Burnt men surrounded her, their smouldering eyes like embers from the fires of Hell, their broken teeth hanging loose in decaying jaws. Saliva and chunks of old flesh dripped onto the ground. Whatever glue had been holding the demons together was wearing away. Their bodies were becoming mush.

But they were still deadly.

And Maddy was surrounded.

The demons closed in.

A burnt man at her rear jolted suddenly and fell to the ground. Then another dropped as well. Something was taking the demons out from behind. Tony appeared in the gap he'd made and reached out a hand to her. "Move it, you daft cow."

Maddy started forward, but more burnt men stepped in her path. It forced Tony to meet her halfway, and he rammed his shoulder into the back of one of the demons and sent it sprawling. Then he grabbed Maddy by the wrist hard enough to almost break it and pulled her back into the group. Everyone continued firing, fighting desperately to keep the multiplying demons at bay.

But the demons just kept coming.

A large primate shrugged off a bullet wound to the shoulder and one to its thigh. The momentum of its surging run kept it moving forward, heading straight for Maddy. Maddy turned to face it, her empty MP5 the only defence she had, but then Tony shoved her out of the way. The primate smashed right into him, knocking him clean off his feet. Several men aimed their weapons, but it was too dangerous to shoot as the demon mounted Tony, and they began to wrestle back and forth, their bodies entwined. Maddy tried to help, but the savage primate swiped its claws at all angles. If she got too close, it would take her face off. Tony had the demon by the throat, keeping it from biting him, but his arms were getting torn to shreds.

Maddy stood frozen.

*I have to do something.*

*He needs me.*

Somebody shoved passed Maddy and launched themselves at the primate fighting with Cross.

Maddy gasped. "General!"

"Not now, woman," said Wickstaff as she squared up to the snarling demon with nothing but a long knife. "I'm a bit busy."

Cross was winded, and he rolled away rather than get to his feet. The primate forgot about him and turned its focus on Wickstaff. It glared at her, lit up by the spotlights of the nearby boats. For a moment it looked like it might run away, but then it leapt at the general with an almighty roar. Wickstaff hopped aside and threw out a leg, kicking the demon in the back of the knees. It toppled onto its side and had no time to recover as Wickstaff dropped on top of it and drove her knife right into its eye socket.

The heavens opened in a downpour as if the skies were applauding her victory. The sound of heavy rain on concrete was like clapping hands. Tony grabbed Wickstaff and yanked her to her feet. "I owe you one, General."

Wickstaff sniffed, raindrops dripping down her face. "Shouldn't that be *Brigadier*, Colonel Cross?"

"Right now, I don't have a fucking clue, but thank you all the same."

"Don't mention it."

Maddy moved up to Cross and touched his elbow to get his attention. "You wouldn't have needed saving if you hadn't saved me first. You're... you're a good man, Tony."

He looked her in the eye, but it seemed like it was a struggle for him. "I try to be."

Wickstaff put a hand out to separate them. "Let's do this later. We need to go."

It was true. While they'd managed to fight off the first wave of demons, multiple shadows were once again slinking out of the dimly lit alleyways. The heavy rain and glaring spotlights were disorientating.

"Everyone, get up those ladders," shouted Wickstaff. "Now!"

A new wave of demons raced through the streets. Everyone at the front formed a line, firing, while those at the rear scurried up the ladders onto the lorry. Once up top, they turned and fired from above, picking off demons as soon as they entered the harsh white glow of the spotlights.

Maddy was up front with Tony and Wickstaff. Tony tried to move her towards the back. "Get yourself up that ladder, love. I've got this."

"Ha! I'm not leaving until everyone is safe."

Wickstaff chuckled. "That's my girl."

"I could use a gun though," she said, strapping her empty MP5 to her belt and then holding out a hand.

Cross pulled a large handgun from his belt and thrust it at her. "I expect it back."

"You'll get it back empty."

The three of them stood their ground alongside two dozen brave but frightened men and women. A wall of demonic flesh hurtled towards them – talons, teeth, and infernal fury all seeking blood. The gunfire started in spatters before becoming a constant drone as multiple rifles, pistols, and shotguns roared.

The demons came in their hundreds.

Too many.

Weapons began to run out of ammo, including Tony's rifle. He held it sideways, ready to fight hand to hand – to *die* hand to hand.

"Get up those ladders," Wickstaff yelled. "Move if you want to live."

The men began to scatter, shoving each other up the ladders and clawing themselves up onto the lorry. It was now so crowded that those already on top had to leap off the other side to make room. Only a dozen people remained outside the barricade, including Maddy, Wickstaff, and Cross. The guardsman, Tom, was there too, shaking like a leaf, but when she looked at him, he gave a defiant nod.

The demons would be on them any second.

They would never make it up the ladders in time. All they could do now was hold the line and hope everybody else got out of there to continue the fight.

*Don't you dare let Portsmouth die.*

Tony licked his lips nervously. "I really wish you brave gals would make a run for it. We don't all need to die here."

Wickstaff popped a shot off from a handgun. "We run without a fight and the demons will be up and over this lorry before the others get a chance to dig in and defend themselves. Not happening. I understand if *you* need to get yourself away though, Colonel."

Tony cackled. "No chance in hell."

The group fired off the last of their ammunition and the cacophony of gunfire spluttered to a stop. They lined up, shoulder to shoulder, and braced to meet the charge. A hundred demons appeared beneath the spotlights, snarling and salivating. Some even spat insults.

"Fight together," said Wickstaff, "and die together. Is there any better way?"

"No," said Maddy, a tear in her eye for the first time since the gates had appeared and shocked her emotions into stasis. It felt good – a release. "My husband's name was Ben," she said. "I really miss him."

Wickstaff stared at her, brow furrowed. Then a sadness washed over her. "My husband's name was Tristan. I miss him too."

Tony grunted. "I had a dog when I was a kid. Used to piss on the carpet."

The demons reached them.

Maddy shut her eyes.

A yellow light bloomed, so bright it flared through her closed eyelids. Her ears thrummed with an almighty *boom*. She opened her eyes and was blinded by light that she thought might have been God. Then she realised Portsmouth had been lit up by an explosion. The entire road was on fire and demon parts lay scattered about. The ones still alive had been stunned into inaction.

Maddy rubbed at her eyes and looked around. She didn't see Tosco but heard his voice. He was shouting down at her from the top of the lorry. "I called in the boats," he said. "We have about thirty seconds before the next strike comes and turns this area into a crater. Come on!"

Beside Tosco were a handful of men. They started firing on the remaining demons in the road and gave Maddy and the others time to make it up the ladders. Tosco grabbed Maddy at the top. "I'm glad to see you're still alive."

She pulled him into a massive hug. "Thank fuck for you!"

"Yeah," said Tony from nearby. He sounded deflated and out of energy. "Good lad."

Portsmouth lit up again as another shell hit.

It was time to go.

---

"What is your goddamn obsession with me?" Smithy was no longer afraid of this demon, Frankie Walker, but utterly annoyed by its dogged pursuit of him. Just when it seemed like he and Harriet might finally get to safety, Frankie had arrived and screwed things up again.

Frankie flicked his fingers like a gangster, and it became an obscene gesture when his index finger flew off and landed in the grass. "You dissed me, blud. I don't take that shit from no one, you get me?"

Harriet looked at Smithy. "You... you know him?"

Smithy moved Harriet behind him. "Yeah, and he's bad news."

"You have no fucking idea," said Frankie, grinning. "I'm going to make you regret the day you were born. I'm going to—"

Smithy lifted his handgun and shot Frankie in the kneecap.

Frankie's leg splayed to the side, but he didn't seem pained by the injury. After a moment, he was able to straighten up again as if nothing had happened. Anger overtook him. "I'm going to ruin you."

Frankie leapt at Smithy and grabbed hold of him. The two began to struggle, chest to chest like ballroom dancers. Harriet yelped, calling for help. Attracting attention.

It began to rain harder, more heavily.

Frankie was strong. Too strong to fight off.

Smithy grunted. "I feel sorry for... sorry for your little brother. Davey deserved better than you."

Frankie roared. "Fuck you!"

"He probably killed himself after he shot you. I know that's what I would do if I had a pathetic wannabe gangster for a brother like you. Who can blame him?"

Frankie roared again. He let go of Smithy to strike him, which gave Smithy room to bring his gun up and whack the demon in the forehead. Frankie stumbled backwards, clutching his face. Smithy lifted his handgun and shot him in his other knee. Frankie slipped on the wet grass and crumpled to the ground like a broken accordion. This time he hissed in pain.

Smithy sneered. "How does that feel, huh? Bet it hurts, innit?"

"Stop it," said Harriet. "Let's just get out of here, Smithy. Please!"

But Smithy was enjoying himself too much. This demon had done nothing but torture him since they had met. Now, finally, he had the upper hand. Smithy pointed his handgun again and shot Frankie in the stomach, folding the demon forward. "You're rotten. You need putting down."

Harriet pleaded with Smithy again, clutching herself against the rain. "Please, I want to go. I want to get to the coach."

"One minute," said Smithy, wiping a hand over his face. "I need to finish this."

*I want to finish this.*

He couldn't leave this place knowing Frankie was still around. He was done being chased. No more.

Stepping right up to Frankie, he levelled the handgun at the demon's ugly, twisted face. Frankie grinned but didn't try to get up. "Always thought I'd go out like this – gunned down by a rival. Born on the streets, die on the streets."

Frankie was deluded. Even in death, he pictured himself as some notorious criminal who would never be forgotten. Smithy felt nothing – no remorse nor anger. This demon in front of him was just a broken thing, a tattered echo of a former life, a scratched record stuck on repeat. Killing this thing would be merciful.

"Go to hell, blud, you get me?" Smithy pulled the trigger and obliterated Frankie's face. The body slumped sideways into the wet grass as rain beat against his ulcerated skin. Smithy blinked. The sun rose beyond the hill, bringing morning with it. He could finally put this night to rest. He turned towards Harriet, squinting through the downpour.

Harriet stared back at him, terror stitched onto her face. Before Smithy could ask her what was wrong, a demon stepped out from behind her. Crimolok – or Vamps. He was still unsure about that whole thing.

"You're a warrior," said Crimolok, gazing at Smithy and then down at what had recently been Frankie Walker, "but he was weak and addled. His gate was closed."

Smithy frowned. "What?"

Crimolok looked up to the heavens, but the rain didn't seem to touch him. It was as though the clouds wouldn't dare offend him. "When my pets came through the gates, they formed tethers. If the gate though which they came closes, they can no longer sustain themselves here on Earth. Soon, such things shall not matter."

Harriet went to move over to Smithy, but Crimolok gripped her around the back of the neck with a massive hand and yanked her backwards. "Not so fast, worm. I am not yet done with you."

"P-Please."

"Let her go," said Smithy. It wasn't an order but a plea.

"If she belongs to you, then perhaps you should have kept a closer eye." With that, Crimolok flicked his wrist and snapped Harriet's neck like a twig. He let her body fall to the ground like a bag of rubbish.

"You bastard!" Smithy raised his handgun and took a shot. Crimolok flinched as the bullet struck his arm, but Smithy had been aiming for his head. He didn't intend to miss again, Marching forward, he fired over and over. Crimolok leapt aside like an acrobat, avoiding every round with ease. Smithy vowed to use every bullet he had until he killed the demon.

Crimolok dived back and forth in the rain, cackling and hooting. Mocking. Smithy stopped firing. While he hadn't counted, he knew his ammunition was nearing an end. He had a pocketful more, but if he stopped to reload, Crimolok would tear him apart.

He crouched down and focused on his senses. He focused on the flickering shadows that were slowly fading with the approaching dawn. He focused on what he could hear – distant moans and a nearby rustling in the grass. He took a deep breath, tensed his body. Waited.

Crimolok leapt at him from the left. Smithy threw himself forward and rolled out of the way. He pivoted on his toes, lined Crimolok up in his sights, and prepared to pull the trigger. "I got you now, bitch."

Crimolok's mouth opened wide in an animalistic roar.

Smithy pulled the trigger.

"NO!" Mass collided with Smithy and knocked him onto his back. The shot went wide. Crimolok grinned, and then retreated backwards into the rain. His cackling laughter seemed to echo off the skies themselves.

"The hell are you doing, man? I had him!"

Mass grabbed Smithy by the front of his shirt and yelled in his face. "You idiot! We can't kill him."

Smithy frowned, but then he realised what he had been about to do. "Shit!"

"You kill him, he gets loose."

"So what do we do then?"

"We make it to the coach and get the hell out of here – and we take Vamps with us."

"You mean Crimolok?"

There was pain on Mass's face, but he nodded. "We can't leave him here. He's coming with us."

Smithy blinked. As he was lying on his back, the rain was hitting him right in the face. "How do you propose we make that happen?"

Mass yanked Smithy to his feet. "I have no sodding idea, but we —" He stopped talking and looked at Harriet lying on the ground.

"It's my fault," said Smithy. "I was too busy getting my revenge to realise she was in danger. I'm a piece of—"

Mass grabbed his shoulder. "We lose people – it happens – but we keep on fighting. Come on, the others made it to the barn."

Smithy took one last look at Harriet, lying in the wet grass like a pale doll. "I really would have liked to have earned that kiss," he whispered. "I'm sorry."

"Come on," said Mass. "It's getting light. We need to move before the demons find us."

They headed for the barn.

---

Mass was running on empty. He was cut all over – deeply in places – and had gone days without sleep. If he didn't get the hell out of there soon, he would pass out. Luckily, safety was in reach. They'd made it to the barn under the cover of darkness, just in time to avoid the dawn. The coach was parked inside the barn and Gemma had the key.

The one big problem was that Vamps was still out there somewhere. They couldn't leave without him. If they got him back to Portsmouth maybe they could do something, maybe they could help him...

"Where's Harriet?" Addy asked. She was over by the barn's door, staring intently at the rain.

"Dead," said Mass before Smithy had the chance to tell them it was his fault. The lad was taking it hard, but the blame belonged to the demons, not him.

"Damn it," said Tox, throwing himself back against the side of the coach. "We wouldn't have made it this far if she hadn't helped us."

Gemma curled her lip distastefully. "You mean when she smashed me in the back of the head with a tin can?"

Addy turned back and grinned. "Yeah, when she did that."

"How's it looking out there?" Mass asked.

Addy peeked out again. "It's quiet. Dawn's arrived, but the demons aren't anywhere I can see."

"What about Vamps?"

"I don't see him."

Smithy shook his head. "He was right out there."

"Must be licking his wounds," said Mass. "Good thing you only shot him in the arm."

Smithy looked around. "Hey, where's David?"

"He never made it back with us," said Addy. "He wandered off in the dark."

"We need to find him. I think he's dying. Crimolok said that when a gate closes it messes up the demons that came through it."

That was interesting, thought Mass, but it was a later discussion, not a now discussion.

Tox shook his head and grunted. "Can we just get on the coach? We need to get out of here. If we find the little demon, we'll get him on board, but he's not a priority."

"I'm not leaving without David," said Smithy. "Anyway, Mass doesn't want to leave without taking Crimolok prisoner first."

Tox and Addy both frowned. "What?"

"He's our enemy," said Mass, "our highest-ranking enemy, and we have a chance to capture him. We can't see it wasted."

Gemma began to laugh. She tipped her head back dramatically and hitched her shoulders. "You people are like the bloody A Team. Don't you ever give up? How many of you need to die before you realise we're all done for? Best we can do is get on this coach and try to eke out a few more days of living."

"Best you can hope for," said Addy, "is a few more minutes before I shoot you in the face."

"You still need me to free the women in the container."

"The women you locked up, you mean?"

Tox groaned. "I almost forgot about them. So, let me get this straight? We need to take one demon prisoner and find another who's apparently our friend, free a load of women from some locked containers, then drive out of here like Mad Max?"

Mass's guts felt like they had sunk down to his knees. The thought of achieving all that made him want to just give up, but that wasn't an option. He put a hand on the coach's front bumper to steady himself and then chuckled. "That's about the size of it, yeah."

Tox loaded a fresh pair of shells into his shotgun and snapped the chamber closed. "Okay, well, I still say we get on board this coach and take it from there. It's all very well wanting to be heroes, but there's no point us dying trying to achieve an impossible mission."

"Amen," said Gemma. "Finally one of you speaks sense."

Addy glared at Gemma and shut her up.

"He's right," said Smithy. "I think we should just get the women out of the containers and head to Portsmouth. There're too many demons here for us to deal with, but if we came back in force, we could capture Crimolok easily."

"If he's still here," said Mass. "This might be our only chance. Anyway, I thought you weren't going anywhere without David."

Smithy sighed. He had lost the peppy spark he'd had when he'd first pulled Mass out of that pit. "I guess I agree with Tox. No point being heroes if it just gets us dead. We'll help David if we get a chance."

Gemma groaned. "Look, I'm unlocking the coach, okay? You lot can continue bickering inside."

Nobody protested, so Gemma pulled out the key and unlocked the door, sliding it aside and folding it. Then she screamed as someone leapt out and grabbed her around the throat. Everyone in the barn raised their weapons, but the person who had Gemma shielded themself behind her. Mass could just about make out a milky-white eyeball peering around her hair. The arm around her throat ended in a hook. A shotgun jutted out from the side of her hip.

Gemma was still startled, but she calmed a little at the revelation of who had grabbed her. "Nas, what are you doing?"

"Protecting what's mine. No one is taking this coach."

"Beg to differ, mate," said Tox, levelling his shotgun. "If you think holding bitch-face hostage will help you, think again."

Addy raised her own weapon. "You should have picked a better hostage."

"Wait!" said Smithy. "We still need the combination from her to get the women free."

"The women also belong to me," said Nas. "They are the seeds that shall blossom in the new garden."

Gemma tried to struggle free. Mass wondered if it was an act. Being taken hostage and getting away with Nas was probably what she wanted. Maybe they were even lovers. Nas was squeezing her throat pretty tightly, though – tightly enough to make her gag. "N-Nas, please, let go of me."

Nas throttled her harder. "Be quiet."

"Nas, I-I can't bre—"

"Be quiet!"

"Let her go," said Mass. "You ain't getting out of here."

"Not alive anyway," said Tox.

"Beg to differ." Nas sneered and let off a blast from the shotgun he was holding against Gemma's hip. Gemma fell to the ground, screaming and clutching her side. Mass thought he wouldn't be surprised if kickback had broken her pelvis.

Addy hit the ground too. Mass ran to her, panic rising in his chest. In the corner of his eye, he saw Nas scramble back inside the coach. The engine rumbled to life a second later.

"He's gonna drive out of here," Tox shouted.

But Mass didn't care. He grabbed Addy and rolled her onto her back. She blinked and stared at him, wood chips in her hair. "I-I'm okay," she said. "Don't let him get away."

But it was too late.

The bus hitched forward, almost crushing Gemma under its wheels. It crashed through the barn door and took off into the field.

Mass leapt up and started firing. So did Tox, Smithy, and Addy. The coach's windows shattered and the long vehicle swerved back and forth.

Then it skidded to a stop. The engine stalled.

For a moment, Mass thought they'd shot Nas. Then he saw the obstacle that had presented itself in front of the coach and caused it to skid.

Crimolok stood tall with twenty demons to his left and twenty to his right. If the gunfire hadn't caused Nas to swerve, he might have mowed right through the line of demons, but the coach had lost too much speed and had been veering at too much of an angle. Perhaps Nas had stamped on the brake out of instinct, but now that the coach had stalled, there would be no driving out of there.

The demons advanced cautiously, looking worse and more abhorrent in the golden glow of dawn. They surrounded the coach, staring in through the high windows. There was no sign of Nas. Mass hoped he wasn't dead yet, because that would mean his pain was over.

Smithy was hiding behind the barn door, handgun at the ready. He looked at Mass. "What do we do? There's probably three-dozen demons out there. No chance of sneaking out."

"And I hate to say it," said Tox, "but we ain't fighting our way out either. I got four shells left."

"I have three," said Mass, having only one shell left in his pocket after having just loaded two into Honeywell's shotgun. "How about everyone else?"

Smithy rummaged in his pocket and brought out a handful of small nine-millimetre rounds. "Looks like I'm good for seven or eight shots."

"I have one shell left, and it's loaded," said Addy, raising her shotgun.

Mass quickly did the math. "Over a dozen shots. Not so bad."

"There's a round left in my hunting rifle," said Gemma, still down on the ground. Her words came out in a breathless rasp. "But I don't think I can fire."

Mass went over to her. As much as he hated her for what she had done – done to Honeywell, Gross, and all the others – he couldn't ignore her injuries. She'd been discarded by a man who she had obviously trusted. In real life, you kept grudges, but war made things less personal. For now, their issues were on hold. He checked her over carefully, being sure not to press too hard on her injured side. "I think you dislocated your hip or something. That shotgun really had a kick. Can you get up?"

"I don't know. Let me—" She placed her hands on the ground and pushed, but she quickly collapsed in pain. "Shite, no, ah, it hurts too much. I-I can't..."

Mass eased her down. "It's okay. Just stay still."

"Fuck her," said Addy. "Who gives a shit?"

Mass sighed. He hadn't lost sight of the fact this woman had killed Gross in cold blood, but right now they didn't need to be turning on each other. "Look, Addy, I know how you feel, but we need to focus on the big issue, which is those demons out there."

"I-I need you to carry me," said Gemma. "I don't think I can make it on my own. Nas has a set of keys for the coach, but mine are still over there on the floor. Just... Help me stand."

"Fuck you!" said Addy. "How does that stand with you?"

Gemma began to cry, a single tear making its way down her cheek. "I've been such an idiot. I'm so sorry. I bought in to all Nas's bullshit, but when it came to saving himself, he threw me aside. I used to be a police officer. I used to be a good person... What I did to you people... I-I can't believe what I've become."

Mass wanted to punch her in the face for the sheer audacity of her apologising for killing his friends less than twenty-four hours ago. Then he thought about the things he had done in the past year and considered what it now meant to be human. "Gemma, I'll help you get out of this place, but it won't be easy. I can't promise you you'll survive, which is why I need the code to free the women now. I need it, in case you don't make it."

Gemma shook her head and began to panic. "If I give it to you, you'll kill me. After what I did, y-y-you're just waiting for a chance. No, I won't give it to you,"

Mass shook his head. "Give me the code and I promise I'll do everything I can to get you out of here. You have my word."

"Your word?"

"Yes. You have my word."

Gemma, still clutching her hip, sat up and stared at him. Despite the grime and hardness of her features, she was an attractive woman. Maybe once she had even been kind. "How can I trust you?"

Mass smiled at her. "We're the good guys, remember?"

Gemma glanced around, searching until she found Addy. Addy's jaw locked in consternation, but after a moment she gave an abrupt nod. It seemed to satisfy Gemma. "The code to the padlock is 1-1-3-4. Just promise me you'll—"

Addy levelled her shotgun and pulled the trigger. An instant later, there was a boom and Gemma's skull exploded across the hay-strewn cement. Mass lost his breath. He reached up and wiped blood from his face, then collapsed backwards onto his hands. "W-What the hell, Addy? What the hell?"

Addy threw the empty shotgun down and snarled. "Bitch had it coming."

"I gave her my word," Mass shouted at her, enraged. Why had she done this? Why had she been so brutal?

"You gave your word, not mine. She killed Gross, have you fucking forgotten? It was over for this bitch the moment his body hit the dirt. I don't give a shit what you think, Mass. This was my decision and you can go fuck yourself if you don't agree with it."

Mass wiped more blood from his face. He stared at Gemma's mangled skull for a moment and then said, "No, you're right. It was your decision. She needed to die."

Smithy was clearly disgusted by the unprompted murder, but he didn't say anything. Strangely, his condemnation made Mass like him even more. The moment Urban Vampires started killing without remorse was the moment they stopped honouring the man they were named after.

Mass picked up Gemma's key and moved over to Smithy. "You still with us?"

Smithy was staring at Gemma's remains, but eventually he met Mass's gaze and nodded. "She had a debt to pay, I get it. I'm just not good with killing."

Mass frowned. "It's the apocalypse. How did you survive?"

"By making it on my own. Less messy that way."

"Lonelier too. Can we still count on you?"

Smithy reached out and patted Mass on his arm. "Long as you're the good guys, I'm with you."

"Let's just say we're the *almost* good guys."

"Probably as close as anyone can get these days. I suppose it will do."

## CHAPTER TWELVE

MADDY WAS LIMPING as she made her way back into Portsmouth's docks, but she had no idea why. Both her ankles ached, but she didn't recall twisting or falling on them. She supposed it was pure exertion that had left her injured, and she considered herself lucky compared to many who made it back in worse shape.

A triage was hastily arranged inside a warehouse behind the port authority building. Maddy and Tosco helped carry Tony there. He had lost a lot of blood from slashes on his arms, and by the time they made it inside he was unconscious and soaking wet from the rain, which had now mercifully stopped.

"He'll be all right," Tosco told her, obviously sensing her concern for the man. "He's just exhausted and has lost some blood. Don't worry."

"If I didn't worry, I wouldn't be human. Until I see him back on his feet, I'm going to worry, okay?" She said it more harshly than she'd intended, and she realised her nerves were taut and her hands were trembling. "Sorry."

"You care about him?"

"I care about everyone." He raised an eyebrow at her and it prompted her to say more. "He's a good man. We need him."

Tosco sighed, looked downwards, and then nodded. "Yeah, we need all the good men we can get."

Maddy didn't like the thought of a man of Tosco's station sulking, but at the same time she liked that he still had emotions – emotions so strong that he could still have a strop. She took one of his hands in hers and moved closer to him. Then she lifted one hand and cupped his face. "There are a lot of good men in Portsmouth. Thank you for coming to help us. I'd be dead right now if it wasn't for you."

He lifted his head and looked at her. "Soon as you guys left, I sent out a team of spotters. Things didn't feel right. Thomas shouldn't have reacted so rashly."

"So, are you finally on the right side?"

He shook his head. "Thomas made a mistake, but that doesn't mean I'm about to join your little insurrection."

She let go of his face and hand and stepped back. "You know about that?"

Tosco smirked. "Commander Klein and I like to share a few glasses of vodka from time to time. He told me to keep an eye on you, but..."

She frowned. "But what?"

He actually seemed to blush then. "But I tend to do that, anyway."

She smiled, then grimaced. "Thomas can't be left to lead here. If you don't see that, then, honestly, you should stop watching my back and watch your own."

"Maddy—"

She turned and walked away. "Look after Cross for me. If he dies, I'll hold you responsible."

"I'm a fleet commander, not a bed nurse."

"You really care about me, be a bed nurse."

She marched away, picking up speed. At first, she didn't even know where she was going, but then she realised she needed to know about the condition of one other person.

She found Tom standing outside the port authority building and raced through the puddles to get to him. He saw her and smiled, although it was a feeble expression that betrayed how rattled he was after almost meeting his death. "Maddy, are you—"

"Where's Wickstaff? I want to check she's okay."

Tom smiled wearily. "She's fine. She went to her office to patch herself up. She wouldn't let anyone else see to her."

Maddy thanked Tom and headed inside the building. The reception was crammed full of people sitting on the sofas and sipping drinks, weary soldiers trying to regather their wits. The corridors, however, were empty, and Maddy encountered no one en route to Wickstaff's office. She couldn't bear the time it would take to knock, so she barged right in.

Wickstaff was standing behind her desk in just a bra, but she grabbed her breasts as though she were naked. "Jesus, woman, learn to knock!"

Maddy couldn't help herself. She rushed over to the general and wrapped her arms around her. "How are we alive right now?"

"Isn't it obvious?" said Wickstaff, her arms out to either side, obviously not knowing where to put them. "I'm unkillable. Every day I wake up and think 'today will be the day', but alas, no, I keep on living. Twenty-eight assassination attempts, multiple assaults at our gates, not to mention the Great Battle, but I keep on surviving. Any more and I'll start developing a messiah complex."

Maddy guffawed. She didn't know why, because Wickstaff's dry wit was something she was used to, but black comedy, at this moment, was exactly what she needed. "You keep surviving because we need you too. We're fucked without you, ma'am."

"Oh indeed, I'm the second coming. Follow me and I shall lead us to the promised land." Maddy went to speak, but Wickstaff placed a finger right on her lips. "I'm tired, Maddy. I was actually thankful when Thomas arrived. I thought I could finally let someone else be in charge, to worry every minute of every day. It wasn't an exaggeration when I said I didn't know how much longer I could keep doing this. I'm tired, Maddy. So fucking tir—"

Maddy leapt forward and kissed Wickstaff on the mouth. While she did so, she wrapped her hands around her naked back and enjoyed the warm throb of her skin. Wickstaff froze with a closed mouth but didn't fight it. Then she shoved Maddy away – not harshly, but firmly. She was breathless as she spoke. "M-Maddy, you mad cow, I'm not a lesbian."

Maddy looked into Wickstaff's eyes and felt like bursting into hysterics. "Neither am I, but... but..."

Wickstaff look utterly perturbed, but then her expression changed. "Yeah, okay, why the fuck not?"

Suddenly Wickstaff was grabbing the back of Maddy's head and yanking her into a fierce kiss, mouths open and tongues exploring. Both women ran their hands over each other like they were desperate to find sanctuary in a desert. Before she knew it, Maddy's shirt was off and tossed on the floor. Both women standing only in their bras, they moved over to the desk, where Maddy hopped up and opened her legs. Wickstaff filled the space between her knees, cupping her face and kissing her all over her neck and shoulders.

There was a knock at the door.

Wickstaff pushed Maddy away, but it wasn't hard or even that persistent. It was just enough so that Wickstaff could see who was entering her office.

Despite knocking, Tosco came right in. His mouth was open to speak, but when he saw Wickstaff and Maddy both standing there in just their bras, he paused. "I-I..." He put a fist to his mouth and cleared his throat. "Excuse me, ma'am, but you're needed outside."

Wickstaff groaned and rolled her eyes. "Am I not allowed a moment to myself?"

Tosco stared at Maddy, glanced at her half-exposed breasts, and then looked at Wickstaff. The way he tried to seem professional while he was addressing his superior in her bra was almost comical. "Y-Yes, ma'am, a moment should be fine. I shall tell General Thomas you will be with him as soon as you're... *able*."

Tosco hurried out of the room, the door almost slamming behind him. Wickstaff remained behind her desk for a moment, then burst out in fits of laughter. Maddy couldn't help but join her. Giggling, the two of them gravitated towards one another until they were once again embracing. This time, instead of desperately kissing, they looked into each other's eyes.

Maddy cupped Wickstaff's face. "Does this mean I can stop calling you ma'am?"

"Yes, I suppose Amanda will have to do from now on. I'm not quite sure what's happening, except it's the most wonderful I've felt in as long as I can remember. It's almost making me forget I might die tomorrow."

Maddy pecked her on the lips and pulled away. "You're not dying as long as I'm around. You're the saviour of Portsmouth, but

I only realised tonight that you're the saviour of me too. The only time I feel happy is when you're around. I think..."

Wickstaff kissed Maddy, long and passionate, then said, "I know. Me too. But let's not say it."

Maddy frowned, her heart suddenly aching. "Why not?"

"Because in this world it seems like a curse."

"Then I'm cursed. I love you, Amanda."

Wickstaff sighed. "Bloody hell, woman. I love you too."

Maddy glowed, her stomach feeling like it was full of sex-crazed unicorns. That wasn't reality though. If she was lucky, there would be more moments like this, but right now Wickstaff had obligations to attend to. "You should go."

Amanda held her for a moment, their noses touching. Then she pulled on her shirt and bid Maddy to do the same. "I'm not going anywhere without you."

With a huge smile on her face, Maddy followed her out of the office all the way to the docks, where they found Thomas surrounded by dozens of his men. Could he not give things a rest for one minute?

Thomas was scowling, but before he had a chance to say anything, the rain-soaked men and women around him began to whistle and cheer. It took a moment, but Maddy realised they were cheering for Amanda.

*Hero*, many were shouting. *General*, said others. They pumped their arms in the air or put fingers in their mouths to whistle louder. It sent shivers down Maddy's spine. General Thomas seemed unnerved. He tried to speak, but Amanda didn't give him the chance. She threw a right hook that connected with his jaw and dropped him like a sack of spuds. The crowd went silent, watching as she then offered a hand and waited for Thomas to recover. Reluctantly, he accepted her help and allowed her to pull him back to his feet.

"You deserved that, General. You want to tell me otherwise?"

"I... It..." He rubbed at his jaw and cleared his throat before trying again. "You were right. You knew something was wrong, and I ignored your advice."

Wickstaff raised an eyebrow. "Advice isn't how I would put it, but I appreciate the acknowledgement. Quite frankly, General, you are the last person I wish to see or speak to right now, so could we do this later, please? I would rather like to get some sleep." Her eyes flicked to the side and met Maddy's. Once again she felt a shiver down her spine.

Despite the knock-back, General Thomas didn't lose his temper. He kept calm – somewhere on the edge of embarrassed. The wolf whistles and chants continued. *Wickstaff, Wickstaff.* For professional men, Thomas's people had lost all control of their emotions.

"I understand," said Thomas. "I lost a lot of good men today, and the last thing I wish is for more hostility. This situation between the two of us is far from over, but for now I would like to call a truce. We have bigger problems."

Wickstaff nodded. "The demons will be back. This was just the start of something. We need to be ready."

"And we will be."

Wickstaff blinked slowly and waved a hand wearily. "But not until I've had some sleep. Good morning to you, General Thomas."

"And you, General Wickstaff."

Wickstaff started heading back towards the port authority building but then she stopped. She looked back at Maddy and frowned. "Maddy, could you accompany me, please? There are things I would like to *discuss.*"

Maddy tried to keep from grinning. Butterflies in her stomach took flight and almost lifted her off the ground. She hurried after Wickstaff – Amanda – and tried to ignore the confused stare of Commander Tosco as she passed by.

*What must he think?*
*Who cares? The world could end tomorrow.*

---

While the demons were busy, Mass told everyone to get to work. If they remained in the barn, they would be surrounded until they ran out of ammo. Then the demons would come in and tear them apart. No, if they had any chance of surviving, it would be by getting the hell off this farm once and for all. Smithy agreed. He had no intention of staying inside the barn with Gemma's dead body.

The odds were still heavily against them though.

The coach outside was surrounded by demons, which was the only reason Smithy and the others were able to move out of the barn. Day had arrived, which meant the cover of darkness was gone. It took only a moment for the mass of demons to remove their focus from the coach.

"Here we go," said Tox.

"Let's make some demon salsa," said Smithy.

"That's disgusting," said Addy. "I like it."

Crimolok towered over the demons, body somehow now contorted to eight-feet tall at least. He stood motionless, allowing them to flow around him. If Mass still intended on taking him prisoner, there would be twenty demons to get through first.

"We make our way to the containers," said Mass. "Don't fire unless you have to. We can't waste a single round."

"I don't have any rounds," said Addy. "I put my last one in Gemma's face."

"I'be got about half a... clippy thing left," Smithy said, wondering if the demons would line up for him so he could shoot them in batches.

Mass sighed. "Use what you have. Don't quit."

Smithy aimed, sighting a burnt man staggering away from the coach. The burnt men were manageable one at a time. Weak and clumsy, their bodies burnt and broken. More than a couple at once, though, and they could make life very hard, and death very easy. Smithy spotted only three primates amongst the pack, which was good news at least. Most had attacked the house last night, which meant many had already fallen.

Mass turned to Smithy and shouted out a warning. Smithy spun to see a demon racing towards him. He was about to pull the trigger, but then he realised it wasn't a threat. "It's okay, it's just Dave."

But the little demon didn't stop running, even when he should have stopped and spoken. Smithy backed up, then realised the demon intended to tackle him.

"Dave, what are you—"

David leapt at Smithy, a fleshy cannonball hitting him in the guts. He was too small to knock Smithy off his feet, but it knocked the wind from him.

Mass lifted his shotgun but didn't fire. "What do you want me to do, Smithy?"

"Don't shoot."

David was growling. He circled Smithy, spitting and gnashing his broken teeth.

Smithy put out a hand. "Dave, it's me. It's Smithy. You don't want to do this. This isn't you."

"David kill. Kill, yes, humans."

"No. No, you're my friend. This is Crimolok trying to control you. He's just... He's..." Smithy glanced around towards the demons that were approaching fast. Crimolok stared through their numbers, looking right at Smithy with a smirk. Smithy turned back to David. "You and me are friends, Dave, but if you need to hurt me, then go on."

David snarled and approached cautiously, as if wary of being tricked. He began to thrash his head back and forth, getting more and more worked up. It didn't seem like the demon was listening. Smithy remained standing there but was anxiously aware of the other demons approaching. Mass and the others got ready to meet them.

"Come on, Dave," said Smithy, beginning to think this wasn't going to work. "It's me. Please don't hurt me."

David hissed and rushed forward. Smithy brought his handgun up.

Mass and the others fired their weapons.

David leapt up and tackled a burnt man that had been about to collide with Smithy. Being clumsy, the burnt man tripped and fell to the ground, where David proceeded to tear its throat out with his tiny claws. Afterwards, he looked up at Smithy with sadness in his eyes. "David bad."

Smithy shook his head. "No, David good. Come on."

Mass took up the front, and the group moved towards the paddock with the containers. They kept the burnt men at bay through speed alone, as they were incapable of moving faster than a stumble. A quicker threat was approaching though.

Smithy planted his feet and fired at the advancing primates, but they moved so quickly that he missed his first two shots. Soon he would be empty, so he decided not to waste any more rounds unless he knew for sure that it worse worth it. He remained standing with his legs apart, handgun pointed ahead – and he waited. Waited.

The first of the three advancing primates broke from its mates and made a beeline for Smithy. It was close enough for Smithy to see the malice in its eyes, the flesh between its teeth. It picked up speed, a galloping beast that would not be stopped.

Smithy's hands were shaking, and he fought to keep his arms raised. He closed one eye – then both eyes – and pulled the trigger. Smithy opened his eyes again and saw the primate tumbling towards him, burning off the momentum of its charge. It came to rest only inches from his feet. A bullet hole smoked between its eyes.

Smithy gasped. "I am awesome."

The horde of demons were following Mass, Addy, and Tox, which left Smithy and David slightly removed from the fray. The demons had obviously assumed the primate would have been enough to take care of him and had kept their attention on the remaining prey. If Smithy wanted to, he could have probably made a run for it in the other direction and made it out of there. His hammering heart told him to do just that, as did a large part of his mind – but there was something inside of him that just would not let that happen. He wasn't running out on the others.

But he did intend on running.

The demons had moved away from the coach and were getting further and further away as they stalked after Mass and the others. It was right there, unattended. Smithy looked down at David and grinned. "Are you thinking what I'm thinking?"

David licked his cracked lips and blinked. "Day bright. Is nice?"

"Yes, it is, my little friend. The day is bright. Do you sense Crimolok? Where is he?" The arch demon was conspicuously absent and Smithy couldn't see him with the other demons nor by the coach where he had been previously.

David placed two rotting index fingers against his temples and closed his eyes. "He is close."

Smithy squeezed the grip on his handgun, reminding himself it was there. There was no sign of Crimolok, and only one place to go. He sprinted towards the coach, knowing this would be the only chance to make it on board. Eventually the demons would spot him out in the open and turn their attack on him. Maybe after Mass and the others were dead. He didn't intend to see that happen though.

When he reached the side of the coach, he felt like he was about to get pranked. It couldn't be this easy, could it? Then he realised his big mistake. Mass had Gemma's key to the coach. "Damn it." He punched the door, and it rattled and slid an inch to the side.

"Your wagon is open," said David.

Smithy poked a hand into the gap and slid the door all the way clear. "Yeah, looks like it. Do you think this is too good to be true?"

David hopped up onto the bus and went into the aisle. He didn't alert Smithy to any danger, so he tested his luck further and went up to the driver's seat. There was blood on the steering wheel, and the windscreen was cracked. Maybe they'd managed to hit Nas with one of their shots. Maybe he had hurt himself when the bus had skidded. Whatever had happened, there was no sign of the hook-handed bastard – but his keys were still in the ignition. Smithy turned them and the engine rumbled to life.

David yelped. "Wagon is angry."

"It's just the engine, Dave. Have you never... Yeah, I suppose this is your first time on a bus. It's okay. The wagon makes a noise, but it's okay."

David nodded. "Is okay. I sit down."

"Yeah, I would do that, because I'm about to take this thing for a spin."

David moved up to the front seat directly behind Smithy, peering through the windows in fascination as the coach trundled forward in first gear. Smithy had never driven a bus before, and he was pretty sure you needed a separate licence. As it was, he swung the large vehicle around in a wide berth, worrying that he might smash into the various outbuildings and equipment lying around the fields. Several times the coach hopped up over debris or crashed down into ruts. Even at five miles per hour the journey was heavy going.

Smithy turned the large steering wheel until he saw the mass of demons through the cracked windscreen. There was no sign of Mass or the others, but he hoped with all his heart that they were still putting up a fight.

*Just hold on, guys, because the cavalry is on the way.*

Smithy stamped down on the accelerator at the exact same time that a sharp hook pressed down against his jugular.

"Turn this coach around," said Nas, whispering right into Smithy's ear. "Or I'll slice your throat."

---

Mass, Tox, and Addy made it into the paddock where the containers were. They were still locked. Were all those women still inside?

"Addy, get these containers open. I hate to say it, but if there's anyone alive in there, they need to help us fight."

Tox raised his shotgun. "My last shell. Wish me luck!"

Mass grunted. "Good luck!"

Tox took the shot and hit a burnt man in the chest. It was enough to drop the thing to the ground.

"I'm out too," said Mass, now holding Honeywell's shotgun like a baseball bat. "Smithy, how 'bout you? Smithy?"

Tox looked around and then frowned. "Shit, where is he? Did they get him?"

Mass ground his teeth and cursed. "Goddamn it."

The demons finally caught up to them. Tox dropped the first by ramming his knife into its skull. He pulled it out again, but it took effort, and by the time he did, another burnt man had grabbed him from the side.

Mass swung his shotgun and cracked it off the face of a burnt man wearing a ragged apron. You didn't see many of them in outfits, and he wondered if the man had once been a butcher. He didn't think about it for long because there was a primate eying him from the pack. Honeywell's shotgun had shattered, the stock barely attached to the barrel, so he threw it to the grass and beckoned the creature with both hands. "Come on, you chimp-ass motherfucker."

The primate leapt and Mass caught it against his chest. The

thing was heavy and strong, and it took all the strength he had to stay on his feet. He grabbed its arms to keep its talons from slicing him, and he rolled his head back and forth to avoid its teeth. Behind him, the sound of metal hinges was interrupted by Addy's barking voice. "Okay, ladies, grab whatever isn't tied down. If you ain't out of this box in three seconds fighting for your life, then you're going to be eaten alive. Come on! Move!"

Mass dared a glance to his right where he saw Tox bringing up his knife and slicing the throat of the burnt man he was fighting with. Then he kicked another that was too close and sent it back into the pack. He saw Mass was in trouble, trying to stay alive against the attacking primate, and he came right over. He raised his knife and planted it in the demon's back. It screeched so loud that Mass's temples throbbed. To shut it up, he grabbed the broken shotgun stock off the ground and planted the splintered end right into its open jaws, shoving it down past all resistance until it was buried deep. The primate toppled over dead.

The women spilled out of the containers, some holding weapons, others making a run for it. Tox, Addy, and Mass moved closer, barely armed and barely standing. More than a dozen demons still approached. It was hopeless. They couldn't kill that many demons with their bare hands. Unless...

"Get inside the containers," Mass shouted. "Back up inside and form a wall. Whoever has anything sharp, make yourself known."

Addy ushered the women back inside the containers. The few who had run for it were now screaming as the demons broke off and took them down, tearing into their backs and ripping out their spines. It was their own fault. The only people who got to live during the apocalypse were those willing to stand and fight.

Mass grabbed a broken mop handle from one of the women. Addy and Tox both had their knives. The three of them stood shoulder to shoulder in the opening on the container, restricting the demon's abilities to surround them. The burnt men were forced to attack in pairs and threes, which allowed Mass, Tox, and Addy to fight them one on one. They took down the first three easily, throwing the burnt corpses to the ground and making it even more difficult for the remaining demons.

Maybe they could do this.

Mass turned to Addy, "Are all the women free?"

"No, there's another six chained up at the back. Who knows how many are in the other container."

"Get them free. We need everyone ready to go if a chance comes along. Remember the code? It's 1-1-3-4."

Addy broke from the front of the container and shoved through the women to the back of the container. A few seconds later, she swore. Then she swore again. "It's not right. 1-1-3-4?"

Mas shouted back over his shoulder. "Yeah. 1-1-3-4."

"It's wrong."

Tox started shaking his head and laughing, even as he lashed out and tried to slice a burnt man with his knife. "The bitch gave us the wrong number. Wow, she was really something, huh?"

Mass groaned. Running was still their best option if the chance arose, but how could they do that if it meant leaving half a dozen innocent women to starve to death in a metal box? Not that there would even be a chance to run now that they were backed up inside the container. The demons still outnumbered them, and his legs were now trembling as if they were empty of blood. He could feel his heart pounding in his chest.

Tox kicked a burnt man back and slipped. He fell to one knee and then rose slowly. "I... I can't keep going much longer. My body is giving up on me."

Mass threw a sluggish punch at another burnt man and also slipped. His legs were so numb. "I know. Just... Just keep fighting until you can't any more."

Addy rejoined them at the front, ramming her knife into a demon's skull. It twisted and fell, taking her blade with it. She groaned and raised her fists. "Shit! Now I'm bound to break a nail."

The demons parted and Vamps appeared in their centre. *No*, thought Mass. *Not Vamps. Vamps is gone. This is a monster. Crimolok.*

Knowing he had neither the strength nor stamina to get out of there alive, Mass tried and go down with a win. He burst out of the container and rushed at Crimolok, planning to tear the monster's eyes out and leave it blind and defenceless. Maybe that would give someone else a chance to deal with him.

Before Mass could make it even halfway, the demons closed in on both sides, crashing down on him like the Red Sea. He got struck from all sides and fell to the ground, covering himself and praying for a miracle.

*I tried my best.*

The demons didn't tear him apart. Crimolok moved forward and stood over him, laughing. "Your friend cries out for you. He begs you to end his pain."

Mass lifted his head, stared at the monster wearing Vamps' face. "Fuck you."

"Come on, don't you want to use your last breath to try to save him? Try to kill me, worm. Amuse me."

"That's what you want. No, you can rot inside my friend's body. He might be in pain, but I know Vamps will be pissing himself laughing knowing you can't do a goddamn thing to get free."

The growling was low and guttural, and Mass felt it in his chest. At first he thought it was coming from Crimolok, but it was further away. And getting closer. He didn't realise what it was until the very last moment.

Oh shit!

Mass clambered up and threw himself back towards the containers. He turned just enough to see a large coach ram into the mob of demons and send them flying. Several fell, crushed underneath the tyres. Crimolok disappeared from view, lost in the chaos. Had he been hit? Killed? What would happen if he had been?

The coach skidded to a stop, barely missing Mass's outstretched legs. He shuffled back on his butt and flinched when hands grabbed him from behind. Addy and Tox were still alive. They had him.

"It's Smithy," said Tox, beaming. "I really love that kid. Let's get on board."

The door to the coach slid aside and Smithy appeared on the step. He didn't look glad to see them. In fact, he looked dismayed. Someone poked him in the back and said, "Move!"

Smithy stepped off the coach, revealing Nas and a shotgun behind him. "He wants the girls," Smithy explained. "If we put the girls on the bus, he won't hurt any of us."

Mass was too weak to do anything. He had an arm around both Tox and Addy, and he couldn't let go. "Do you not see what a monster you are? Cam told me you used to be a good man. A father."

Nas flinched. "You do not talk of such things. My journey along God's path has been difficult for a reason. Only through loss can we understand true strength."

"Then I should be strong enough to crush you," said Mass. "And you can be sure that I will. I won't let you get away with this."

"Just put the girls on the coach."

Addy sighed. "Let's just do it. At least they'll be alive and away from this place. We aren't going to make it."

There were demons scattered all about the grass. Many were still, but some were moving. Before long, enough would recover that they would once again attack. Mass turned to one of the frightened women and sighed. "Get on the bus. We'll come for you later, I promise."

The women hurried onto the bus, moving to the back and huddling together. They were broken creatures, willing to do whatever they were told so long as they were not hurt. Mass wondered if they could ever become people again. Harriet had managed it somehow.

"What about the girls in chains?" asked Addy.

Nas sneered. "Animals yet to be broken. You can keep them."

"No! You leave them here, they die."

"So be it. They are of no use to me."

Addy shook her head. "Please. Let me free them and put them on the coach. They'll behave, I'm sure. If you're really a man of God, you wouldn't leave them to die."

Nas glared at her with his one good eye. He nodded curtly. "Fine. The combination is 9-1-2-1."

"9-1-2-1," Addy muttered. "Okay, great." She hurried into the back of the container and unlocked the chains. The women there rubbed at the ankles with relief. "Get in the coach. We'll rescue you later."

Mass thought the women might argue – clearly higher spirited than the morose women already on the coach – but they eventually formed a line and headed on board.

"What about the other container?" Mass enquired. "Are there any women inside that one?"

One woman just entering the bus turned back and shook her head. "We all huddled together in the same one. Everyone is here."

Mass nodded. Okay. The women were all safe. At least they had achieved that much. With any luck, they would overpower Nas and leave him in a ditch somewhere at the side of the road.

Some of the girls on the coach screamed. "There's a demon inside."

Smithy half turned, the shotgun still at his back. "That's just Dave. He's with me. Come on, mate. Get off the bus."

David scampered along the aisle and then hopped out onto the grass. He looked confused.

Nas shoved Smithy forward and stepped back onto the coach. He kept his shotgun pointed, ready to shoot him in the back.

Mass glanced aside and saw burnt men getting to their feet. There was also a primate with a broken leg. Once Nas and the coach left, they would be back to square one. Mass was too tired to run. Too tired to fight.

Smithy had a pissed-off grin on his face. "Hey, Mass, you want to know something?"

Mass frowned. "What?"

"This guy really knows how to push my buttons." It made no sense, but, rather than explain it, Smithy threw out his arm and struck a red circular button beside the coach's door. It slid shut with a *hiss* and knocked Nas's shotgun aside. Addy leapt forward and grabbed the barrel, snatching it out of Nas's hands. Then the tables turned.

Addy held the shotgun in her hands, and Nas, sensing he was well and truly screwed, grabbed the door and forced it shut, keeping a shield between him and the shotgun. Smithy grabbed the door and tried to force it open, but the two of them reached stalemate.

Several burnt men were on their feet, slowly coming around to face Mass and the others. "We need to get out of here."

"Yeah," said Smithy. "On this goddamn coach. Open up, you piece of shit."

"The world will never be yours," Nas cried. "Heathens! You are forsaken and you do not even know it. This world has been reclaimed."

"Shut up," said Smithy. "You're a dickhead."

"We need to move," said Mass. He was still leaning on Tox, but since Addy had moved away from him, it was getting harder and harder to stay standing. The best he could hope for was to limp out of there. But it would have to be now. They didn't have time to fight to get the door open.

Smithy swore, and he looked like he was about to give up, but he was then startled by Nas's face hitting the glass. Behind him, the women who had been shackled were beating at him with their fists. It forced him to let go of the door to defend himself.

Smithy finally yanked the door open and Nas toppled off the steps and into the mud. He immediately went to get up, but Addy hit him with the stock of her shotgun. Blood trickled from his forehead and his eyes rolled about in his skull. He lashed out at her with his hook, but missed and ended up burying it in the dirt. Addy pointed the shotgun at his head, but Mass reached out to her. "Don't waste the ammo. We might need it."

Addy looked over at the approaching demons and understood. She lowered her shotgun and made it onto the bus. Then she turned back and said, "Well, what are you waiting for?"

Smithy put a hand on David's back and ushered the tiny demon back onto the bus. The women inside whimpered, but they accepted his presence. Mass climbed on board and heard Smithy reassuring them.

Tox grabbed Mass's waist and started helping him down the aisle. "Hell of a couple of days, huh?"

Mass's vision was spinning. He wanted, more than anything, to be back at Portsmouth. No more being out in the field. He just wanted to be safe. "I fucked up so bad, Tox. Everyone is dead."

"Not everyone," he said. "And we have a busload of innocent women who will be thanking you later."

"But "

"No more thinking, Mass. You've earned a little silence, so leave things to the rest of us."

Mass clambered onto a seat near the front. The comfort was amazing, his heavy body sinking into the worn cushion. Almost immediately he began to fall asleep. It was only Nas's screams that kept him alert. He could've looked out the window to see what was happening to the man, but it was better to imagine it. Hopefully it hurt enough to make the man see how misguided he had been. The world had no room for zealots. Religion was dead.

The soft grumble of the engine and the vibrations through the seat was finally enough to make Mass close his eyes and try to sleep. They were getting out of there. They were going home.

## CHAPTER THIRTEEN

Tox took the driver's seat, which allowed Smithy to take a breather. While he was nowhere near the state Mass was in, with his torn throat and bloodshot eyes, he was utterly exhausted. He took a seat with David, who stared out the window with fascination, and toyed with the yellow scarf around his sliced forearm. It made him think about Harriet. He had barely known the women, yet it hurt his heart that he never would. She had been damaged and afraid, but brave and decent. He wondered how many people like that were still alive.

Were they really heading back to Portsmouth? Were there people there? Safety? Could he finally get off the road and stop surviving? Start living? It seemed impossible. The end of an endless nightmare.

The women were all huddled at the back of the coach with Addy watching over them, but when he peered back at them, none made eye contact. What must they have been through? It made him happy that Nas and all his followers were dead. He had watched the man get torn apart by the burnt men and the primate. His hook had come loose and tumbled into the mud. Once the demons swarmed over him, it was the only part of him left.

"We go safe place?" David asked. One of his eyes seemed to have died in its socket. It no longer moved when the other one did. How much time did he have left? Was there any way to help him?

Smithy nodded. "Yeah, buddy. The fighting is over now. We're going to a safe place."

David smiled, all his teeth now gone. "Good. David happy."

Smithy welled up with tears. He didn't know whether it was the tiredness, the relief of surviving, or if he was sad for this little demon who had somehow become his friend. David had had multiple chances to run, but he had come back every time. David was as much a warrior as anyone on this coach.

To keep himself from weeping, Smithy got up and headed for the front of the bus. He passed by Mass, who had fallen asleep within a minute of sitting down, and carried on until he was up front with Tox.

Tox was rolling the large steering wheel back and forth as he manoeuvred away from the containers. They hadn't yet made it away from the demons, but they no longer felt like a threat. After being smashed to pieces by the coach, they were battered and broken too. Both sides were licking their wounds.

"We lost a lot of good people," said Tox, glancing only partially at Smithy, "but I'm glad we were able to pick a few up. Those women will need all the help we can give them, but you're going to be welcomed like the hero you are, Smithy. If Addy hadn't found you, I don't think any of us would've made it."

"We all did our bit," said Smithy. "I think we would have failed without any one of us."

Tox smiled. "I think so too. That's why it's so important that we stick together. Portsmouth is a safe place, but only because we fight to protect it. You up for that?"

"I've been fighting since this thing began. I'm just glad I'll get to do it beside other people."

"You won't ever have to fight alone again, Smithy. You know why?"

Smithy shook his head. "No, why?"

"Because you're an Urban Vampire. Welcome to the family."

"I'm not quite sure what that means, but thank you. I'm grateful you people found me. I'm just sorry you lost so much."

Tox nodded. "I suppose that's war. It never gets any..."

Smithy frowned. "What is it?"

Tox lifted his foot off the accelerator and let the coach lose speed as it neared the edge of the field. "Look!"

Smithy stared ahead and slightly to the left. A man crawled along the ground, legs broken and trailing behind him. "It's Crimolok."

"No," said David, calling from a little further up the aisle. "Crimolok is not here. He is not inside my head."

Smithy and Tox looked at one another, each clearly trying to figure out what that meant. Then it made sense, and realisation dawned over them both.

"I'll go wake up Mass," said Smithy.

---

Mass had to fight to open his eyes because his lids were so heavy. The way Smithy was shaking him and talking to him was not with the urgency of danger, but it was urgent. Something important was happening and Mass needed to see it.

"W-What is it, Smithy? I can barely move."

"I know, mate, but you have to stand up and see something. I'll help you."

Smithy put his arms under Mass and lifted him from. His entire body ached, and his left knee refused to bend, which meant he had to hop and shuffle towards the front of the bus. Tox was at the steering wheel, looking back at him with a grim expression. For some reason, he had stopped the coach.

"Tox, we need to get out of here. Why aren't we moving?"

"Look! Look who's out there."

Mass squinted and peered through the windscreen. At first he saw nothing but grass and a long wooden fence. Then he saw a figure in the grass. Crimolok was dragging himself along, and he was massively injured. "We've got him. We've got the bastard. Get him on board. The bastard is coming back to Portsmouth with us."

Tox winced at him.

"What is it? Why are you looking at me like that?"

Smithy spoke from beside him. "It's not Crimolok. It's Vamps."

"What? How do you know?"

Smithy pointed back towards his demon pet, David. "I have a demonic radar with me. He can't sense Crimolok, which means—"

"Which means that's Vamps out there," Tox finished.

Mass readjusted his grip on Smithy. "Take me out there. Take me to him."

Smithy didn't argue. He reached up to the dashboard and took the shotgun Addy had left there when she'd boarded. Then he opened the door and helped Mass down the steps before carrying him across the field to where his best friend lay in a tangle of his own limbs. Once Smithy got him close enough, Mass told him to go.

"You sure, man? This might be a trick or something."

Mass shook his head. "I don't care. Just leave me."

"Fine, but I'm leaving this with you. Two shells." He handed Mass the shotgun and went back to the coach.

Mass tried to use the shotgun like a walking stick, but it was slightly too short. He was too tired to stay upright even if it had worked. The only thing he could do was drop to his knees and drag himself up beside his friend. The rain had let up, but the whole world was soaking wet.

Up until then, Vamps hadn't noticed the coach, or Mass and Smithy walking towards him. Now he flinched and turned to look at Mass. His eyes were full of pain and confusion – but they were *his* eyes. Vamps was staring back at him.

Mass grinned despite the tears rolling down his cheeks. "Hey, gangster, looks like you got your ass beat."

Vamps stared at him like a stranger for a moment, but then a smile slowly spread itself across his lips. "You should see the other guy."

The two of them fell at one another, grabbing each other in their arms and hugging as fiercely as their broken bodies would allow. "I missed you, Mass. I miss you all. Ravy, Gingerbread. I just want to go back."

Tears dripped from Mass's chin. "Me too, man. Me too."

"But we can't ever go back, can we?"

Mass squeezed his best friend harder. "No, mate, we can't."

The two of them broke apart and looked at one another. Vamps' face was no longer distorted like it had been, but cracks in his skin and painful blisters showed the strain of Crimolok's presence.

"Are you dying?" Mass asked, fearing the answer. Knowing the answer.

But Vamps shook his head. "No. I can feel him in me, healing my body. He's not doing it on purpose, but his... his energy is too powerful to contain. I can feel it knitting my bones back together. He hates it. He wants me to die so he can escape, but he can't do anything to make it happen. If he frees himself, I think he'll end up even more trapped somehow. Like in purgatory or something."

"Do you know his thoughts? Can you tell me anything that can help?"

Vamps shook his head. His voice was pained, but he was clear and precise, as though he'd been waiting a thousand years for a chance to talk. "I-I only hear what he allows me. He tricked me into closing a gate. I thought I could use his power to close them all, but he wanted me to do it. He wanted me to close the gate so he could bubble up to the surface and take control. The gates aren't evil, Mass. They're seals, meant to keep evil from invading the Earth, but Crimolok broke them and they opened. They still have power over him though. They call him back to Hell and dampen his power. He needed them to invade, but now they hurt him every single moment that passes. By closing the gates, we make him stronger, and he's been getting stronger since he got here. Soon, even trapped inside my body, he'll be unstoppable, but if I die... I don't know, but he wants to get free real bad. I have to keep him inside me."

Mass placed his forehead against Vamps' and asked, "How can I help you, man? Tell me how."

"You can't. Just get out of here before he comes back. I don't have long. Soon, it won't be me again."

"Does it hurt? Being a passenger in your own body? Does it?"

Tears cut through the blood on Vamps' cheeks. "It's like acid being injected into every cell of my body, and it never stops. It never lets up even for a second. The evil inside me... it's hollowing me out. But it don't matter, man. I'll hold on as long as I can so I can watch you beat the fucker. Keep fighting, Mass. Don't stop. He can be beaten, I know it. For that, I'm willing to suffer for a million years. The pain don't matter."

"You always were a badass. I love you, man, you know that? You were always the best of us."

Vamps closed his eyes and smiled. "Love is what separates us from them. It's the one thing Crimolok can never understand about us. Maybe if he'd ever felt it himself, he wouldn't have been cast down."

Mass had the feeling Vamps knew things that no human was ever meant to know, but he was in too much pain to explain then. Perhaps they couldn't even be explained. "I want to take you with us. We can help—"

Vamps shook his head. "No, man. You can't help me. It's my burden. The pain, the suffering, it's only worth it if you get out of here and keep fighting. Kill some demons for me, yeah?"

Mass wiped the tears off his face. "I'll kill a hundred."

"Good man. I'll see you around, okay?"

Mass grabbed the shotgun and used it to push himself to his feet. He looked down at his friend, a broken mess, and tried to comprehend the agony he must be in. The agony he willingly endured to help the rest of mankind. It broke Mass's heart. "How long do you have left until he's back?"

"I don't know. A few hours maybe. Believe me, I'll make the most of it. Two broken legs is almost ticklish to me now."

It was a joke, but Mass didn't find it funny. He raised the shotgun Smithy had left him. "I don't care what we have to do to win this, Vamps, but you're the best friend I ever had."

Vamps nodded. "Ditto."

"And that's why I have to end your suffering."

Vamps opened his mouth to speak, but Mass pulled the trigger and shot him in the face. Then he emptied the second shell into his chest to make sure there was no chance of Crimolok *healing* him. It was all it took to make his friend, and his friend's suffering, disappear.

Mass collapsed backwards into the grass. The smoking shotgun fell into the grass beside him and he began to sob. He sobbed so hard his chest hurt. No one approached him for several minutes, but when someone did, it was Addy. "Hey," she said in a soft, gentle voice. "You okay?"

He shook his head.

"I listened to what you said, you know." She sniffed. She'd been crying. "Back at the house?"

Mass looked at her but said nothing.

"I decided to keep living. That's what Gross would have wanted. We've all lost people we love, but we keep on fighting because it's the right thing to do. We can't let the bastards get away with this."

"I shot... I shot my best friend in the face."

She chuckled. "Friendships are complicated. I reckon he would have done the same for you."

"He was in so much pain. Every second was agony. I don't care what happens next, but I couldn't go on knowing that. I... *couldn't*."

"Yeah, well, maybe things will work out okay. Shit doesn't seem to have hit the fan yet, does it? Perhaps nothing bad will happen."

Mass considered it. He had shot Vamps and killed him, but there had been no explosions of hellfire or demonic fury. He had killed his friend and nothing had happened. Maybe they really would be okay. Maybe...

The sky lit up as though a thousand suns had suddenly entered the Earth's orbit. An almighty wind arose from nothing and rocked the coach on its axles. The distant trees swayed. The world itself seemed to howl.

Addy licked her lips and peered around anxiously. "I really shouldn't have said anything."

"Let's get back on the bus," said Mass, reaching out for her support. "Whatever it is, we'll deal with it."

Addy helped him up and they got going.

---

The first thought that came to mind when Smithy saw Mass shoot his best friend in the face was *hypocrite*. The second thought was that he probably shouldn't have left him that shotgun.

Mass had made it very clear that killing Vamps would be a bad idea, so what the hell had just happened? There had already been a blinding light and an almighty gale, so some kind of bad shit was clearly about to go down. He doubted it would end with a herd of galloping unicorns.

Addy helped Mass back onto the bus. Smithy said nothing. The guy had made his decision and now they all had to live by it. No point arguing over something that couldn't be changed.

Smithy put a hand on Tox's back. "We should get out of here."

Tox nodded and switched the engine back on. Then he switched it back off. He was staring ahead, transfixed by something in the distance. Smithy turned his head to see what was the matter. He gasped. Then stared in silence for a minute more. A new gate had opened, so big and so tall that it filled the entire horizon. A mammoth, world-swallowing gate. And something was coming through.

Smithy punched Tox on the shoulder. "Yeah, step on it, mate. I don't feel like sticking around."

"Yeah, me neither." Tox floored the accelerator and turned the wheel. The coach slid on its rear wheels and fishtailed. It missed the opening in the fence and instead flattened a large section of it. The large tyres were undeterred, and they steered over the rotting wood with ease, biting into the gravel road that led away from the farm.

Then they were moving, gaining speed steadily and moving away from the rapidly growing gate behind them.

Addy moved to the front. "Was that what I think it was?"

"I have no idea," said Tox, "but I don't think we should stop to take pictures."

They made it onto the main road a few minutes later. Smithy could still see the throbbing light of the gate behind them. It was hidden by trees and the undulations of the land, but the glow it gave off made it all the way to the clouds. If it had been night, then perhaps it would have spread across the entire country.

What the hell was it? What could be the meaning of a gate many times the size of any other? This was all because Mass shot Vamps. Why the hell had he done it?

Mass was back on his feet, although he was as pale as a sheet and suddenly seemed like a frail old woman. His large biceps seemed to hang off his bones. "Take this road here."

Tox glanced at him. "Why?"

"Because our brothers are this way."

Tox followed Mass's direction for a couple of minutes and then sped up on a clear A-road heading south. "We're heading back to where we started," said Tox. "The toilet block where we parked the truck."

"No," said Mass. "We're heading to where Honeywell and the others died. I want to take them home."

Smithy frowned. "You lost friends here?"

Mass nodded. "This is where it all started. Gemma set a trap, and we walked right into it. I lost a lot of good men. They deserve to be buried in Portsmouth."

"Okay. I'll help you get them. This coach has luggage bays on the one side. Maybe we can place them inside."

Mass patted him on the shoulder. "Thank you."

Ahead, a dark mass came into view on the road, and there were stains on the concrete. Eventually they revealed themselves to be bodies rotting in the morning sun.

"Okay, stop here," said Mass. "This is them."

Tox slowed the bus and then stopped beside the scattered collection of bodies. Mass got Addy to help him off the bus. Smithy went after them. It was hard to tell how many bodies littered the road because they'd been blown to pieces. Arms and legs lay strewn about. Blood slicks stretched from one side of the road to the other. Whatever had happened here, it'd been brutal.

Mass stepped away from Addy, clearly wanting to do this on his own. He moved slowly towards the bodies and then knelt down beside them. "I'm sorry," he said. "You were older and wiser, but I thought I knew best. Tell you the truth, I was never fit to lead – not when men like you were around. You were a good man, and I know you were a good father. My own father was a piece of shit less said about him the better – but meeting you, and hearing the way you talked about your son, it gave me hope. I hope that one day there'll be more dads like you caring about more kids like Dillon. If I hadn't met you, I might have given up, and I regret the fact I'll never tell you how I wish I'd had a dad like you."

Smithy didn't want to interrupt, but he feared that time was against them – that if they didn't move soon, something would catch up with them. "Mass? Do you want me to start moving them onto the coach?"

He turned to Smithy and nodded. "Yeah, thanks."

In a strangely surreal moment, the road suddenly spat at Smithy, a patch of concrete breaking apart right at his feet.

Then something struck the coach.

Smithy ducked. "Someone's shooting at us. Fuck!"

Mass was still weak, but he managed to scramble towards the bus. Smithy stopped by the door and helped him up the steps. "Who the hell is firing at us? Is it your friends from Portsmouth?"

"No. People from Portsmouth doesn't shoot at other people."

Smithy ducked as another bullet hit the coach. "Then who?"

"I don't know." Mass climbed the steps onto the coach, then looked back at Smithy with his eyes wide. "Shit. Shit. Shit."

"What? What is it?"

"The other men." Mass shook his head in disgust. "Harriet told me that four of Nas's men had left the farm to go siphon the petrol from our lorry. What the hell are they still doing here?"

Smithy ducked back on board just as Mass started yelling at Tox to get them out of there. Tox didn't waste time and started the engine. The coach began to roll.

Demons spilled out into the road. One second the way ahead was clear. The next, a wall of rotting, rancid flesh erupted from the hedges. Where the hell had they come from?

Tox swore. "People are shooting at us and now there are demons. Grand!"

"Guess we know why those men have been stuck here," said Mass. "Look, they're up there on the verge. They must have been surrounded for a day at least. They're desperate."

Mass saw three men peeking out from between a thick hedge on the hill. They had switched from firing at the coach and were now firing at the burnt men emerging from the opposite bank. The demons were everywhere. Four dozen at least. What had suddenly brought them? Had Crimolok summoned reinforcements? Were the demons amassing again, ready to wage war a second time?

They needed to warn Portsmouth. They needed to tell them what was coming. About the giant gate.

There was a *ping* as another bullet hit the coach, then a second one shattered a side window. The women at the back of the bus screamed. Smithy gripped the back of Tox's seat as he fought to keep his balance. The coach rocked back and forth as it accelerated erratically. "Why are they shooting at us?"

Tox turned the wheel hastily to the side. "Because we're driving off with their only means of escape. Maybe if they'd asked nicely, we would've given them a lift."

Demons filled the road but Tox didn't brake. He sped up. They crashed into the first and the bus hitched up as the wheels crunched over its body. Then they hurtled into the main pack. More side windows were shattered. A primate leapt up into the broken windscreen. Smithy shot it in the head with one of the last bullets in his handgun.

The men on the hill fired at the coach again, trying to keep it from leaving. Everyone inside ducked.

The demons thinned out ahead, falling beneath the coach or leaping away before the iron chain wrapped around the front bumper seared their flesh.

"We're getting out of here," yelled Tox. "Hold on to your—"

Suddenly Tox slumped over the steering wheel and hissed in agony. The coach lurched to the left. Smithy saw blood coming from his hand. He'd been shot, a round taking off several fingers as they gripped the wheel.

Something exploded, and the coach lurched again, this time even more violently. Smithy tumbled into the aisle. The screeching that followed told him one of their tyres had burst, either from crushed demon bones or another shot fired by the men on the hill. Tox tried to fight the steering, but with only one hand, he didn't have the strength. Smithy tried to get up and help, but the bus tilted and threw him back down.

Then gravity betrayed them all and the bus was spinning. Smithy was vaguely aware of branches and vines whipping at the sides of the coach, but mostly he was aware of falling. The windows shattered all at once and the coach's interior turned sideways, and there was the sound of twisting metal and breaking glass.

Then silence.

Smithy lay still, lodged between a row of seats. He checked himself for injury. Miraculously, he didn't seem to be hurt. But what about the others? He peered around the coach's interior, which was partly shaded by the bushes and trees that had come through the windows like probing fingers. Several bodies moved, and the silence was broken by multiple moans. Addy was nearby, staring at Smithy like she didn't know where she was. Her face was bleeding.

"Addy, are you okay?"

"W-We crashed."

"We went into the ditch. I'm okay. How about you?"

She paused for a moment, probably to see if anything hurt. Then she spoke. "I'm okay."

"Good. Can you help the women at the back? I think a couple of them might be injured."

Addy climbed out from her seat. "I'll go to them. You check on everybody else."

Smithy clambered towards the front. It was disorientating with the aisle being to the side and the seats now forming the floor. He had to clamber over them like stepping stones, heading for the large square of light that must have been the windshield.

A demon leapt out at him.

"Jeez, Dave, you scared the hell out of me."

"Our wagon died."

Smithy laughed. "Yeah, it really did. You okay?"

David nodded.

"Okay, help me find the others."

Mass was only a few seats away. He wasn't in any pain, but his leg appeared to be trapped. He'd slipped into the footwell, and the seat in front had snapped free of its rivets and fallen across his knee. "I'm fine," he kept on saying. "Check on the others. Is Tox okay?"

"I'm fine," said Tox from somewhere up ahead. "It's just my hand. Lost a couple of fingers."

Mass sighed. "We're cursed. That's the only explanation for all this shit. We need to get everyone off this coach. Looks like we'll be walking to Portsmouth."

Another *ping* as a bullet hit some part of the coach. Smithy ducked instinctively. "No! Those dickheads are still shooting at us."

"And they aren't the only problem," Tox shouted. "There're still demons out there. I can see them coming."

"Cursed," said Mass. "We're fucking cursed."

Smithy disagreed. "When you consider how many life or death situations we've survived in the last twenty-four hours, I would say we're pretty goddamn lucky. Come on, let's get you out of there."

Mass shook his head. "Just get whoever you can and get out of here. Someone needs to warn Portsmouth about that gate. They need to prepare."

"Sorry, mate, but I'm an Urban Vampire now, and I think that means not leaving a brother who needs help."

Mass raised an eyebrow, revealing a thick pink gash that was strangely bloodless. "This is bigger than any of us. General Wickstaff needs to know what's coming. You need to get out of here, Smithy."

No way. He couldn't do it. He couldn't cut and run on these people. He looked around for an answer, and he saw it smiling back at him. "Dave! Do you think you could find a big city called Portsmouth?"

He frowned as if he didn't understand the question. "Follow signs?"

"Yes, can you do that? Portsmouth."

"Cannot read words."

Smithy grimaced.

"Boats," said Mass. "Portsmouth has a dock and ferry terminals. Most of the road signs have little boats on them. He can follow the pictures."

"Boat pictures," said David. "Yes, can follow. Why do follow?"

Smithy put a hand on David's shoulder and put his face closer to his. He needed to know the demon understood. "Because you need to take a message there. You need to talk to the person in charge."

"General Wickstaff," said Mass. "General Wickstaff."

David pursed his lips and spoke slowly. "Wick... Staff."

"Yes, that's it!" said Smithy. "You need to find her and tell her all about what happened at the farm. You need to tell her about the giant gate that's opened there."

David nodded. "Yes. David tell and people ready. Ready when fighting comes."

Mass smiled. "For a demon, you're pretty smart, David. You get that message to Wickstaff and you'll be saving a lot of lives."

David smiled. "Want to do. Thank you."

"Then go," said Smithy. "And if I never see you again, I hope you're okay. You're a good friend."

"Friend. Smithy's friend."

Smithy squeezed his shoulder. "Best friend. Now go, get out of here, Dave. Follow the boats, remember?"

David nodded. "Boat pictures. Yes. Goodbye."

Smithy watched the little demon scurry away, dodging between the seats and exiting out of the windscreen. Then he turned to Mass. "What's your policy on allowing demons to join the Urban Vampires?"

Mass chuckled. "I'm sure we could use a mascot."

"Time's run out," shouted Tox. "Our ugly friends have arrived."

Shadows passed over the sides of the coach, demons surrounding them. Their hisses and moans began to increase as they savoured their prey. Addy moved up to join Mass, and a moment later, Tox moved away from the front to be with them.

"Urban Vampires for life," said Mass.

"For life," said Tox and Addy.

"For life," said Smithy.

Mass nodded. "Let's kill some demons."

# CHAPTER FOURTEEN

THE LAST WEEK had been tense. General Thomas had kept to his word and caused no more problems at Portsmouth. His men were respectful to the local militia, and friendships were even beginning to form. It was looking, more and more, like things might just work out. Portsmouth had an army.

The only exposed thorn was the fact Wickstaff and Thomas were still yet to form an agreement on how to move forward. The last week had seen a ceasefire, not a treaty. Maddy feared his desire to lead would soon, once again, raise its ugly head.

But that wasn't what Maddy wanted to think about right now – not while she was half-naked in Amanda's office.

The two women hadn't been able to keep their hands off of one another for days, and it was no doubt starting to get around that the general and her aide were seemingly closer than ever. Wickstaff had proclaimed she didn't care, and if Maddy was honest, neither did she. Diane had found the whole thing hilarious when she'd told her. "Sleeping your way to the top, you slut," she had said with a grin on her face. Maddy had blushed. But she only felt alive, or anything approaching happy, when she was with Amanda.

They were currently lying on the small sofa that took up one side of the office. Maddy was lying on top of Amanda, both of them topless, and she was kissing her forehead, her cheeks, her everything.

"You know," said Amanda, "for someone who claims not to be a lesbian, you sure seem very enthusiastic about kissing me."

Maddy grinned. "I can stop."

"Please don't."

"So you never... you know... you never had feelings for another woman before either?"

"I've spent my career surrounded by men, but no, I haven't. It's rather remarkable, isn't it."

"It's weird," admitted Maddy. "I didn't even know I was falling in love with you until..."

"Until you pounced on me in my office?"

"Yeah, that."

Amanda lifted her head and kissed Maddy's collarbone, which she had recently discovered she loved. "I didn't realise it either, but this whole time you have been my rock in the ocean. You're the only thing that keeps me from drowning."

"You think Portsmouth is ready for this? It could be quite the scandal."

Amanda chuckled. "It might give them something else to think about besides dying, so I say let them gossip."

There was a knock at the door.

Maddy leapt up. "Shit, shit."

Amanda smirked. "Calm down. It's not like you're going to get in trouble. You're shagging a general."

"I know, but I don't have my clothes on. Damn it, where did I leave my blouse?"

"It's under the desk. Go on, hide underneath while I see who's at the door. It might be fun."

Maddy rolled her eyes. "You're terrible." Then she scurried around to the back of the desk and crawled into the foot well. She had to cover her mouth to keep from giggling. She heard Amanda dress herself and then cross the office to the door, just as the visitor knocked again.

She heard General Thomas introduce himself and groaned. "General Wickstaff, I was wondering if we could talk."

"Oh, um, of course, General. Right now might not be the—"

"Please, I have something I need to get off my chest."

"Very well. Please, come in."

"Thank you."

Maddy saw shiny shoes clomp across the floor from the gap beneath the desk. As fun as hiding might be, Thomas was not a man who enjoyed games. She prayed he didn't discover her hiding.

"What can I do for you, General Thomas?" Amanda asked. "Would you like a drink?"

"No, no, thank you. I just came here to apologise and ask you to accept my resignation as general."

Amanda spluttered. "I-I'm sorry? I think I misheard you."

General Thomas chuckled. "You didn't. I am stepping down immediately once you accept my resignation."

"Why?"

"Because my position in Portsmouth is untenable. My own men hail you as a hero and, quite frankly, I can't disagree with them. The only option is me stepping down or trying to wrest power from you. I fear I would come off the worst if I were to go up against you."

Wickstaff cleared her throat. "Is this some devilish trick? It seems very unlike you."

"I'm tired, Amanda. I've been sending men to their deaths for the best part of a year. I helped liberate Asia only to have my victories claimed by the Germans. I think I came here to gain the recognition I deserve. I wanted to be the hero who rescued the United Kingdom, but I realise now that I'm not that person. You are. Whatever has happened, I have always fought for our survival as a species. My heart has always been devoted to my men, and I don't want to risk any more lives than I need to. I've had my victories and now you need to gain yours. When I saw them all cheering you on the docks, I realised how old I've gotten. Let me retire while I still have the respect of my men."

Maddy had to cover her mouth to keep from gasping. This was the greatest news ever. It sounded like Thomas was not just stepping down, but stepping out. Would he spend the rest of his days with his feet up and out of the way?

*Please let it be.*

"I won't force you to do this, General," said Wickstaff. "I'm sure there's a way we can work together."

"Not without endangering lives, I fear. I'm not being forced to this, Amanda. It's what I want – welcome it even. Let me be old."

There was movement, which Maddy sensed was Amanda shaking her adversary's hand. "I'll keep you permanently stocked with brandy and whatever else you need."

"Now that sounds like a victory. Thank you, Amanda. I'm just sorry we had to get here in the way we did."

"I don't hold grudges, General Thomas, and you will always be a valued and respected man. You have my word."

Another knock at the door. Maddy wrapped her arms tightly around her knees, trying to make herself smaller. She had managed to get her bra on before Thomas had come inside, but she was still topless. The last thing she needed was a crowd.

It was Diane at the door, and it sounded like Tom was with her. The two of them had been working together a lot recently since Wickstaff had added the young guardsman to her personal security team. "General Wickstaff, General Thomas, I have and urgent matter to bring to you."

"Yes," said Amanda, "what is it?"

"We've captured a demon as you requested. Well, sort of."

"What do you mean?"

"It kind of gave itself up. It says it needs to talk to you."

"Talk to me? What on earth?"

Thomas huffed. "It's a ploy to get close to you, surely. Diane, you're usually very cut-throat about these things, aren't you?"

"Yes," said Diane. "I was about to shoot it in the face, but then it said the message was from a friend of ours. Mass."

Wickstaff fell silent. Mass and his team hadn't been heard from in over a week, and they never stayed out that long. Quick in and outs was how they survived. Everyone at Portsmouth had been fearing the worst. Especially since demons had now been spotted all over the place, gathering, once again, in force.

"Is Mass... Is he alive?" Amanda asked.

"This demon said so, although he's hurt. I couldn't work out everything the demon said, but it sounds like Mass and his team were in a bus crash."

"Where is this demon? I want to speak with it."

"Don't be reckless," said Thomas.

"I'm not being reckless. I can handle myself against a single demon, no matter what it's planning."

"I assumed you would think that," said Diane. "That's why we brought the demon here. It calls itself Dave"

Thomas spluttered, "Dave?"

"Yes, Dave. Tom, could you bring it in, please?"

Maddy tried to see underneath the desk. This wasn't something she wanted to miss. As it was, she would just have to listen. There were sounds of something small shuffling into the room, chains rattling. Diane would have taken precautions, and the demon was likely in handcuffs.

"Hello, yes, General. Wick... Staff, yes?"

"Yes, I am General Wickstaff. What do you have to tell me?"

There was a squawk of a radio, and the conversation was interrupted. Tom was the one who spoke after receiving the message. "There's a pack of demons approaching the gate. Nothing we can't handle, but we should be there to monitor things."

"Go," said Wickstaff. "Both of you get a full report and bring it back to me."

"What about... Dave?" asked Diane.

"General Thomas and I will be quite all right. I've known larger six-year-olds."

"This could be a trap," said Thomas. "Be careful."

"I always am. Diane, Tom, get going. Report back to me ASAP."

Maddy heard shuffling feet and the closing of the door. She smelt the stink of rancid flesh.

"What do you have to tell me... Dave?"

"Message from Smithy and Mass."

"I don't know anyone named Smithy."

"Urban Vampire, yes?"

Wickstaff cleared her throat. "Mass sent you? Could you describe him?"

"Large man, small hair."

Maddy frowned. She didn't know whether to laugh or cry.

"Yes, well, I suppose one might describe him that way. Where is he? Is he hurt?"

"Yes. All hurt. Wagon break. Wagon fall. Men and demons nasty fight. Send help."

"Yes, of course. Do you know where we can find this... wagon?"

"Many walking. Farm and fields. Dave see."

Thomas grunted. "Needle in a haystack."

Wickstaff shushed him. "David, you shall show us the way, yes?"

"Yes. I show. Follow boats backwards."

"Okay. Thank you for reporting this. I shall see that you are—"

"More tell," said the demon. "More message."

"Okay, speak."

"Big light, you see?"

Maddy knew what the demon was referring to. The horizon had been glowing orange at night, something far in the distance. The assumption was that some giant structure was burning – a power plant, perhaps.

"What do you know about the light?" Amanda asked.

"It is gate. Biggest gate you see. All the way to clouds and birds. Giant gate. Danger come. Mass give message and David give."

"Could it be true?" said Thomas. "A new gate?"

"Is true," said the demon. "Yes, gate, yes."

"Okay," said Wickstaff. "One thing at a time. We need to find Mass. In the meantime, I need you to stick around a while longer, Thomas. I need you to help prepare Portsmouth against an attack while I go out and bring home my boy."

"Don't be a fool. You're needed here."

"That's the benefit of having two generals in Portsmouth. We can afford to lose one."

"I strongly advise you stay. You can't put the fate of a small group of men above the whole of Portsmouth."

"That's where we differ, General. I value one life the same as all lives. If you start leaving men to die then the whole thing falls apart. I'll assemble a team and leaving at once. I'll take an army if I have to."

"Those men will be needed here if we are attacked. It's the wrong call."

"It's my call," said Wickstaff firmly.

"Well, maybe it shouldn't be."

There was a sudden *punching* sound, followed by what might

have been someone gasping. Maddy didn't know what had happened until she saw the blood dripping onto the floorboards. It crept towards her, moving through the narrow cracks in the floorboards. She opened her mouth to scream, but covered her mouth and held her breath.

"Why kill friend?" asked the demon, sounding genuinely confused.

"I didn't kill her," said Thomas. "You did."

There was a gunshot, and this time, Maddy did let out a squeal. The demon's corpse hit the floor, and she waited to see whether Thomas had heard her scream.

"Help! Guards, I need help."

Maddy heard rushing footsteps followed by the door swinging open. Voices she recognised spoke – Thomas's own guards. Then Thomas spoke. "General Wickstaff needs help. The enemy sent an assassin and the stupid woman fell for its tricks. Damn you, Amanda. Damn you. What are you pair waiting for? Get help."

The footsteps retreated.

Maddy could see a shadow on the floor that she knew was Amanda's body. She couldn't hide any longer. She stood up slowly and faced the room. General Thomas saw her and gasped, but she ignored him. She stared down at Amanda and knew she was dead. Her throat was slashed wide open. Somewhere on his person, Thomas had a knife covered in her blood. The demon was dead too. It was a tiny thing, almost like a child. A bloody hole split the centre of its chest.

"What did you do?" She muttered it at first, but then she roared. "What did you do?"

Thomas was shocked stiff, and she knew it was because he had no idea what to do. Then he rushed at her, gun raised above his head. Maddy saw it coming down towards her temple, but it was too late. The floor came up to meet her, and she landed on her face beside Amanda.

---

"Maddy, wake up."

For a moment, Maddy thought she was buried. She opened her

eyes and it was still pitch-black. Then light spilled into her world and gave her a headache. A face stared down at her. It was Colonel Cross.

"T-Tony?"

Tony smiled. "Yes. Keep your voice down."

She looked left and right. She was lying in bed. Her bed. "W-What happened?"

"You don't remember?"

She thought a moment, then felt like being sick. "Amanda. Amanda! He fucking killed her. Thomas is a murderer."

Tony's eyes flickered, and he seemed sad – disappointed even. "So it was him. I was really hoping it wasn't. Diane told me that the demon wouldn't have hurt a fly."

"D-Diane came to you?"

Cross nodded. "Apparently, Wickstaff had mentioned trusting me to be a good man. She came to see me earlier to tell me Wickstaff was dead and that General Thomas had taken charge. The whole thing sounded dodgy, and Diane said there was no way the little demon had done it."

Maddy shook her head. "The demon came to give Amanda a message. Thomas killed them both and said it was an assassin. Then he hit me."

"He's going to have some men come by later and kill you. I know because one of those men came and reported it to me. They all liked Wickstaff and they know that you and she were… close. It's not adding up for a lot of people. Still, some of those men will be by later to take care of you, but you're not going to be here."

"W-What? Where then?"

"Kielder Forest Park." He smiled, seeming to understand how little that made sense. "Before bringing the demon to Wickstaff, Diane questioned it for almost an hour about everything it knew. One of the most interesting things it mentioned was a group of survivors in a forest up north. They have a castle."

"A castle?"

"A pretty perfect place to live nowadays, wouldn't you say? Anyway, you have a boat ticket waiting for you. I'm getting you out of here."

"How? If Thomas wants me dead, he'll never let me out of here."

"That's why we need to be quick about it. Can you get out of bed?"

She moved her arms, then her legs. "Yes."

"Get up then!"

Maddy got out of bed and realised she was still topless. Cross stared at her a moment and then glanced away while she grabbed a blouse from her closet. Once dressed, she hurried with him to the door.

There were two guards outside, but neither tried to stop her. "This is Carl and Martin. They're here to make sure you don't escape, but after reflection they've decided to do the opposite. They're heading north with you. So are another thirty Portsmouth men who Diane has arranged to keep you safe."

"W-What about Diane? Is she coming?"

"I tried to convince her but she wouldn't have it. She said she needs to stay here and keep people safe. For what it's worth, I'll be doing the same."

Maddy deflated. She was getting more and more frightened by the second. "You aren't coming either?"

"I'm the only person who can stick close to Thomas. Things are going to get tricky here, and I want to be around to try to keep things from falling completely to shit. Don't worry, my allegiance is no longer to Thomas. I used to respect his vision of the big picture, but he lost that when he killed Wickstaff for his own gain."

"I'm going to kill him. Take me to him."

"No, he's surrounded by guards. He's waiting to see where the chips fall. You might get your chance one day, but not tonight. Come on."

Tony and the two guards led her outside onto the docks. There, she found a military uniform waiting for her along with a baseball cap. "Put it on," Tony said.

She got dressed quickly, keeping her own clothes on underneath. Then the small group hurried across the docks towards the quayside. There, as always, several massive warships waited. "Which one?" she asked. "Who is taking me on board?"

"A friend," said Tony.

"A friend?" And then she saw him. Commander Tosco stood beside a stack of containers, hiding in their shadows. Guards looked down on their meeting from several perches, but it must have merely looked like a pair of officers with their guards having a chat.

"Commander Tosco," said Tony. "How's the water tonight?"

"Smooth. Perfect conditions for a pleasant trip." He looked at Maddy. "How you doing?"

She shook her head, wanting to cry as the death of Amanda weighed on her. "Not good, Tosco. Not good at all."

"Well, let me get you out of here and then we can talk about it."

"Why are you doing this? If Thomas finds out, he'll have you shot."

"I'm not coming back," said Tosco. "I'll be with you all the way."

Maddy shook her head. "But why? All you've worked for…"

"It was time for me to pick a side. Come on, *The Hatchet* is waiting for us."

Maddy turned to Tony and didn't know what to say. She wanted to kiss him, but that would only hurt her heart, because the person she wanted to kiss most of all was now dead. "What are you going to do now, Tony?"

"I'm going to find your friends. Sounds like they're in trouble."

"You're going to find Mass?"

He nodded. "He sounds like a man we could do with having around."

"He is. Find him and tell him what happened, and… keep Diane safe."

"That girl can look after herself, but I promise I won't let anything happen to her."

"Then I guess this is goodbye."

He smiled. "For now. Good luck, Maddy."

"You too."

Maddy turned to Tosco and let him lead her to *The Hatchet*. It was time to leave Portsmouth. Time to find a new home. And then she would come back and kill Thomas.

*Hell hath no fury like a woman scorned.*

# RESURGENCE

Damien stood on the battlefield with his allies. Harry, Stephanie, Nancy, and a demon with his ward. It was not how he had ever seen his life going, but somehow he had become a war hero.

Indiana was free, the Hoosier Army victorious today against the last-known demon army. There had been six gates in the state and now all six were closed. Damien had discovered an ability to close them by touching them. No one was required to commit suicide.

They had lost thousands of people today, but they had died for this moment. This moment where the demons were finally beaten. Word was coming in from nearby states of similar victories, but their wars were separate. Indiana was the first state to declare itself free of demons, and there was an army over ten thousand strong at the ready to keep it that way.

"We did it," said Stephanie. "We beat them."

"In our corner of the world, yes," said Damien. "The fight isn't over yet though. Our previous battles were easier than this one. The demons were... confused, but today they were back to their old selves."

"Yes," said the large demon lord, Sorrow. "They are once again under the thrall of the Red Lord. He has returned from wherever he has been. His final attempt to rid this world of humanity will soon come."

"So we need to be there when it does," said Harry. "I still have some fighting left in me."

"Damn straight," said Scarlett. "I'm up for killing the big bad."

Damien turned to Sorrow. The demon had a weak connection to Hell – and as such, one to the Red Lord as well. "Where is he? Where do we need to be to beat him?"

Sorrow furrowed his thick brow. His jet-black wings flapped behind him. "England."

Nancy flinched. England was a painful place for her. Her children, Kyle and Alice had died there. Damien put his arm around her. "No time to lose, right? Are we all game?"

Everybody was. They were all ready for the final battle. They joined hands, closed their eyes, and opened a gate with ease. It was no longer a difficult task. Damien was a path walker, and these were his totems. "Say your goodbyes and get what you need. This will be a one-way trip."

Ted was tending to Jackie's grave in the meadow at the bottom of the hill. It was getting late, and he would need to leave now if he wanted to have dinner with the others. He could barely believe he had been here six months already. It was home.

And he hadn't been idle during that time. The castle was now surrounded by a wooden palisade, and the woods had been cleared for a hundred metres in all directions. They had dug a moat and installed stakes along it. Everyone now had a bow and arrow and some skill in using it. Crops were growing in the nearby fields and livestock had been collected from adjacent farms. They had survived long enough that they were now starting to live.

But he never slept at night. He always lay there, ears wide open and listening for the next attack. That no demons had approached the castle since Caligula had attacked was a miracle. It felt like too much of one to take for granted. The war for mankind wasn't over yet. The scouts still detected demons and there was still a gate about twenty miles north. The enemy was hurt but not finished. And they didn't have enough people or supplies at the castle to risk taking the battle to the enemy.

They needed help.

A wind rose up, gathering leaves. Ted's nose detected a metallic twang that reminded him of blood, and a shiver raced its way along his spine. The air felt wrong, like the moments before a storm arrived.

"Time to get back behind the wall, I think. Something ain't right."

The nearby woods lit up suddenly, and Ted was sure the attack had finally come. He had known it would, eventually. A gate had appeared, and soon demons would spill through it and overwhelm them all. They had been living on borrowed time.

Angry, enraged, and afraid, Ted picked up his hammer and stalked towards the trees. The more demons he killed, the less that the others would have to face.

The first demon approached, a massive being with impossibly black wings that seemed to capture the light and consume it. Some kind of a leader like Caligula had been. He would focus on trying to kill that first instead of the... *humans* that were with it.

What was this? Why were two dozen humans carrying rifles coming out of a gate with a massive demon? What was going on? Who were they?

An average-looking young man stepped to the front. He waved a hand as if to show he was friendly and then said, "Are you alone?"

Ted's eyes narrowed. "No, and if you came here looking for trouble, you'll have a fight on your hands."

The young man grinned. "It looks like we came to the right place. My name is Damien. I came here to help. I have fighters with me and we brought gifts."

Ted frowned, and nothing happened for a few moments until a pair of tough-looking men dumped a pair of massive crates on the ground. Then they opened them to reveal a stack of high-powered assault rifles and an endless trove of ammo.

Ted ran his eyes over the group. There were thirty men at least, all carrying weapons and wearing armour. "Who the hell are you people?"

"We're guardian angels," said a young girl moving to the front of the group. "We're here to help end this war against the demons once and for all, but first" – she grabbed her tummy and did an awkward wiggle – "I really need to use your toilet."

Ted blinked, utterly confused, but then he pointed an arm up the hill towards the castle. "You'd better follow me."

# WANT FREE BOOKS?

Don't miss out on your FREE Iain Rob Wright horror starter pack. Five free bestselling horror novels sent straight to your inbox. No strings attached.

CLICK HERE TO GET YOUR 5 FREE BOOKS

## PLEA FROM THE AUTHOR

Hey, Reader. So you got to the end of my book. I hope that means you enjoyed it. Whether or not you did, I would just like to thank you for giving me your valuable time to try and entertain you. I am truly blessed to have such a fulfilling job, but I only have that job because of people like you; people kind enough to give my books a chance and spend their hard-earned money buying them. For that I am eternally grateful.

If you would like to find out more about my other books then please visit my website for full details. You can find it at:

www.iainrobwright.com.

Also feel free to contact me on Facebook, Twitter, or email (all details on the website), as I would love to hear from you.

If you enjoyed this book and would like to help, then you could think about leaving a review on Amazon, Goodreads, or anywhere else that readers visit. The most important part of how well a book sells is how many positive reviews it has, so if you leave me one then you are directly helping me to continue on this journey as a fulltime writer. Thanks in advance to anyone who does. It means a lot.

**Iain Rob Wright** is one of the UK's most successful horror and suspense writers, with novels including the critically acclaimed, THE FINAL WINTER; the disturbing bestseller, ASBO; and the wicked screamfest, THE HOUSEMATES.

His work is currently being adapted for graphic novels, audio books, and foreign audiences. He is an active member of the Horror Writer Association and a massive animal lover.

**www.iainrobwright.com**
FEAR ON EVERY PAGE

*For more information*
www.iainrobwright.com
author@iainrobwright.com

Copyright © 2019 by Iain Rob Wright

Cover Photographs © Shutterstock

Artwork by Stuart Bache at Books Covers Ltd

Editing by Richard Sheehan

All rights reserved.

No part of this book may be reproduced in any form or by any electronic or mechanical means, including information storage and retrieval systems, without written permission from the author, except for the use of brief quotations in a book review.

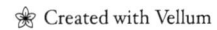

❦ Created with Vellum

Printed in Great Britain
by Amazon